Praise for Cynthia D'Alba

An emotional, complex and beautiful story of love and life and how it can all change in a heartbeat.

—DiDi, Guilty Pleasures Book Reviews on *Texas Lullaby*

Highly recommend to all fans of hot cowboys, firefighters, and romance.

—Emily, Goodreads on *Saddles and Soot*

This author does an amazing job of keeping readers on their toes while maintaining a natural flow to the story.

—RT Book Reviews on *Texas Hustle*

Cynthia D'Alba's *Texas Fandango* from Samhain lets readers enjoy the sensual fun in the sun [...] This latest offering gives readers a sexy escape and a reason to seek out D'Alba's earlier titles.

—Library Journal Reviews on *Texas Fandango*

[...] inclusions that stand out for all the right reasons is Cynthia D'Alba's clever *Backstage Pass*

—Publisher's Weekly on *Backstage Pass* in *Cowboy Heat*

Texas Two Step kept me on an emotional roller coaster […] an emotionally charged romance, with well-developed characters and an engaging secondary cast. A quarter of the way into the book I added Ms. D'Alba to my auto-buys.

—5 Stars and Recommended Read, Guilty Pleasure Book Reviews on *Texas Two Step*

[..]Loved this book…characters came alive. They had depth, interest and completeness. But more than the romance and sex which were great, there are connections with family and friends which makes this story so much more than a story about two people.

—Night Owl Romance 5 STARS! A TOP PICK *on Texas Bossa Nova*

Wow, what an amazing romance novel. *Texas Lullaby* is an impassioned, well-written book with a genuine love story that took hold of my heart and soul from the very beginning.

—LJT, Amazon Reviews, on *Texas Lullaby*

Texas Lullaby is a refreshing departure from the traditional romance plot in that it features an already committed couple.

—Tangled Hearts Book Reviews on *Texas Lullaby*

[…]sexy, contemporary western has it all. Scorching sex, a loving family and suspenseful danger. Oh, yeah!

—Bookaholics Romance Book Club on *Texas Hustle*

Also by Cynthia D'Alba

Whispering Springs, Texas

Texas Two Step: The Prequel (digital only)

Texas Two Step

Texas Tango

Texas Fandango

Texas Twist

Texas Bossa Nova

Texas Hustle

Texas Lullaby

Saddles and Soot

Texas Daze

Single Title Novellas

A Cowboy's Seduction

Texas Justice

Big Branch, Texas (Kindle Worlds)
Kindle Format Only

Cadillac Cowboy (Hell, Yeah!)

Texas Ranger Rescue (Brotherhood Protectors)

Texas Marine Mayhem (Brotherhood Protectors)

THE MONTGOMERY FAMILY TREE

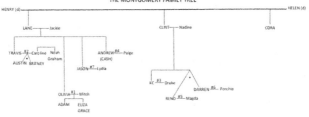

CAPITAL NAMES denote MONTGOMERY SURNAMES

- Denotes twins

#1 – Texas Two Step   #4 – Texas Twist   #7 Texas Lullaby

#2 – Texas Tango   #5 – Texas Bossa Nova

#3 – Texas Fandango   #6 – Texas Hustle

TEXAS TWO STEP

Whispering Springs, Texas

CYNTHIA D'ALBA

Texas Two Step

By Cynthia D'Alba

Copyright © 2012 Cynthia D'Alba and Riante, Inc.

Second Edition 2017

Print ISBN: 978-0-9982650-6-3

Digital ISBN: 978-0-9982650-7-0

ALL RIGHTS RESERVED. No part of this book may be reproduced or transmitted in any form whatsoever without written permission from the author—except by a reviewer who may quote brief passages in a review to be printed in a magazine, newspaper, or on the web. For additional information or to obtain permission to excerpt portions of the text, please contact the author via email at CYNTHIADALBA@GMAIL.COM

This is a work of fiction. The characters, incidents and dialogues in this book are of the author's imagination and are not to be construed as real. Any resemblance to actual events or persons, living or dead, is completely coincidental.

Cover Artist: Scott Carpenter

Editor: Heidi Moore

Dedication

It's been said it takes a village to raise a child. In my case, it took a slew of friends, family and critique partners.

To MA Golla for her unfailing support and belief in my ability to write.

To Leigh Duncan, who read more incarnations of this story than one critique partner should have to.

To Delilah Devlin, Shayla Kersten, and Elle James aka Myla Jackson who were always available to chat, read or push me on when I needed it.

To my editor, Heidi (Moore) Shoham. Thank you for taking a chance on this debut author.

Last, and without doubt the most important, to my husband, Phil, who suggested I try my hand at writing and then gave me unwavering support.

Chapter One

The woman stood on tiptoe in the baggage-claim area of the Dallas/Fort Worth airport looking for all the world like someone who'd been sent to collect the devil. Mitch Landry had expected Wes or one of the other groomsmen to come for him. Instead, his gaze found a statuesque blonde arching up on her toes, a white T-shirt with Jim's Gym in black script stretched across her lushly curved breasts and long tanned legs extending from tight denim shorts. His heart stumbled then roared into a gallop.

Blood rushed from his brain to below his waist. His nostrils flared in a deep breath, as though he could smell her unique fragrance across the crowded lobby.

She hadn't looked in his direction yet, which gave him an unfettered opportunity to study her without having to camouflage his reactions.

No make-up covered her creamy rose complexion, not that she needed any. Not then and not now. No eye shadow was required to bring out the deep blue of her eyes. Nor did her mouth need any enhancement. Her lips radiated a natural pink, although the bottom one grew redder as her upper teeth gnawed on it.

Six years had passed since he'd seen Olivia Montgomery, but he'd swear she was more beautiful today. She had an appeal that came only with age and maturity. A smile edged onto his mouth. He was surprised—pleasantly surprised—to admit how glad he was to see her.

He watched as her glare bounced around the room, searching faces until it fell on him. As a look of resignation flashed across her face, she frowned.

His smile faded. Not exactly the reaction he'd hoped for.

IF THE BURNING ACID IN HER STOMACH WAS ANY indication, Olivia Montgomery Gentry was not happy. This was not how she wanted to look when she saw Mitch Landry for the first time in six years. Her stomach pitched and her hands fisted when she got her first view of him in the DFW luggage area. Damn Emily and Wes and their last minute wedding emergencies.

Olivia had been at her gym when her best friend—and this weekend's bride—Emily, had called frantic over a wedding snafu. Someone had to go to the airport and pick up the best man and would Olivia be a dear and run to DFW?

Olivia had knocked her head against the wall at the request and begged Emily to send someone else—anyone else—pleading work and appointments and any excuse she could dream up to avoid being alone with Mitch Landry.

She couldn't face him…not yet. But nothing could dissuade the determined bride, who'd appealed, cajoled and blackmailed. As the deal cincher, she'd sprung the you're-the-maid-of-honor guilt trip and Olivia's resolve had collapsed like a cheap lawn chair.

With no time for a shower, she'd made do with a quick sponging off, a fresh pair of shorts and a clean T-shirt. Leading this morning's vigorous kickboxing class had left her long hair in a sweaty mess, which had given her no option but to slick it up into a damp ponytail.

Thanks to Emily's last-minute notice, Olivia had raced across town, lucky not to add another speeding ticket to her growing collection. Typically by mid-morning at DFW airport, all the closest parking spots were occupied. Today was no exception and she'd found herself in the last row of the most distant lot.

Mother Nature had decided to ignore the calendar, which clearly indicated the season was spring, and launched summer a little early. The morning temperature had vaulted to ninety-three with a forecasted high of ninety-nine by afternoon. By the time Olivia had hoofed it across the blistering asphalt parking lot under a bright and vicious scorching sun, her minimal powder and blush had melted in the heat. Her clean shirt had molded to her body like an entry in a wet T-shirt contest.

A blast of cold from the airport's air conditioning had smacked Olivia's sweat-dampened neck when she'd blown into the baggage claim area. Chills snaked down her spine and she shivered, unsure if the shiver was due to the shot of cold air or the anticipation of seeing Mitch again.

Arching up on her tiptoes, she scanned the crowd. Years had passed since she'd seen him, but she remembered every inch of his six-foot-four-inch body.

Sometimes at night, if she closed her eyes and concentrated, she could still feel his naked body spooned around hers. Hot chest flesh and chiseled abdominal muscles pressing against her back. Strong thighs cupping her legs. A muscular arm wrapped tightly around her waist, making her feel secure.

She forced her shoulders down and locked her jaw. She didn't—couldn't—allow her thoughts to wander into those memories. They were too painful, like having a tooth filled without Novocain.

Her gaze met his blue-eyed stare and her gut tightened in response. Her lungs seized, making breathing almost impossible. She gritted her teeth, angry at herself for being unable to calm her racing heart.

Sometimes life wasn't fair. This was one of those times.

Mitch sported a natural tan, not the sprayed-on kind many Dallas wanna-be cowboys boasted. Sexy stubble dotted his cheeks, one that made her ache to run the palm of her hand along his chin. His long dark hair, tied at the nape of his neck, begged to be freed. Her fingers twitched, ready to slide through his silky strands as they'd done many times before. Of course, she'd have to remove his ever-present Stetson before she ruffled his hair. Olivia doubted there was a woman in the world who wouldn't enjoy taking the hat off this cowboy's head. Hell, even the wrinkles in his shirt and jeans looked sexy. In short, Mitch looked as though he had been ripped off the cover of a western romance.

She, on the other hand, looked like someone who'd been yanked from a *Sweating with the Oldies* video. Self-consciously, she touched her hair, tucking a stray piece behind her ear. Not only wasn't life fair, sometimes it outright sucked.

The smile on his face slipped as their gazes met. For a moment they just stared at each other, then his lips pulled into a toe-curling grin and she sighed. He lifted his chin in acknowledgement and strolled toward her, a carry-on in one hand and a garment bag in the other. Olivia's stomach flipped and her heart dove into a roller-coaster freefall.

Thick thigh muscles bulged through his jeans as he walked. A white oxford shirt stretched taut across broad shoulders. Brown cowboy boots clacked on the tile with each step.

A number of female heads turned as Mitch walked past. She wasn't the only one who noticed this Texas cowboy.

"Livie." Mitch dropped both pieces of luggage and grasped her hands. His weren't the soft, manicured hands of a counterfeit cowboy. His were the callused, weathered hands of a working rancher.

The roughness of his skin against her palm produced erotic images of what those thick, rough fingers felt like on other places of her body. The region between her thighs tightened to a throb.

He pulled her close and kissed her cheek. Stubby bristle on his jaw scraped her skin. Pressing her nose against his face during the kiss, she savored the unique mixture of woodsy cologne and Mitch's raw masculine scent, a scent she'd long ago stored in her memory. Behind her navel, her gut tugged. The kiss was chaste, but that meant nothing to her heart, which ramped up to a dangerous gallop, or to her insides quivering in anticipation.

"You look...amazing." He stepped back, his gaze lazily moving down, then back up her body.

Still the flirt. He hadn't changed a bit, except to become more handsome, if that were even possible.

"You're a liar, Mitch Landry, but thank you anyway." Her fingers twitched to tighten the grasp. Instead, she dropped his hands. His touch was more than she could bear and yet still everything she wanted. She nodded at the pieces of luggage riding around on the conveyer belt. "What are we looking for?" she asked in an attempt to get control of both the situation and herself.

"Stay here. I'll grab it." In a moment, he returned with a rolling suitcase.

"I had to park a mile off." She snagged his carry-on and whipped toward the exit. "Wait here. I'll get the car and pick you up."

"Don't be ridiculous. How far out are you?"

With a roll of her eyes and a shake of her head, she said, "Last row, last spot."

He chuckled. "I don't miss the big city and all its headaches."

Did his statement mean he didn't miss her either? Was she one of the headaches he associated with Dallas? Was the memory of their love a *something* he wanted to forget?

Apparently—or at least it seemed to her—Mitch had moved on with his life and left their love in the past. She hated to admit a small part of her wanted him to still want her, to regret the way they'd left things. Part of her wanted him to fall at her feet, begging for forgiveness.

That wasn't going to happen. She slammed the door to her heart. Time for her to relegate Mitch to her past and move on, much as it seemed he had.

"This way then," Olivia said with a toss of her head toward the exit.

Outside, the Texas heat sucked the cold airport air from her lungs. The strong odor of hot asphalt scented the air. People tugging rolling bags and crying children hurried past them, eager to get out of the broiling sun.

She forced herself to project a relaxed composure,

one she didn't feel in his presence. "How have you been, Mitch?"

Good. Her voice sounded calm, cool and collected, nothing like the tempest swirling inside.

He dipped his head and arched one eyebrow. "So, we're going to pretend that nothing happened six years ago? Just two old friends meeting up after a long absence?"

She gave a shrug she prayed he'd interpret as nonchalance, when in reality her reaction to seeing him again was anything but. They stood on the curb and waited as a line of cars passed, then stepped down into a crosswalk and made their way to the parking area. Her walk was brisk, but with his long legs, Mitch had no trouble keeping up.

"Livie. Stop for a minute."

She took a couple of more steps before she paused and turned toward him. "What?"

"I wanted to say I'm sorry." He draped the carrying bag over the arm pulling the luggage and lightly brushed his fingertips along her cheek. "Sorry for all the stupid things I said six years ago. Sorry for being such a horse's ass. You were special and I did care about you. And I'm really sorry I didn't tell you that a long time ago."

He gave her a smile that shot a pang into her stomach. "Tell me you're not still angry at the actions of the immature jerk I was back then."

As she flinched away from his caress, she fought unwelcomed tears blurring her vision. She'd believed she'd cried all she could over Mitch years ago. But her skin burned where he touched as if she'd been hit with a hot branding iron. "Of course not," she lied. "That's all in the past. Never give it a thought."

Embarrassed at her lack of emotional control, she

resumed her death-march pace, trying to outrun her feelings and his touch. After a few yards her steps slowed until she stopped. She turned to face him again. He looked like dinner to a starving man—or in her case, woman. Her stomach muscles quivered. "Listen, on a different subject, I was so sorry when I heard about James's death. He was too young to die. Your poor mother." She re-tucked a hank of hair behind her ear. "Parents aren't supposed to bury their children. I mourned with your family even though I couldn't imagine what everyone was going through. God, I'll miss him. He was a wonderful friend to me."

His expression sobered at the mention of his late older brother. "Those days were hell on everyone. Thank you for sending cards and flowers to Mom. I know she appreciated them."

She resumed walking toward the car. "How are your parents?" she asked with a glance in his direction.

The smile that curved his lips softened his face. "They're doing much better…now. Losing James almost killed them. But then one day my parents were back. No idea what was the magic key that restarted them. And really, I don't care. I was just relieved to see traces of the parents I'd always known." He touched a stray piece of her hair that'd escaped her ponytail and was moving in the breeze. "By the way, they said to tell you hi." He shifted the hanging bag back into his free hand and tossed it over his shoulder. "I wish you'd have come for his funeral. James was so fond of you."

"You know I adored James too. I wish I could have been there. For your mom and dad…and your brother. And you too, of course." Her nose began an irritating burn she always experienced with unshed tears. Her throat throbbed with pent-up emotion. She didn't dare look at him now. She suspected her face would say more than she was willing to tell.

"Sure. I understand."

They walked in silence for a couple of minutes. Nearby, a car alarm screamed. Planes leaving DFW roared overhead.

"I wasn't lying earlier. You do look great. Are you working out?" he asked, pumping his eyebrows in exaggerated movements. "Walk in front of me so I can enjoy the view."

Even though a thrill ran through her, she rolled her eyes. "You are so bad," she said, then gave her hips a little wiggle. "But yeah. You could say I work out. Remember Jim's Gym on West Highfield? I bought it." She waved a hand at the logo on her shirt. "Decided not to change the name."

"So you own Jim's?" He looked at her, his eyes wide with surprise. "That's great, babe. You like running a gym?"

Hearing him address her by his old pet name produced a jolt to her heart. She pasted on a smile. "It pays the bills." When he chuckled, she added, "Yeah, I do. I like working with people, helping them reach their goals. Plus, I've expanded the place. Added a separate spa area for facials, manicures and such. I have an incredible staff I adore. All in all, it was a good business decision."

"You don't miss being on your parents' ranch and your barrel racing?"

"Sometimes," she admitted. "But most days I'm too busy to miss the ranch or the riding. Besides, they're only an hour from us, so we…er…I can go out there anytime."

She ventured a quick glance at his expression. Had

CYNTHIA D'ALBA

he noticed her slight verbal stumble? His expression was unchanged, so apparently she'd dodged that bullet. She hoped he didn't ask much more about her riding or the ranch. The why and when she quit riding wasn't on the table for discussion. He didn't seem to know about her accident and keeping him in the dark about the details suited her fine.

Neither spoke again during the remaining trek to the car. Olivia just wanted to focus on how good he looked. How much she still wanted him and missed him was there too, but she tried to ignore those messages. She honestly had no idea what was going on in his mind.

Scorching heat from the sun poured down. Tiny beads of perspiration popped on her head and itched as they trickled through her hair. What she wouldn't give for the Stetson in her closet right now.

Pointing a remote, she popped the trunk of a black Mercedes Benz.

Mitch tossed in his bags as well as the one she carried. "A Benz, huh?" His gaze raked over the car. "Business must be good. Congrats."

"Thanks." Oven-degree heat rolled from the car when she opened the door. After waiting a minute to let out as much hot air as possible, she slid onto the toasty leather of the driver's seat. "But this isn't mine." She started the car then lowered the temperature controls on the air conditioning. "Belongs to one of the trainers at the gym. My car was blocked in and Mark loaned me his."

Mitch tossed his hat onto the back seat before sliding into the passenger side. He looked around and whistled. "Nice ride."

"Yep. Nice guy too." Moments later, she paid the toll at the south exit and turned east onto Highway 183.

"Emily said to drop you at Grayson Mansion. Do you need to stop anywhere first?"

"Like where?"

"I don't know. Armani store? Walmart? Williams Feed and Tack?"

To her relief, he chuckled at her joke. The deep sound vibrated around the car and straight into her heart.

"Nope. Got everything I'll need this weekend." He cleared his throat and angled his body toward her. "So Livie, are you really happy living here in the big D? Don't you miss the ranch life? The riding? The early morning chores? The nosy small-town gossip?"

Her fingers tightened around the steering wheel and she kept her gaze glued on the traffic ahead. Every glance at him produced a sucker punch to her gut, and she didn't want him to know how much seeing him physically pained her. "I'm as happy here as much as anywhere, I guess. My business does well. I have friends, so…" She shrugged, pulling the car's shoulder strap tight across her chest.

"How's the Lazy L doing?" she asked, referring to his family's cattle ranch.

"Actually, pretty damn good. Had some bad years with drought and some freaky winter weather, but we kept her going. Now if beef prices would just get back up."

The pride and enthusiasm in his voice left no doubt how much he loved being part of the family cattle business. With him way down in south Texas and her in Dallas, a big spread of Texas geography separated them.

"Glad it's working out then."

She looked at the back of his head as he stared out the side window, seeming to study the landscape as it whizzed by. The ends of his hair were distinctly lighter than the roots, visible now that he'd removed his hat. She suspected his hair had been lightened and his skin tanned from the daily sun exposure of working on his ranch. She'd seen him wear a cowboy hat so many times, and she could picture him on his horse, his hat saturated with sweat, the ends of his long hair soaking up the sun's rays as he rode behind the cattle. Now that she thought about it, she couldn't remember ever seeing his hair this long. He'd once told her he always kept his hair short to make the south Texas heat bearable. And while she liked his new look, she had to admit she missed the old one.

"Haven't had time to keep up with the old crowd. You never did get married, right?" His gravelly voice jerked her mind from reminiscing.

"Wrong. I did." His question surprised her, but if the shock on his face was any indication, her answer was an obvious bombshell. Her gaze snapped back to the road.

"You did? How come I didn't know that?"

She shook her head while saying, "I don't know. It wasn't a state secret or anything."

"So you're not Olivia Montgomery?"

"Of course I'm Olivia Montgomery. I just added Gentry to the end. I married Drake Gentry. I don't think you ever knew him."

"I didn't. Will he be here this weekend?"

"No."

He gave her left hand a pointed stare. "Are you still married?"

She shook her head. "Divorced." A pang of regret settled around her heart, regret about hurting Drake, a wonderful man who'd been her rock when she'd needed stability the most. He'd been there for her and she'd let him down so many times in so many ways.

"Hmm."

"Hmm? What does that mean?" She glanced toward him, wondering why his opinion was suddenly so important. At almost thirty, she ran her own business while raising a wonderful son single handedly. Why did Mitch's opinion still mean so much to her?

His fingers drummed on the arm console between them. "I'm just surprised. Your marriage caught me off-guard."

"So I gathered. Why? Did you think no one would marry little old me?" she asked, lifting one eyebrow in a challenge.

He chuckled and placed his forearm on the back of her seat, letting his elbow dangle in the opening between the seats.

His deep-throated chuckle reverberated through her again. The muscles in her jaw clenched at the zap of energy tingling through every nerve.

"Don't be a goose." He tapped a knuckle on the side of her head. "Any man would be fortunate to have you as a wife and a fool to give you up. I...I'm just surprised no one told me, especially my mother. They talk, you know? My mother and yours."

She nodded. "I know." She also often talked to his mother but some secrets were best left alone.

"Since Caleb left for school, and without James to help, keeping up with all the ranch work means odd work hours. Up early, to bed early. Like I said, I haven't really kept in touch with old friends." He caressed her cheek again with a rough finger. "Like you."

Her heart leapt into her throat at his touch. The muscles in her stomach seized. She turned her singed cheek away from his touch. "No problem. I've been busy myself."

"What happened? To your marriage, I mean."

Frowning, she exhaled loudly. "Nothing happened. Drake and I are still good friends. Better friends than lovers, I guess."

Mitch had been stroking her neck with a finger. His finger stilled at the word lovers. "Is he in Dallas?"

The hair in her ponytail tugged at the roots when she shook her head. "No. He's in Wyoming on an archeological dig. Something about dinosaurs."

Definitely time to change the subject from marriage. She did not want to venture into Mitch's marriage and divorce from Joanna St. Claire. The fact he'd married Joanna, or anyone else, a mere six months after their break-up still squeezed her heart almost to the point of breaking.

And she certainly didn't want to talk about, or even remember, the phone call from Mitch explaining the marriage. The pain of his betrayal had almost killed her. It'd certainly driven her to make some questionable, if not outright bad decisions. But the choices he'd made about his life had affected the choices she made about hers, and now she had her own secrets to keep.

She ordered her mind not to think about that phone call years ago, but that worked as well as saying don't think about pink elephants. In her mind, she was there again, sitting in stunned silence as his words tore her heart and her future to shreds. The anguish from that night scalded her eyes with tears she couldn't shed…at least not right now. When she was alone, she would allow herself to remember. Then, and only then, she could cry.

Yes, the last thing she needed this weekend was deep, heartfelt talks. She blinked hard and lifted her chin.

"So," he said, dragging out the word. "Are you seeing anyone now? This Mark person maybe?"

Laughter erupted, mostly in relief at the change in subject. "Well, I'll admit, Mark is quite the stud, but Nancy—that's his wife—frowns on him dating other women."

As she'd hoped, Mitch laughed. "Who is this nice guy who would lend you his Mercedes?"

"One of my trainers. Ex-Dallas Cowboy linebacker."

"Great. He must bring a nice clientele to your gym."

"He does." A smile spread on her lips at how the addition of Mark had boosted her bottom line.

"You didn't answer my question though. Are you seeing someone?"

"No one right now. You?" When she glanced toward him and their gazes locked, Olivia felt as though she were drowning. She gasped in a breath, and then turned back to the road, switching lanes with a quick jerk of the wheel.

He shook his head. "Not much. As I said, most of my days start about five in the morning and end about seven at night. Sometimes as late as midnight." He rested his hand on her headrest. "Hard to cram a social life in there."

When she thought of Mitch with another woman her heart cleaved in half, but she had to be realistic. They'd had their shot at a relationship and failed. And with a marriage apiece, they'd apparently found other people to fill the void.

The front pocket of her shorts vibrated, startling her. As she dug out her cell phone, she swerved. Damn. If she put even a ping in the paint of Mark's car, he was going to kill her. After steadying the car, she glanced at the number display. Jim's Gym. She flipped open the phone. "Hello?"

"Momma?" a high-pitched voice asked.

Switching the phone to the ear farthest from Mitch, she said, "Hi, Adam. I asked you not to call me unless it was important."

"But it is," the tiny voice whined.

"Okay. What's the problem?"

"Nancy's making me take a nap. Tell her I'm too old for a nap."

Mentally, Olivia shook her head in maternal frustration. They went through this almost every day at naptime. "You know the rules. When I'm not there, Nancy's in charge. You do what she tells you. Got it? Now, let me talk to her."

Each word was chosen with extreme care. Mitch would hear every word of her end of the conversation. It'd be impossible for him not to. But he didn't need to know anything about Adam. In fact, she'd be happy if Mitch went home neither hearing of nor meeting her son.

"Nancy," the little boy yelled.

Olivia flinched at the volume of her son's voice.

"Momma wants to talk to you."

Clicking and clacking sounds reverberated through the receiver as the phone passed from her son to the assistant manager at Jim's Gym.

"Hi, Olivia. What do you need?"

Olivia paused, thought, and then chose her words carefully. "Adam called me about your plans for the afternoon." She shot a furtive sideways glance toward Mitch, who was watching her. She stifled the urge to shiver under his intense gaze.

Nancy drew in a deep breath and let it out slowly. "*So sorry*, Olivia. I thought he was already asleep on the cot in your office. I'll handle the little troublemaker."

Olivia laughed softly. "Okay. I'll see you both in a

little while." She clicked the phone shut and slid it back into her pocket.

"Problem at the gym?"

"What?" Guilt stilled her body. "Oh, no. Not really. Everything's fine."

She wheeled into the hotel's drive and pulled the lever to open the trunk. Uniformed bellmen immediately opened both doors. A third bellman unloaded Mitch's luggage onto a cart.

Olivia slid from the car and glanced toward the valet holding her door. "I won't be staying. Just dropping off."

"I'll meet you at registration." Mitch handed the luggage bellman some folded bills from his wallet and watched for a moment as the man rolled the cart toward the lobby. Mitch walked around the car to Olivia. "Thank you for the ride."

His voice was formal and distant, and strangely, she was relieved. She needed some emotional distance between them to survive the weekend.

"You're welcome, Mitch. I'll see you tonight."

After he gave her a quick kiss on the lips, he tapped his finger on her nose, winked and walked away.

Olivia touched her lips with her fingertips. Her heart tattooed painfully against her ribs. Exactly like old times. Some flirting, a few laughs, and then an exit without a backward glance.

She watched him enter Grayson Mansion through revolving doors then momentarily shut her eyes. Not again. She steeled her resolve. She wouldn't let him get to her again.

The wedding obligations were for Friday and Saturday only. Two days. She was mature enough to handle Mitch Landry's presence for that long.

MITCH TIPPED THE BELLMAN AND SHUT THE DOOR TO his suite, grateful for the quiet. Exhaustion was kicking his ass. He'd been up most of the previous night with a difficult calving. But saving the mother and her calf was worth losing a night of sleep. If he wanted to be the least bit sociable tonight, he needed a short nap.

Stripping off his clothes, he headed for the cream-colored, marble-tiled shower in the lavish bathroom befitting the luxurious suite décor. As he stepped under the hot, pounding water, he couldn't stop thinking about Olivia. Seeing her at the airport had thrown him for a loop. Of course, he'd known he'd see her this weekend. He simply hadn't prepared himself for seeing her the minute he stepped from the plane. He grimaced. He hadn't looked his best when they'd met, but damn, she looked good.

Most of their conversation was a blur, but two facts stood out in his mind—her divorce and her current single status.

He frowned as he rubbed the soap bar over his tight-ening chest. How had he not known about her marriage? His mother and hers had been college sorority sisters and gossiped all the time.

Did his mother know? Of course, she did. She had to. The question was, why hadn't she mentioned it? A subject for their next conversation.

Olivia wasn't seeing anyone. That thought made him smile. Their break-up had been painful...for both of them.

He shoved his face under the showerhead and let the pounding water bounce off his head. He hated that he'd hurt her, but hell, at the time he'd thought he was doing the right thing. One of these days he'd learn not to decide what was best for everyone else and do what was best for him, regardless of how selfish that sounded.

He stepped from the shower and rubbed a thick towel over his body. An inkling of jealousy ticked his psyche as he remembered the phone call from someone named Adam. Her voice had been affectionate during the telephone conversation, even when it seemed as though she wasn't happy with whatever Adam was telling her. Who was this Adam person? He sorted through his memories of her circle of friends for the name. He didn't know an Adam, did he? None came to mind.

Slipping between the soft sheets, he hoped his mind would turn off and his eyes would slam shut as soon as his head hit the pillow. No such luck. Instead, memories of Olivia circled his brain as though set on a continuous loop. Her laugh...her smile...her kiss.

She'd looked great, hell, more than great. He'd underestimated his reaction to seeing her again. He wanted her. Desired her. Craved her touch.

With a groan, he punched his pillow and rolled to his side. She, on the other hand, seemed cool...friendly but distinctly cool.

He flopped onto his back and threw his arm over his head. Of course she was cool. Hadn't he been the utmost ass when he'd left her? He covered his eyes with his arm and groaned at the memory of that phone call about marrying Joanna. Guilt gnawed inside, driving the acid up the walls of his stomach.

Even though he would be in Dallas until Monday, his wedding duties would only tie up Friday and Saturday, leaving him all day Sunday free. Would it be possible to make it up to her with a little fun and extra attention this weekend? Maybe they could even recapture some of the old magic.

This weekend was all the free time he had. He had to go back to the ranch and his life there. She would return to her life here. Their lives would go on as before, but it would be nice to part as friends and be able to leave his guilt in the past.

SEVEN HOURS LATER, OLIVIA THREW THE CAR INTO park and checked her face in the rearview mirror. Lips red, no telltale chocolate hiding in the teeth, nose powdered. She studied her face in the mirror. She could see guilt etched in every wrinkle, every shift of her eyes. Hopefully, no one else would look that close tonight.

A diamond-covered heart locket around her throat glittered in the fading evening sun. She lightly stroked the gift Mitch had given her on her twenty-second birthday. Prying it open with a fingernail, she looked down at the man's face on the left and her son's face on the right. Carbon copies. Had she made a mistake wearing the necklace tonight?

When she'd dressed, she'd hesitated before fastening the locket around her neck. Would Mitch read anything into her wearing his gift? Was she subconsciously sending him a message?

No, she wasn't. The locket was the nicest piece of jewelry in her collection.

And not looking her best tonight would be criminal, the imp on her shoulder whispered.

Her breathing was quick, not panting, but shallow and rapid. Nerves had that effect on her. Closing her eyes, she leaned her head against the seat and concentrated on slowing her breaths, calming her nerves and stashing her tractor-trailer load of guilt in the far recesses of her mind.

After a couple of minutes, she drew in a deep breath, let it out slowly then opened the driver's door. She stood, letting the black silk dress slither down her body until the hem skimmed the skin above her knees. The sliding silk caressed her overheated skin inch by inch, stirring up the butterflies in her stomach. She pressed her palm against her abdomen and waited for the nervous tension to abate. As she straightened the diamond locket necklace, she strengthened her resolve.

Facing a firing squad had to be easier than facing an old lover.

As she hurried through the lobby to the Promenade, her three-inch strappy heels clacked on the white and black tile of the foyer. Hosiery and she were not close friends. Heck, they were barely acquaintances. Normally, she avoided wearing stockings when she could, but for tonight, thigh-high black silk stockings made a sexy swoosh sound as she race-walked. She liked it.

"Sorry," she called to Emily as she hurried to join the other members of the wedding party.

Emily waved and then turned to a tall, reed-thin woman standing beside her. The pinched-face woman clapped her hands for attention. "Okay. Listen up. We'll go through this a couple of times. I suspect most of you know what to do, but please pay attention."

The gossiping and whispering undertones stopped with the handclap, and the bridal party stilled, listening to the wedding planner's instructions.

"Bowing to tradition of bad luck, the bride and groom have decided not to walk through the wedding. Olivia?" The wedding planner looked around, eyebrows raised.

"Here." Olivia dropped her purse into a chair and hurried forward.

Wolf whistles from the groom and his groomsmen produced a wide grin on Olivia's face and a reassurance that her dress selection was exactly right.

"Good. Emily would like you to walk through her paces as the bride. She'll take your place as maid of honor, that way you'll know your role tomorrow." Her gaze scanned the group of men. "Now, where's Mitch?"

Mitch stepped from the herd of men leaning against a wall. Dressed in a black pinstriped suit, dazzling white shirt, red tie and black cowboy boots, he could have been the groom from the top of a wedding cake. If the facial expressions of the other women were any indication, several of them would have volunteered to help clean the icing off his boots…while he was removing the rest of his duds.

His long black hair from this morning had been trimmed. Shorter, but still long enough to make Olivia's fingers twitch to run through the strands. Her heart swelled with a familiar emotion that, until today, she'd thought dead. She licked her lips as her hands clenched into fists.

For Olivia, Emily was family. Olivia adored her three brothers, but she'd always dreamed of having a sister to gossip with, practice hairstyles on, shop with, and all of the other activities Olivia imagined sisters did together. Meeting Emily in first grade was like finding her lost sister.

When Olivia had found out Mitch would be the best man, she could have made her excuses and skipped being in the wedding. Emily would have understood, but the idea of not being with Emily on the day she married was inconceivable. Olivia had assured Emily that Mitch being in the wedding wouldn't be a problem. After all, they'd both moved on with their lives.

But she'd been wrong. Seeing him, touching him, even hearing his laugh was tearing her to shreds. Now she was being asked to play bride to his groom.

Her nails made half-moons in the palms of her hands. Why couldn't he be fat and bald instead of tall and hunky?

Chapter Two

"Mr. Landry, Wes has asked that you stand in for him during rehearsal. Okay? Good." The wedding planner didn't wait for an answer.

Mitch's gaze met Olivia's. He arched an eyebrow as if to ask if she was okay with this.

Olivia shrugged one shoulder. Did she—or he—really have any choice but to go along with the bride and groom's wishes? Any reaction other than cheerful participation would put a damper on the whole weekend and her best friend's wedding—something Olivia wasn't going to do. Stiff upper lip and all that nonsense. She would get through this weekend and get back to her routine on Monday.

Mrs. Peters clapped her hands again. "Okay, people. Let's get started."

The bride and groom each had five attendants. As Mrs. Peters walked the first two bridesmaids down the aisle demonstrating the pace, Emily slipped up alongside Olivia. "I am so sorry I had to send you to pick up Mitch this morning. Wes couldn't find any of his groomsmen to go. I swear. You were my last resort."

"I didn't mind," Olivia lied. "I knew I'd see him this weekend anyway, so it wasn't a big deal." If her name had been Pinocchio instead of Olivia, her nose would now be a tree.

"Thanks for being my stand-in tonight. I know it's foolish to be so superstitious, but…" Emily bumped her shoulder into Olivia's, "…I'm taking no chances."

With a lump in her throat, Olivia hugged her friend. "Not a problem," she lied again. "I'm glad to help. Besides, you and Wes are made for each other. Nothing could jinx y'all."

"I wish Adam could have been the ring bearer. He'd have been darling in a mini-tux. But I know that's impossible."

Tamping down the panic that rushed at the mention of her son's name, Olivia took a quick glance around to ensure Emily and she were far enough from the others not to be overheard. She managed a stiff smile and whispered, "I do too."

"You still haven't told him, have you?" Emily didn't have to spell out for Olivia who the *him* was.

Olivia shook her head. "I can't. Too much time has passed, and well, maybe it's better to let sleeping dogs lie."

"I hate I don't live in Dallas anymore. I miss you and Adam so much. He is growing up to be so handsome, not that I'm surprised with his gene pool." Emily clasped Olivia's hand and gave it a squeeze. "Thank you for not hating me for letting Wes ask Mitch to be his best man. I couldn't tell him he couldn't without explaining why not. And I haven't—and won't—tell him anything until you tell me I can. I promise."

Before Olivia could reply, Mrs. Peters clapped her hands. "Bride. Maid of honor. You're not paying attention."

Olivia and Emily exchanged embarrassed glances and the grins of guilty children.

"Sorry, Mrs. Peters," Emily said.

"Sorry, Mrs. Peters," Olivia echoed and stifled a smile. She and Emily had received many such reprimands back in their high school days. They hurried over to where the wedding planner stood waiting.

"I want you both to walk with me down the aisle," Mrs. Peters explained. "That way you can get a feel for the speed I want you to enter the room for the ceremony and…" she looked at Olivia, "…since you aren't actually practicing your role tonight, you can see exactly where you need to stand tomorrow. Then I need you, Olivia, to walk in again as the bride so the attendants can practice turning as a group. Got it?"

When they nodded Mrs. Peters said, "Great. Let's go."

Mrs. Peters walked the bride and her maid of honor down the aisle at the pace she wanted them to proceed during the actual wedding. As soon as Emily stepped into the designated maid of honor's position, Olivia hurried to the back of the room to be the stand-in bride.

"Now," Mrs. Peters announced to the group, "the attendants will continue facing toward the audience and not turn until the bride reaches the front and stops. Then you will all turn as a group toward the couple. Start walking," she said to Olivia. Olivia had taken one step when Mrs. Peters thrust a bouquet of silk flowers in her hand. "For practice in handing off."

Olivia gave a nod of understanding and tried to swallow, but her mouth had become the Sahara Desert.

The white silk roses hissed as the petals scratched against each other in her shaking hands. Her breathing dropped to a shallow, rapid pant. She prayed she wouldn't pass out from lack of oxygen. As she made her way toward her make-believe groom, she wobbled the first couple of steps before she got control of her trembling legs. The walk down the aisle toward Mitch felt surreal, almost painful. Could this weekend get any worse?

To Mitch's right, Wes stood as rigid as a statue. Mitch understood. His stomach was queasy and he wasn't even the real groom.

Livie took her first step down the aisle. The black silk dress accentuated her curves, shifting with each swing of her hips. The diamonds in the necklace laying in her soft cleavage—his birthday gift to her seven years ago—winked as the heart locket jostled with each step.

Mitch hardened at the sight of Olivia walking toward him carrying a bridal bouquet. He tilted his head toward one shoulder and then the other, trying to loosen the stiffness in his neck. Although he wore a custom-made shirt, the collar was strangling him. He resisted the urge to tug it away from his neck. The shirt felt two sizes too small. The material squeezed every-where—his shoulders, his chest, across his gut. He moved his shoulders around in a circle, thinking—hoping—the motion might loosen the material at the neck and back. Nothing helped. If anything, the damn shirt shrank more with each step Livie took toward him.

Tiny tingles pricked his toes. He wiggled them. His new cowboy boots seemed to have also shrunk, cutting off the blood supply to his feet. Discreetly, he stomped one foot, then the other. It didn't help. The tingling continued.

Olivia stopped after taking a couple of steps. The white flowers shoved in her hands shook slightly before she began again.

Mrs. Peters stepped alongside her. "You're walking a little too slow. I would say most girls would rush down the aisle to him." With a wink, she tilted her head toward Mitch.

Heat infused Mitch's face. Wes slapped Mitch's shoulder with a loud guffaw. The rest of the wedding party tittered.

Mrs. Peters looked at Emily and raised her voice. "Tomorrow, you'll want to walk at about this pace." With measured steps, she walked about halfway down the aisle. "Got it?"

Emily nodded.

"Let's start again."

Olivia started her walk down the aisle at a pace that put a smile on the wedding planner's face.

Mrs. Peters flashed a thumbs up and returned to her position near the door. "Much better," she shouted from the rear of the room.

A band tightened around Mitch's chest as Livie walked toward him. Each breath required concentrated effort. Figuratively and literally, this woman from his past took his breath away.

Her long blonde hair had been secured into a twist at the back of her head. As she moved, the glow from the overhead lights sparkled off her hair. Her modest dress highlighted every curve of her body. The sexy swoosh of silk stockings teased him as she neared. He swallowed hard. Mitch's heart got a beat faster with each step she took, until it raced as she stepped beside him.

She smiled and all those years fell away. Six years ago, this wedding could have been for them. He'd tried to forget her. Tried to move on without her. Tried to love another woman. But getting past a love like theirs had proved damned impossible. What an egotistical fool he'd been to decide what was best for her, instead of grabbing the best thing that'd ever happened to him.

Together they turned toward the wedding's chaplain.

Following Mrs. Peters' tutelage, they walked through the gestures of holding hands, handing over the bridal bouquet and retrieving the rings from the maid of honor and best man.

"At this point," the chaplain said, "I'll pronounce Wes and Emily husband and wife and tell him he can kiss his bride."

Mitch turned toward Olivia, smiled and pulled her into his arms. Her hands rested on his chest. Confusion and maybe some trepidation infused her eyes. He dipped his head and brushed a kiss across her lips. When she didn't push away or try to avoid the contact, he kissed her again, taking it deeper, allowing himself the pleasure of touching her, kissing her again. Her lips were hot and soft, and after a brief moment, they parted, allowing his tongue to slide into her warmth.

She tasted like sin and fine whiskey. Past and future.

His whole body grew hard and tight with need for this woman. Not just any woman, but this woman. The love of his youth. The woman he'd once believed to be the love of his life. Was this love relegated to stay in the past or did it have a part in his—no, their—future?

She swayed closer, her hands sliding up and over his shoulders. Warm fingers stroked his neck, then into his hair. She answered his kiss with long, soft strokes of her tongue.

For six years, he'd been a walking, talking zombie. A hollow version of himself, lost in the day-to-day running of his ranch. Living, but not alive. Under her touch, he felt as though he'd awakened after a long sleep. Blood surged his veins. His heart leapt like a deer over a fence.

He grew harder against her soft belly. Desire flamed inside him. Between them. Needing more, he jerked her tight against him, her full breasts flattening against his chest.

Loud whoops and a firm slap on the back broke Mitch from the kiss. He stared into Olivia's dazed eyes, her face flushed, her lips swollen and luscious. Her tongue darted out to lick her upper lip and then she swallowed, her throat lifting and falling with the action.

The chaplain coughed. "Like that, but maybe not as, um, long."

Wes snorted and Emily let out a giggle.

Mitch ran his hands down Olivia's naked, soft, warm arms until he could grasp her hands. Squeezing them once, he stepped back into his role as stand-in groom. He hoped that kiss wasn't a mistake on his part. He hoped she got his message. *Give us a chance, Livie.*

Mrs. Peters clapped her hands. "One more time, people."

OLIVIA DIDN'T NEED TO LOOK OVER HER SHOULDER TO know Mitch watched her walk away. She could feel his gaze on her backside. Forcing herself to stroll up the carpet as though she was kissed mindless on a daily basis, she put a little wiggle in the walk. Maybe she could still make him regret losing her.

Why did she kiss him back? Dumb question. She

knew the answer. Because his kiss could make a nun question her vows.

I cannot let him get under my skin again. Come Sunday, he's gone. Be sensible. Think with your head, not your heart, or rather your raging libido.

Emily met her about halfway up the aisle and they linked arms. "Whew. That was some kiss. I hope my honeymoon is half that hot." Emily fanned her face with a hand. "Are you okay?"

Olivia bumped her hip against Emily's and laughed to hide her own reaction. "I'm fine. Don't worry about me."

The third run-through went the same as the first and second, except for the deep, soul-searing kiss. It was only after everyone swore to Mrs. Peters they knew their places and their roles that she dismissed the wedding party for dinner.

"Wow. What a slave driver," Emily whispered to Olivia. "But she's the best, and since I don't live in Dallas now, I needed someone like her. Thanks for being my feet on the ground here."

Olivia nudged Emily's shoulder. "She was great. Very organized. Tomorrow will go without a hitch. I feel it."

Emily smiled. "It doesn't matter. I'm marrying the love of my life tomorrow. That's all that matters to me."

The love of her life. Did Emily have any idea how incredibly lucky she was? Did she realize how many women would give anything to not only find but to marry the love of their life?

Olivia had once believed Mitch Landry to be the love of her life. But the love of your life doesn't leave you with assurances it's for the best because you're too young to get married. He doesn't walk away because he's not ready for marriage, only to marry another woman a short six months later.

The memory of his phone call to explain his marriage still turned her inside out. His voice had been strained, emotionless, almost clinically cold. She hadn't argued. Hadn't told him why he shouldn't marry Joanna. She'd let him say what he'd needed to say and then she'd hung up. The next day, she'd changed her phone number and tried to get on with her life. Their baby was growing inside her and needed her to be strong. Without Adam, she might have curled into fetal position and died from the pain.

Wes leaned between the two women. "Let's see," he said, "which lady do I have a date with tonight?"

Both women laughed as Emily laced her fingers through his. "Baby, I'm your date for the rest of your life."

He kissed her knuckles. "Lucky me," he said then hurried off with his fiancée for the rehearsal dinner.

Olivia smiled as she watched them, their faces aglow with love. She was happy for her friends, but a twinge of jealousy stabbed her heart. She'd had that kind of love once, or at least thought she had, but she'd let it—him— go without a fight. More than once she wondered if maybe she should have fought for a future with Mitch. Would he have come running if he'd known about Adam? She'd thought about her decision to let him go, knowing she didn't want him to want her because of Adam. She wanted him to want—no, need her.

She sighed. After tomorrow night she'd have to let him go again. Would it be easier this time than it'd been last time? Somehow, she doubted it.

Mitch stepped up beside her, took her fingers and pulled them into the crook of his arm. Trapped between the heat of his palm and the hard muscles of his forearm, her hand burned. She tried to pull away but he tightened his grip to keep her firmly in place.

"You look beautiful," he whispered in her ear. "Thank you for wearing the necklace. Did you put pictures inside?"

The combination of warm breath in her ear and the softness in his voice sent chills rippling down her spine. Everything inside her tightened. Reflexively, she touched the locket then shook her head. "No," she lied. "Never did." She shivered and he gave her hand another light squeeze.

"You okay?"

She nodded, unable to force words past the knot in her throat. *Oh Mitch, if I could tell you everything, would you understand? Would you hate me? Would you have come if I'd called?*

Mitch was her past and she needed to keep reminding herself of that reality. Until today, she'd been positive her love for Mitch had died years ago. As she walked beside him, touching him, smelling him, her heart inflamed with feelings, she feared she was no longer in control of her emotions. Heck, she was pretty sure she was close to out-of-control. And right now, she wasn't sure how she felt about that.

Together she and Mitch followed the rest of the wedding party to the staircase leading down to the hotel's wine cellar. Shoes thumped on thick carpet. Voices filled with laughter and joy echoed off the walls as the wedding party trooped down to an area designed to hold far fewer people than were currently filing in.

Olivia stepped through the door with Mitch close behind, the palm of his hand scorching her lower back through the silk of her dress. Her heart throbbed painfully in her throat. How could she possibly swallow food around the boulder resting there?

She stepped forward, trying to put some distance between them, but he moved swiftly, matching her step for step, staying close, continuing to touch her.

She glanced at the single, round table set with fresh flowers, candles and seventeen place settings of fine china. Seventeen chairs crowded around a table meant for fifteen. Flickering flames from the candles tossed dancing shadows along the walls and on the ceiling. All in all, an incredibly romantic setting with extremely cozy seating.

A setting she did not feel safe sharing with Mitch Landry.

Too close.

Too intimate.

Too painful.

Before she could escape to the far side of the table away from him, Mitch pulled back a chair. He tipped his head toward the table and said, "I believe we're supposed to sit here."

Olivia looked at the china then noticed the place card with *Ms. Olivia Montgomery Gentry* mocking her from above the plate. Her gaze slid to the right. Mr. Mitch Landry.

What she said was, "Oh, okay."

What she meant was *damn it.*

She sat and Mitch took the chair next to hers. She scooted to the left. He followed. His thick, muscular thigh pressed against hers. She pulled her legs together and broke contact, but not for long. Within seconds, he was pressed against her again.

She didn't need the heat from his leg to remind her he sat beside her. His unique spicy cologne filled her nose. The taste of him remained on her lips, in her mouth. Her back still burned from the branding of his palm. Her fingertips stung from his touch. Her body was on fire. Her nerves were arcing like a clipped electrical wire.

Hotel staff poured champagne into the flutes on the table. She didn't need any champagne tonight. She was already drunk on Mitch Landry.

The food must have been good. The Grayson staff was known for excellent cuisine, but one would never know from her plate. She barely touched her steak or the vegetables, or even the turtle cheesecake, her absolute favorite dessert. Mostly, she moved the food from one side of the plate to the other. The food she did put in her mouth tasted like Mitch's tongue. Every aroma smelled like Mitch, dark and sexy.

She was in heaven…and hell.

Mitch slid his chair back and stood. He rapped his water glass for attention then rested his hand on the back of Olivia's chair. His fingertips brushed the nape of her neck. She pressed her thighs together as arousal dampened her panties. She glanced down, wondering if anyone besides her could see the material of her dress moving with the pounding of her heart or the arteries in her neck pulsing rapidly at the simple brush of his fingers.

Mitch cleared his throat. "Wes. I was with you the night you met Emily. At the end of the evening you said, 'Mitch, I'm going to marry that woman'. I thought you were just drunk."

Everyone laughed and Wes said, "I was."

Mitch smiled. "But obviously not too drunk to recognize the only woman who could live with you the rest of your life." He lifted his champagne glass. "Many years of love and happiness. Cheers."

"Cheers," the group repeated and drained their glasses.

Flutes were refilled and the toasts continued, each toast a little more bawdy than the last as the collection of empty champagne bottles grew.

By the end of the third round of toasts, Mr. Benton, Wes's father, stood. "The night is young, but Wes's mother and I are not. Eat, drink, have fun, but don't be late for the wedding."

Both sets of parents along with the chaplain said their goodbyes and left the immediate wedding party sitting in the wine cellar with six more bottles of Cristal Champagne. After downing two more bottles and one final round of toasts, the party broke up.

Olivia breathed a sigh of relief. She'd done it. Made it through the evening without making a blathering fool of herself. One night down. One day and night to go. She might make it yet without melting into a puddle of sexual frustration at Mitch's feet.

A reluctance to leave offset her relief the evening was over. Part of her—the part she considered to be her sane side—demanded she rush to the safety of her home. A larger part—the bubbling cauldron of sexual frustration —wanted desperately to stay close to Mitch. This weekend would be the last time she'd see him for a long time, maybe forever.

She wasn't ready to let go. Not yet. Just a few more minutes. There was nothing demanding her attention at home. Adam was well cared for, spending the night with her assistant manager, Nancy and her husband, so she didn't have to pick him up.

The two factions battled inside her brain like a tennis match.

Mitch grabbed Olivia's hand. "Can you stay a while?" His voice was deep and seductive, sending wave after wave of heat pulsing through her body.

She pursed her lips. "I really should be going." She heard the equivocation in her voice and wondered if he'd heard it too.

"C'mon up to my room. Let's talk. It's been too long since we've had any private time." He squeezed her hand. "Besides, it's still early."

Talk? About what? She hesitated. Was he finally going to apologize for ripping her heart out and running a herd of cattle over it? That'd be nice, almost as good as falling at her feet and begging her forgiveness.

Her mind hiccupped. Adam? Adam couldn't be the subject of their conversation. He didn't know anything about her son—at least he'd better not. Everyone who knew had sworn to keep the boy a secret from Mitch, and she planned to keep it that way. Plus, he was a little too calm for someone who'd had a bombshell dropped on him.

When she hesitated, he said, "I don't bite." He flashed her one of his patented smiles designed to weaken any woman's defenses.

"Yes, you do," she retorted.

He grinned. "Yeah, but you liked it." His face grew serious. "Stay. Just for a while. I'd like to catch up. I've missed you, Livie."

She tried to stir the embers of pain and anger she'd suffered when he'd left her. Tried to stoke the fires of hate to propel her out the door. Nothing worked. Sexual desire overrode the dissenting voice in her head. She didn't want to go. It was that simple…and maybe that complicated.

In a couple of days he'd go back to the Lazy L ranch and her life would continue here in Dallas. Separate lives. A huge swatch of Texas dividing them. Tonight was her chance to be with him, touch him, get passed the emotion that held her heart in a death grip.

She nodded. "Okay. Just for a little while."

"Great." Mitch placed a quick kiss on her knuckles before letting go to lift two unopened champagne bottles. "Hate to let these go to waste."

"Criminal," she said, picking up two clean flutes off the tray.

His plush suite was huge, almost as large as her entire house. Her heels sank into thick flesh-toned carpet.

Mitch slipped off his jacket and tossed it casually on the back of a chair. He'd loosened the knot in his tie but left it hanging around his neck. "Want me to open a bottle?"

She glanced at him then to a pair of French doors. "Sure," she said and headed across the room to the double doors. She opened one and walked out onto a private balcony. Fresh floral scents wafted up from a rose garden below. She drew in a deep breath, enjoying the bouquet.

Leaning her hip against the railing, she looked up at the stars. They twinkled more than usual tonight. Everything around Mitch appeared brighter, better, tastier. Would being with him everyday be like that, or was it only now and only tonight? Was his life always this easy, this charmed?

Her life started at four every morning, and sometimes she didn't get to bed before eleven. In between was filled with sweaty workouts, financial demands and a five-year-old son who needed her as much as her business did. She hadn't had a date or a night out with friends in months.

Was his life similar? Early mornings, hard work all day, then a late night after taking care of all the ranch business?

She thought about his ex-wife. She'd never been able to see Joanna St. Claire as a rancher's wife, at least not a working rancher's wife.

Mitch had jokingly referred to his brother, James, as the gentleman rancher, because his brother had loved the idea of ranching, but not the actual dirt and grime that went with it. James had had the business aspect of ranching down to an art, keeping the cattle breeding records, maintaining the financial records, the social glad-handing with bankers. His boots had been expensive and rarely scuffed.

Mitch, on the other hand, loved the daily ranching grind. Loved getting his hands dirty and his jeans dirtier. She'd seen his boots on many trips to the Lazy L Ranch. They were sturdy, scuffed and usually muddy.

A socialite like Joanna St. Claire would have fit into James's gentleman-rancher world like a hand in a glove. Joanna living and thriving in the bloody, muddy world of real ranching seemed out of character for the sorority sister Olivia had known in college.

The pop of a champagne cork caused her to turn toward the living room. Mitch poured the bubbly wine into two glasses. As he started across the room toward her, he reminded her of a mountain lion tracking a new born calf—gleaming predatory eyes, a lean body with muscles bunching and releasing as he walked toward her. Unlike the mountain lion's prey, maybe she didn't mind all that much being caught tonight.

Her heart throbbed in her throat as he neared. Heaven help her, she wanted him now as much as she had years ago.

Mitch joined her on the balcony and passed her a champagne flute. A slight tremor shook her fingers as she grasped the stem.

"It's beautiful out here," she said, biding time. Time to get her raging desire under control. Time to remind herself that *if* anything happened tonight, it would be a one-time deal. Mitch was her past, not her future.

No matter what her mind said, her heart heard only blah blah blah and ignored it.

"Yeah," he said, but his gaze never left her face. "Beautiful." He leaned his hip on the railing next to her. A cougar settling in for the kill.

Olivia's cheeks burned under his constant stare. The fervor of his gaze melted her last ounce of resistance. She took a sip of champagne and hiccupped.

He laughed softly. "I remember how much you loved champagne. You used to giggle when the bubbles tickled your nose as you drank." The tan lines on his face deepened when he smiled. "You had the sexiest laugh. Used to drive me nuts."

Her bones liquefied beneath his smoldering look and words. The region between her thighs ached with desire. Her breasts throbbed with longing to be touched, stroked, sucked.

Oh Lord, she wanted him, more than she'd wanted anything in a long time. She'd cared deeply for her ex-husband, but never, in all their lovemaking, had Drake brought her to this point with a mere look and a few words.

Why couldn't she have Mitch, if only for tonight? Yes, probably not the best idea, but as long as she went in with her eyes open she could be the one who walked away. With more than four hundred miles of vast Texas landscape separating them, there'd be no weekend quickies in their future. No dates. No reconciliation. No future.

Eyes open. Reality realized.

No reason to bring up Adam, or Mitch's marriage, or anything else that might put a damper on their short time together.

"To old and dear friends," she said, clinking her glass against his.

"To lovers reunited."

She dipped her head in silent agreement.

He drained his glass in one long gulp.

She downed about half her champagne and moved back into the suite's living room. Mitch followed.

"Nice room," she said, slipping from her shoes then digging her toes into the carpet pile. She turned in a full circle, taking in a décor that screamed expensive. She shut her eyes as the walls undulated around her. A low groan escaped her lips. Maybe she'd spun too quickly.

"You all right?"

His deep voice resonated inside her mind. If only she could store his voice in her memories, be able to hear him by shutting her eyes and concentrating. Be able to call on it when she was alone.

"Olivia?"

She opened her memory vault and stuffed in her name spoken in his rough, rumbled voice. She shivered as a bolt of sexual lightning rippled through her.

Nervously she chewed her bottom lip. "I spun too fast. That's all."

"Uh huh. Come on," he said, holding her arm. "Sit down." He pulled her onto the sofa.

Her bottom hit a cushion. She bounced. And giggled.

His deep throated chuckle gave her chills. He refilled their glasses. "What shall we drink to?"

"Friends with benefits?" She was tipsy, but not from the champagne. At most she'd had maybe three or four flutes. Her intoxication came solely from Mitch, his closeness, his touch, his scent.

He smiled and nodded. "Friends with benefits."

She finished her drink then sat the glass on the side table. Resting her head on the back of the sofa, she said, "You look good, Mitch. Really good. Life on the ranch must agree with you."

He snaked his arm under her head and around her shoulders. "It's good…now. The first couple of years were difficult. After James died, everything seemed to land on me at one time. But I missed you terribly."

Years she'd waited to hear him say those words. Years.

And tonight, she wanted to believe him.

Needed to believe him.

Did believe him.

"I missed you too." And to her surprise, she meant it.

The cushions on the sofa shifted as he slid closer. The heat from his chest roasted her skin as he leaned over her. His seductive pull drew her toward him. She had no doubt that she wanted him. But she feared that making love with him would chisel a hole in the wall she'd built around her heart after his betrayal.

Deep inside she knew she should run home, lock her doors and never look back. She should leave now, before it was too late…before he kissed her, because she worried—no, she knew—if he kissed her, she was lost.

Looking deep into his eyes, she met his gaze and held it. God help her, but she craved his kiss, his touch.

The sapphire blue of his irises deepened as his desire flared. She licked her lips. Lost her ability to think logically, to remember all the reasons making love with Mitch was a bad idea. She swallowed and fought her emotional panic as nervous quivers strummed in her gut. Once again, she licked her lips, preparing herself for a kiss she knew would come. A kiss she simultaneously craved and feared.

Chapter Three

He kissed her and the world stopped revolving. She swayed into him. Ran her fingers into his thick, wavy hair. Stroked his tongue with hers. Tasted the champagne inside of his mouth. Sucked gently on his tongue. Soaked him up like an arid desert in an unexpected rainstorm.

Olivia could have blamed the dim lights, or the romantic setting, or even Mitch's raw animal magnetism for her response to his kiss. Instead, she admitted she wanted this night, this man, his touch, his kiss. All of her fantasies started this way.

Could reality be as good as her imagination?

What would it be like to be with him again? Make love with him again?

There was curiosity, but that wasn't what was driving her response to his kiss. Desire ran rampant through her veins. A soul-deep lust consumed her.

Their love story was history, so she'd waste no time planning a future that would never come. She'd take what he offered, take what she wanted. Here and now, not a future. Tonight was all there was. She'd not walk away from his arms until she'd gotten what she needed.

Mitch's mouth scorched her lips as he took her mouth with a rough passion that left no doubt of his intentions. He pulled the pins holding her chignon and threaded his fingers through her hair, holding her head in place as he plundered her mouth with his tongue.

Returning his kiss with a fervor matching his, she allowed the all-consuming yearning to fill her. The desire to touch him, be close to him, make love with him over-whelmed her.

She flattened her hands against his chest. His heat seared through the shirt's material and burned into her flesh. She stroked hard muscles sculpted from years of physical labor. His nipples stiffened to her caress. The soft cotton of his shirt teased the nerve endings in her palms.

He leaned his huge body over her and cupped her breast in his work-roughened hand. He squeezed and flicked her now distended nipple.

Ripples of sexual longing echoed through her. She moaned into his mouth and, arching her back, pressed her breast firmly into his palm, wordlessly begging for more.

Mitch gave her what she wanted, fondling and stroking her breasts until she wanted to rip her clothes off. She groaned, burning with a frantic desperation to feel skin against skin.

Olivia slipped the buttons on his shirt through the holes with ease. She separated the shirt's edges until she could feel the crinkle of his chest hair and the direct hot flesh of his chest beneath her hands.

The tantalizing scent of Mitch filled her nose. She'd probably smelled the same cologne on other men, but the cologne's interaction with Mitch's body chemistry produced a bouquet unlike any other on Earth. She lowered her head to his chest, first kissing then flicking her tongue on his turgid nipple before wrapping her lips around it. His skin was a dichotomy. Sweet and salty. Dangerous and comforting. Past and present.

There'd be no turning back for her now. She'd had a sample of her addiction, and she had to have more.

When she sucked his nipple between her lips, he groaned and slid his hand under the hem of her dress. Her abdominal muscles danced and jerked when his thick fingers touched her inner thigh.

He stroked fingers along the inside of her thigh, the silk of her stockings tickling and enflaming her flesh at the same time. "Your silk stockings drive me wild," he said, nibbling along her chin. "Your skin was always silky and smooth. I love to touch you. I've always loved to touch you. I loved the way you moaned and twisted at my touch. The way your eyes would glaze over when I stroked you." His hand moved higher, stopping at the top of the stocking. "But tonight, I want—no, need—to see you in these stockings. These stockings, my necklace and nothing else." His voice was coarse and guttural and harsh.

Olivia quivered at his words. Emotional fires she'd suppressed since finding out she was pregnant with Adam flared. She'd believed them stomped out and dead. She'd been wrong. She was dry tinder to his lit match.

He stood, took her hand, pulled her to standing.

Her legs were weak and rubbery, threatening to collapse under his relentless assault.

Gazing intensely into her eyes, he said, "I want you. I want to be deep inside you. If you want to stop, say it now, because in a minute I don't think I'll be able to stop."

He waited. Gave her time to say no. Gave her time for rationality to return.

But she didn't want rational thoughts. Didn't want to think about tomorrow, or the next day, or the next. Didn't want to let go of all the sensations surging through her.

She'd made up her mind when she'd unbuttoned the first button on his shirt. For her, there was no going back.

She shook her head. "Don't stop. Please."

He placed both hands on her shoulders and turned her around. Tossing her long hair over her shoulder, he kissed the nape of her neck, giving little nibbles with his teeth and soothing each bite with his lips and tongue. Each kiss, each touch of his tongue made her inside boil with pent-up lust. Her panties were wet with desire.

He unzipped the dress. The silky material slithered down her enflamed body and pooled on the floor. The exposure of her hot body to the air-conditioned room launched shivers down to her toes. Behind her, Olivia heard his sharp intake of breath.

Did he like what he saw? Her body had changed a great deal since they'd last been together. She wasn't twenty-three anymore, not to mention the lasting effect pregnancy and childbirth had on her body.

She hesitated before she glanced over her shoulder, prepared to jerk her dress back if the need arose.

Mitch stepped back, caressing her with his eyes. "My God, Olivia. You are beautiful. Turn around."

Wearing only a black bra, thong, thigh-high stockings and her three-inch heels, she turned, proud her hours of hard work gave her a toned body. But inside, she was still the insecure college girl wanting to impress a guy. She fought the urge to cover herself.

His gaze met hers before raking down her body and back up. His eyes darkened and glittered with desire. His nostrils flared as he studied her.

His reaction was all the encouragement and assurance she needed.

She stepped to him, slid her hands under his shirt, pushed the fabric off his shoulders, let it fall to the floor. She rubbed her hands along his neck, the tense muscles in his shoulders, his upper back, thrilling to the touch of hot sinew under her fingertips. A flesh-covered furnace searing her fingertips with each touch.

Groaning, he pulled her tight against him and took her mouth in a forceful kiss, thrusting his tongue between her lips, filling her mouth with his presence, his taste. Wedging one knee between her legs, he pressed his solid muscular thigh against the stiff bud of her sex. The rough material of his slacks in contrast to her silk stockings sent jolt after jolt of adrenalin singing through her veins.

The juncture between her legs throbbed for relief. She moaned and ground herself against his leg. He grasped her waist, lifted her, held her intimately firm against the hard ridge in his slacks.

He wanted her. Even if he hadn't told her, she'd known. Even if he only wanted her for tonight, then tonight it would be. For the first time in years, she was alive and sexy and desirable.

Jerking her mouth from his, she kissed his neck, using her lips, teeth and tongue to caress his salty skin.

"Wrap your legs around me," he said in a strained voice.

She locked her ankles around his waist and thrust her

aching center against the bulge behind his zipper. They were as physically close as two clothed people could be. His large hands scorched her bottom as he dug his fingers into her flesh, holding her in place, rocking her against him. She groaned at the torture of being close but not close enough. He was driving her insane with desire.

He locked his mouth to hers, carried her across the room and kicked open a door. The door banged against the wall. He laid her on his turned-down bed, the satiny sheet cool to her heated flesh.

"Don't move," he growled. "I want to enjoy the view."

Instead, she rolled to her side and rested her head in her hand. "I don't think so. I think it's time I had a turn looking."

His lips curved into a slow, sexy smile.

"As you demand." He toed off black cowboy boots and kicked them toward a closet door. He unfastened his slacks and pulled the zipper slowly down.

Each click of the zipper notched her heart rate higher.

When he shoved his slacks and underwear to the floor in one move, she sighed and licked her lips in appreciation. Riding horses and herding cattle had done for him what men paid her trainers big bucks to achieve —thick, contoured muscles and rippled cording in all the right places. Her gaze ate up his chest, his taut, flat abdomen, his… She licked her lips again. He was bigger than she remembered.

Her insides quivered with lust and need. "Mitch Landry, I want you." She got to her knees and crawled to the edge of the bed. "Come here."

He grinned. "Yes, ma'am."

Taking his hard arousal in her hand, she slid her cheek from the head to the base, relishing the velvety feel, inhaling his musky scent. Then, wrapping her lips around the head, she took him into her mouth, pulling him deep. Her taste buds exploded with his salty tang. If she had the rest of her life, she didn't believe she could ever get enough of him.

"Oh, God. That feels so good," Mitch grasped out on a low groan. Fingers slid into her hair, pulling the strands taut, holding her head as he drove in and out. Then he was gone.

"Unless you want this over quickly, I can't take any more of that right now."

Olivia smiled. Her tongue darted to lick her lips, savoring his taste.

"My turn," he said as he removed her bra before taking one breast into his mouth. He sucked her full flesh, using his teeth to scrape her rucked nipple, then soothing the scrape with his tongue.

She arched her back in response. Needing more. Demanding more.

"Harder," she commanded. "Suck harder."

He ignored her demand. Instead, he tortured her by moving his mouth to her other breast, tweaking and rolling her stiff nipple between his finger and thumb. Lightning sparks rumbled from the top of her head to the soles of her feet. She whimpered in response to the cool air when his mouth left her breast. The sound seemed to drive him on.

He pressed his lips on her stomach, ran his tongue around her navel before tickling the inside with the tongue's tip.

Her abdominal muscles contracted and quivered in response. The only sound she could hear was the drum-

drum-drum of her heart in her ears. She rested her
hands on his head, stroking fingers through his soft
strands.

Slipping a hand between her damp thighs, he cupped
her, pressing his thumb to the rigid nub of her sex, trig-
gering waves of energy pulsing through her. She gasped
and arched her back in response. His hot breath whispered across the skin of her inner thigh seconds before
his mouth covered her thong. He sucked through the
thong's silk, almost bringing her to climax with his
mouth. She jerked on the bed, clinging to the sheets with
her fists, her nerve endings alive and sparking. He
grabbed her thighs, pushed them wider, held her in place
as he used his mouth to torture her.

Too soon. Too soon. Not yet.

As if he could hear her thoughts, he moved his
mouth from her thong and ran his tongue down the
inside of her thigh until it met the lace elastic of her
stockings. His gaze lifted to hers. "The stockings stay
on," he said, then hooked his fingers at the side straps
of her throng. "These don't. Lift your hips or I'll rip
it off."

She smiled but didn't lift her hips.

He ripped the damp silk and tossed it on the floor.
Raising her foot to his mouth, he kissed the arch, then
her ankle, leaving more sizzling kisses on her silk-encased
calf. He ran both hands under her knees then pulled her
to the edge of the mattress before draping her legs over
his shoulders.

"Mitch," she gasped. "You don't have to…"

"Shh. This for me."

The minute his mouth touched her swollen flesh, she
bucked, digging her heels into his broad shoulders.
Torture. Unbelievably sweet torture as he kissed and

sucked her throbbing center. His tongue traced her rigid nub. His mouth was ravenous on her flesh.

Her ability to think shut down. Basic animal instincts ruled her thoughts, her actions. The satin sheet knotted in her fists as her head rolled from side to side.

And then his mouth was gone, leaving her unfulfilled and wild with lust. Her legs slid down his arms to rest on either side of his hips. One thick finger dipped inside, stroking her swollen walls. A second finger joined the first, thrusting in and out in rapid secession. Olivia's breath was a pant, a groan, then a pant again.

"Mitch, I don't know how much I can take," she said through gritted teeth. "I can't hold back."

"Then don't. I want to watch as you break apart in my arms."

She shut her eyes.

"Don't shut your eyes," he ordered. "Look at me. I want you to know it's me, it's us together again."

The tension inside twisted to an almost painful level. She forced her eyes to open and look at him. He stared at her, a serious expression covering his face.

"Let go," he whispered. "Let go. I'll catch you."

She went over as flashing multi-colored lights danced behind eyelids she couldn't keep open. Wave after electrical wave coursed through her as the climax overtook her.

Limp, she lay spread on the bed, Mitch between her legs, the rough hair of his legs abrading the soft tissue of her inner thighs.

Heat infused her body as Mitch lay on top of her. Hot flesh pressed against hot flesh. She arched into him, wrapping her legs around his thighs.

"God, Livie," he said in a breathy voice, "God, Livie, I need you. I've missed you."

"I'm here, Mitch. Don't make me wait any longer," she said, then kissed his mouth.

He jerked away, wrenched open the drawer of the bedside table and grabbed a small package. His actions were frenzied and hurried as he ripped open the condom and put it on. With one thrust, he plunged deep inside her body.

Olivia gasped. She looked into the face of the man she'd loved all these years. She stared at him, trying to memorize all the curves and angles for when he was gone, and she had no doubt he would leave. She stored his scent, his taste, his touch, his voice.

"Okay?" Mitch's face held the concern his question asked.

She forced her breathing to slow, drawing in deep breaths until she no longer gasped. She blew out one long breath and smiled. "I am now."

He pulled slowly out of her. "No one has ever replaced you...could ever replace you."

Emptiness permeated every cell of her being.

"Nothing has ever felt as good as loving you." He thrust into her. "Nothing." His face hardened as his jaw clenched. "I'm sorry, babe. I can't hold back much longer."

"Then don't. Let go. I'll catch you," she said, repeating his words back to him.

He plunged into her again and again, the sheen from his sweat glimmering on his brow. She met him stroke for stroke, rocking her hips to meet the rhythm he set. He shoved both hands under her bottom, lifted her to meet his thrusts. With each stroke, he hit her swollen sex nub, driving her again higher and higher.

Her fingernails raked his back as she approached the brink again.

In answer to her pleas and moans, his hips pistoned faster and harder, giving her everything she needed. She came again. Ripple after delicious ripple rumbling through her body. In the next instance, he followed, groaning softly in her ear.

He collapsed on top of her. "Give me a minute. I'll move," he gasped into her ear.

She wrapped her arms across his back, soaking in the feel of his weight, storing away memories for the cold years to come. "Don't hurry. You feel good."

And so right. How could they—he—have thrown this away?

COLD AIR BLEW ACROSS MITCH'S FACE AND NAKED chest. He reached for Olivia to pull her close, to steal some of her warmth. His hand came up with only a cold sheet. No Olivia. Opening his eyes, he searched for her, but found only an empty space in his bed.

Certain she wouldn't have left without saying good-bye, he searched his suite until he found her wrapped in his robe on the balcony, staring into the sky. Backlit by the moon, she stood in profile, reminding him of a goddess statue. The perfect jut of her nose. Her sensual lips in a pout. Her breasts, full and luscious, rising and falling with each breath. She took his breath away.

Once he'd loved Olivia with a passion so intense it had scared him. Tonight, as they'd made love, he realized the infinite depth of his feelings, but now he was no longer afraid. With maturity came understanding. A love like theirs didn't come along every day. It was special. Unique. Something to be cherished, not taken for granted. How could he have wasted such a treasure? A youthful mistake, for sure. But he was no longer the naïve boy he'd been.

Would it be possible to find their way to each other again, find the love? He believed—hoped with all his heart—that they could.

Was it too late to start over?

He remembered something his mother had said to him. *It's never too late to love. And never too late to forgive and find happiness.*

At the time, the divorce from Joanna had been fresh and his emotions raw. He'd assumed his mother had been talking about his failed marriage and Joanna's miscarriage. Since he'd been in no mood to accept advice, he'd nodded and replied, "Right, Mom."

Now, looking at Olivia in the silvery moonlight, his heart so engorged with love he could hardly speak, he understood what his mother had been trying to tell him.

"Livie."

She turned toward him. "Mitch."

He held out his hand. "My bed is empty without you. I missed you."

She gave him her hand and a smile that didn't begin to camouflage the sadness in her eyes, a sadness he didn't understand. He pulled her close and kissed her, putting all his feelings into his kiss, his touch. Tonight, actions were safer than words. He wasn't ready to put his feeling into words. This time—unlike the night they'd broken up —he'd choose his words with more care and caution.

Her soft arms twined around his neck. Holding her in his arms felt right, like coming home after a long trip.

Her mouth challenged his for control, kissing, nipping, licking, sucking. He didn't need to hear her words. Her actions conveyed her desire.

He slipped the knot from the robe's belt. Sliding his

hand under the silk to her warm shoulders, he pushed the material off. The robe landed in a heap at her feet. Silvery moonbeams glided across her smooth skin. Forever wouldn't give him enough time to look at her.

He took her hands and placed them on the concrete railing of the baloney. Moving behind her, Mitch pressed his chest against her soft back. "You are so beautiful in the moonlight," he whispered, then kissed her behind her ear. "Spread your legs for me. Take me back inside you."

At his words, Olivia leaned on the railing and parted her legs, arching her bottom toward him. Her sex glistened in the moonlight from her arousal fluids. He kissed her shoulder then ran the tip of his tongue down her back. She moaned on a sigh. He dropped to his knees and drew in a deep breath, inhaling the scent of her essence.

He put his hands on her inner thighs and applied gentle pressure. "Wider."

Her feet slipped farther apart. Using his thumbs, he separated her folds and ran his tongue alongside her sexual center. He filled his mouth with her sweet nectar while his thumb rotated and stroked her clitoris until he felt the muscles of her thighs begin to quiver. This time he was going to make her wait and come with him. When he stopped she wiggled her bottom.

"Don't stop. I'm so close."

He chuckled. "I know, but this time we're going over together."

She turned her head until their eyes met. Her fingers flexed against the hard railing. "Fine, but hurry."

After snatching a condom from the robe's pocket, he quickly sheathed himself and stood. He grabbed her hips and drove deep into her. Her breath left in a gasp then she moaned, moving her hips back to meet him.

"Harder," she said with a groan.

He slammed into her again and again, his balls slapping against her flesh.

"Don't. Leave. Me. Again," he said, each word accentuated with a driving thrust.

She cried out as her muscles squeezed him with her orgasm, milking his own powerful release. He rested his cheek on her back, struggling to catch his breath.

The second time was as emotionally powerful as the first, if not more. Olivia met his demands and made some of her own. This time, when he climaxed, he understood the depth of his love for this woman, how much he wanted Olivia to be a part of his life. How much he needed to be with her, every day, every hour.

Later, as he drifted into a sated sleep, his last thought was he had to convince her that she needed him as much as he needed her.

OLIVIA TOOK ADVANTAGE OF MITCH'S SLEEPING STATE to study the dark, thick eyelashes resting on his cheeks, eyelashes most women would kill for. How unfair was it that men got such incredible lashes while women curled, mascaraed, glued on fake lashes—anything to get the look of the lashes Mitch sported with no effort.

She lightly brushed his hair off his face, tried to store mental photographs of every detail. The telltale pale of his forehead where his cowboy hat rested glistened in the soft moonlight kissing his face. From his nose down, there was a slight tanning where even the best Stetson couldn't block the relentless Texas sun.

A little snore escape his parted lips, making Olivia

grin. She remembered that snore. There were nights when she couldn't sleep and would've given anything to hear his snore beside her, feel the warmth from his hot body, take comfort from him being near. Nothing—nor anyone—had ever dulled the ache for him she carried deep inside.

There wasn't anything she wouldn't have done for him, including giving him up when he'd asked her to. She'd wanted to tell him about the pregnancy, but the timing could not have been worse. Then fate had continued to cause a domino effect of events that kept her from telling him about their baby.

Thinking about her son jerked her guilt front and center again. She slipped from the bed and put Mitch's robe back on. Mitch would have been—hell, could be—the best father in the world, but she couldn't risk Adam's future on it.

She moved quietly from the bedroom into the suite's living room, where she paced and debated and cursed fate. Each time she reached the balcony, she was sure she should tell Mitch everything. By the time she'd walked back to the suite's bar, she was positive she and Adam were doing great without him, or any man. Besides, who knew how he would react to the fact she had a son.

The carpet blurred as tears burned her eyes.

Damn it, Mitch. Joanna might have been a long-time friend, but did you have to be the good guy and step up to the marriage plate with her?

Why blame him, you chicken, she chastised herself. *You could have told him.*

And if she had, even more stress and turmoil would have been heaped onto the chaotic mess that had come with James's death. She couldn't do that to Mitch.

James dead. Joanna pregnant with James's child.

CYNTHIA D'ALBA

Mitch stepping up to marry his childhood friend, Joanna. Doing what he thought his brother would have wanted.

Or at least Joanna had said she was pregnant. No baby had ever been born, and from what Olivia had heard no abdominal baby bulge had ever been noted. Joanna had miscarried the baby early in the second trimester. Remembering her own pregnancy, Olivia realized her pregnancy pooch hadn't become obvious until she was well into her sixth month, so maybe it was possible that Joanna had been pregnant.

Had there ever been a baby, or had the pregnancy been one of Joanna's elaborate schemes to get James to marry her, only to have it backfire when he died? Mitch's mother, Sylvia Landry, had always been convinced of the latter.

Years later, Sylvia had confided to Olivia's mother that if she'd been of sound mind, she never would have let Mitch marry Joanna. But once the deed was done, everyone had tried to make the best of the situation.

Marrying a Landry had been Joanna's goal. Without James, that left her good friend Mitch. Maybe Olivia should have spoken up, stopped the marriage, told Mitch everything, forced him to—

Stop it. You made the best decision you could at the time.

"Livie?"

Startled, she stumbled into the coffee table and clasped a hand over her jumping heart. Hastily, she dried her eyes on the arm of the robe and turned toward him. "I think I'd better go."

He went to her and wrapped her in his arms. "What is it, sweetheart?"

For just a moment, she allowed herself to soak in the heat from his arms, allowed herself to feel the joy of being held by him again. Then she forced herself back to reality. "Nothing's wrong. Really." She pushed against his chest.

His touch, so gentle and caring, was a caustic acid to her soul, bubbling all her guilt to the surface. Tonight had been a mistake. She'd been a fool to think she could walk away unscathed.

"Stay the night." He kissed her ear. "I'll make it worth your while," he said with a crooked grin.

She shook her head. "I can't, Mitch. I have to get home."

"Why? Stay."

This time she shoved hard enough to force him to take a step back. "I really have to go," she repeated, her voice coarse with unshed tears. She had to get out of there, and fast.

She untied the robe, letting it glide down her arms onto the floor. Wearing only her locket, she snatched her dress off the floor and wiggled it up her body. She shoved her feet into the pointed stilettos, her toes howling in protest.

"I'll see you tomorrow," she said, hurrying to the door. "Good night, Mitch."

"Wait." He stalked across the room, his long legs eating up the distance between them. Slamming his palm on the door, he held it closed. "You want to tell me what is going on here? Tonight was incredible. We connected as though we'd been apart for a day, not years. Don't tell me you didn't feel it too. Now you're charging out of here like the hotel's on fire. What happened? What'd I do wrong?"

All of her strong bravado momentarily faltered. Her shoulders sagged. The air rushed from her lungs on a sigh. Recapturing her resolve, she stiffened upright. "It was wonderful. You were wonderful. Tonight was wonderful. Can't we just leave it at that?" *Let me go, please.*

"No, damn it, we can't. Tell me what's going on."

She lifted one shoulder in a casual shrug, an indifference she didn't feel. "Nothing's going on." She cupped his face in her hands. His prickly whiskers stabbed into her palms. She stood for a moment, enjoyed the feeling of holding his unshaven face before she sighed and swallowed the gallon of tears threatening to overflow at any minute. "Let me go. Please. Don't make this harder than it already is."

Please, please push me out the door. Please don't be nice. Please don't ask me to stay again. I only have so much strength.

She leaned forward and kissed him and let her hands slid from his face. He caught one hand and brought it to his mouth, placing a kiss in her palm, branded her as sure as any of his cattle.

"Stay with me tomorrow night. Bring a change of clothes. I want to spend as much time with you as I can."

Her mouth drew into a grim line. "I'll try."

He captured her face between his hands and kissed her. "Tomorrow night."

OLIVIA RACED HOME THROUGH QUIET EARLY MORNING Dallas streets. The stoplight in the intersection turned red and she braked. Argh. Why waste electricity to stop her at a red light when there was no traffic.

Frustrated and furious with herself, she banged her fist on her steering wheel. She was a fool. An idiot. When she ran out of creative ways to describe the lunacy of her actions, she flipped on the radio, praying the music could shut up her internal voice. After one chorus of "I'll

Always Love You", she flipped it back off and hit the gas. That was no help at all.

Stupid. She'd thought she could handle sex with Mitch. Truly believed she could get him out of her system. That a little fling couldn't hurt either of them.

Ha!

Streetlights glistened in rainbow colors when viewed through her tears.

What a sad joke she'd played on herself. Not only had tonight not dampened her feelings for Mitch, now they were as deep and solid as oak-tree roots. She'd never be over him.

But being with him wasn't an option either. She'd accepted a life without Mitch years ago.

They'd each made life-changing decisions in difficult situations. He'd never forgive her for the decision she'd felt forced upon her by circumstances outside her control. Sometimes she wondered if she could ever forgive him for making the decisions that had altered the course of her life and their son's.

She swiped at her damp cheeks with the back of her hand. If he learned about Adam… Well, she didn't think she could bear his disappointment in her…and worse, the hatred in his eyes she was sure would be there. Would he love Adam enough to want to raise him, or would Mitch hate her enough to try to take Adam from her?

It didn't matter. No one, not even Adam's father, would ever come between her and her son.

Chapter Four

Not every woman could pull off wearing a dress the color of a bruised face after a good bar fight. Olivia could and had. The strands of her blonde hair shimmered under the lights. Her eyes sparkled as reception guests made toast after toast to the newlyweds. Some women secretly resented when friends got married, jealous the friend had found love when they hadn't. Olivia's face displayed only genuine joy for her friends.

Mitch hadn't had an opportunity to talk to her before the wedding, but when she'd started down the aisle during the procession, his heart had pounded against his chest like a bull trying to get to a heifer. Her gaze had captured his the minute she'd started her walk and never let go. He could have looked away, broken off the connection, but he didn't. The closer she came, the tighter the knot in his gut had clenched until he wondered if his face reflected the pain. God, she was beautiful. While she might not admit it aloud, her actions told him everything he needed to know. She wanted him as much as he desired her.

Mitch would have sworn he didn't have a jealous bone in his body. However, as Olivia made her way through the reception crowd, greeted and hugged individual guests, he had to resist the urge to rush over, wrap his arm around her shoulder and claim her as his own.

He drained a flute of champagne and exchanged it for a fresh glass from a passing waiter.

"You want to tell me why you're glaring at the maid of honor," Tony, one of the other groomsmen, asked.

"I'm not."

Tony chuckled. "Bullshit. You haven't taken your eyes off her since she walked into the rehearsal last night. And what was with that rehearsal kiss? Wes suggested someone throw a bucket of water on the two of you."

Mitch arched one eyebrow. "Someone needed to show Wes how to do it."

Tony hooted. "She's one hell of a woman, isn't she?"

"Emily? Yes, she is. Wes is one lucky bastard."

Tony playfully slugged Mitch's arm. "Not Emily, but yeah, she's great too. Olivia. Wes's been trying to fix us up for the last month or so. Wanted me to escort her for the wedding, but I'd already asked someone. That's going nowhere, so…" He shrugged, snatched a champagne flute off a passing tray and downed it in one long gulp. "I think I'll give Olivia a call next week."

Both men looked at the woman under discussion. She stood with the other bride's attendants holding up flutes in a salute for the photographer. The sweet smile she'd worn during the wedding was gone, replaced with a broad and wide grin that lit up her face. She threw her head back in a laugh and the sound carried across the large reception hall.

Mitch sat his glass on the nearest table and looked at Tony. "No, I don't think you'll be calling her next week."

Tony laughed. "Man, you're hundreds of miles away. Me? I'm right here in Dallas. Which one of us stands the best chance of seeing Olivia next weekend?"

Mitch walked off with Tony's laughter still ringing in his ears.

"Mitch." A large woman dressed in blue grabbed his arm. "I'm Teresa Miller, Emily's mother."

Mitch shook the hand she offered. "Yes, I know, Dr. Miller. It was a lovely wedding."

He took a step back to move on, but Dr. Miller insisted on regaling him with stories of growing up on a cattle ranch in Wyoming, delaying him long enough for Tony to make his move. By the time Mitch could politely excuse himself from the woman's clutches, he found Olivia on the dance floor in Tony's arms. Mitch's hands rolled into fists of annoyance as Tony swept Olivia around the room in a grand gesture, then dipped her low to the floor, his mouth mere inches from hers. The edges of Mitch's vision reddened with rage. He snatched a flute of champagne off the tray of a passing waiter and downed it in one gulp. The cold liquid did nothing to cool him.

After that dance, every attempt to locate Olivia met with failure and a growing frustration. Either she was on the dance floor in the arms of another man, or another wedding guest intercepted him and wanted to talk.

Reining in his impatient nature—and his jealousy— he talked and smiled and drank, all the while keeping Olivia within his sights. Whether she was in his immediate area or not, she was planted firmly with one goal in his mind. He wanted her back in his bed, the sooner the better.

As music faded from one song and the DJ transitioned into the next, he spotted Olivia making a hasty retreat from her dance partner. When she headed for the bar, Mitch decided he'd had his fill of champagne and followed in her wake.

"I'll have a beer," he said to the bartender. "Whatever you've got in a bottle will be fine."

"Good thing you're not driving tonight," Olivia said, rolling a cold bottle of water over the back of her neck.

Mitch turned toward her and arched an eyebrow. "And why is that?"

Olivia intercepted the hand-off of the beer from the bartender. "I'm not sure mixing champagne and beer is a wise idea. However, I've been too busy to drink. I'm parched. This looks wonderful. Mind?" She took a long swallow from the dewy bottle and sighed. "Just what I needed." She fanned her face with her hand and added, "All the dancing, you know."

He took the bottle from her and set it on the bar. "I know. I saw you. Surely you saved one dance for me?"

She hesitated.

The first notes of Tim McGraw and Faith Hill's "Let's Make Love" drifted from the speakers.

As the music filled the room, he smiled and held out his hand. "They're playing our song."

She hesitated a moment longer, then returned his smile with one that rocked him to his toes.

His blood thickened, forcing his heart to pump the molten lava through his veins.

"Okay," she said with sigh. "But only one dance. These shoes are killing my feet." She took the hand he'd offered and led them onto the dance floor.

"Darlin', feel free to take them off…or anything else for that matter."

She chuckled then pressed her body against his, draping her arms around his neck. Her luscious breasts flattened against his chest. As though sharing one mind, their breathing became synchronized. He looked down into her face, trying unsuccessfully to see into her mind through her eyes.

He momentarily hesitated. The daily ranch work had left the palms of his hands rough and dry. Would that matter to her? Would his palms snag the soft material of her dress?

She held his gaze and smiled. "Dancing works better when we both hold on."

The corners of his mouth twitched with laughter. He'd missed this woman. He just hadn't realized how much until this weekend. He wrapped her snugly in his arms and pressed her tight against him, or at least as tight as two people could be in public while still clothed.

Every cell of his body was aflame with desire. The soft silk of her dress allowed his roughened palms to slide smoothly to the small dip in her lower back. He grew hard against her abdomen. Their bodies fit like two pieces of a jigsaw puzzle.

They swayed to the music, seemingly unaware of anyone or anything else around them.

She licked her lower lip, pulling it between her teeth.

He growled deep in his throat. Angling his head, he kissed her. When she sighed, he drew her breath into his mouth. Her breath was his breath of life. He needed her. He knew that.

Her beer-flavored kiss made him long for privacy and a soft bed. The shiver of her body assured him she'd been as affected as he by this simple kiss.

The song came to an end. He held her long after the final notes faded. Everything about being with Olivia again fit like puzzle pieces. What had been fragments of a picture was now a fully formed vision of what they could have together. She filled a hole inside him he hadn't been aware existed until this weekend.

"Olivia?" The bride's voice jarred him out of his thoughts.

Olivia startled. Her head snapped toward the voice. "Emily. What's wrong?"

Emily smiled. "Nothing. I wondered if I could talk to you for a minute."

As Olivia stepped from his arms, a rush of cold air filled the space where she'd been. His arms dropped to his side, empty and aching to be around her again.

"Sure." Olivia glanced at Mitch. "Thanks for the dance. In case I don't get a chance to talk to you later, it was good to see you this weekend." She gave him a quick kiss.

Mitch retrieved his beer and watched as the two women linked arms and walked out of the reception. He tipped the bottle to his mouth. If she thought she could escape so easily, she didn't know him at all.

"THE WEDDING WAS BEAUTIFUL, EMILY."

Emily looked over at Olivia. "This is the happiest day of my life. It'd have been impossible to pull off this wedding without all your help."

Olivia lifted one silk-covered shoulder in a shrug. "You're my best friend. You know I'd have done anything to make this day special." She placed her hands on Emily's shoulders. "I've never seen Wes so happy. The look on his face when you walked down the aisle was the look of a man in love. He had the biggest grin. I know you guys will be happy."

Emily turned and hugged her. "Thank you again. When I asked you to be my maid of honor, well, I knew I was asking a lot. I worried that being around Mitch might open up old wounds. It wasn't fair to you. I know that. But I couldn't get married without you. Was it just awful?" Emily's face wrinkled into a mask of concern. "Are you okay?"

"I'm fine." When her answer didn't erase the worry from Emily's face, Olivia added, "It wasn't as much of a problem as I'd feared. Don't worry so much about me. This is your day. When are you and Wes making your grand exit?"

"Now. Before we left, I needed to thank you one more time for all you did to help."

Olivia placed a light kiss on Emily's cheek, cautious to not leave lipstick. "You've said it, now go. Enjoy Hawaii."

With a final wave, Emily hurried to her new husband, leaving Olivia alone and more than a little melancholy. As happy as she was for Emily and Wes, the green-eyed monster tore at her insides.

Emily and Wes faced the thrill of starting a new life together, the comfort in finding a soul mate, the promise of love and honor until death, the confidence this person —this life mate—would always be there for you, come whatever.

Olivia wanted all that too. The love and honor. The wonderful confidence of a husband's love. The lifetime commitment.

Because of her choices, her decisions, Olivia didn't know if she'd ever have that kind of security in a relationship. But Adam was worth any price. She could never regret her decision.

"You should be ashamed of yourself." The familiar deep southern voice whispered in her ear.

She couldn't stop her lips from twisting into a smile. Her pulse beat bass drums in her ears. "Why's that?"

"You outshone the bride today."

Olivia chuckled. "I don't think so, but…"

She turned toward Mitch and mentally sighed at the sight. Tall. Tan. Muscles hard as bricks. A small scar on his chin. Masculine sexuality oozing from every pore. He was too handsome and he knew it.

"Thank you for the compliment."

Mitch leaned against the wall, his hands tucked into the pockets of his tux pants. She let her gaze roam from his black cowboy boots to his dark blue eyes, storing his deliciousness in her memory file cabinet. She lifted an eyebrow and whistled. "You should wear a tux every day."

He laughed. "A little overdressed for riding the range, but I guess I could amend the dress code. Have a feeling my foreman and cowboys might complain, however." He stepped away from the wall, pulled his hands free and placed them on her shoulders. "You have an overnight bag in your car?"

His light touch bore into her shoulders like a ten-ton weight. Or it could have been her guilt bearing down on her. She shrugged out of his grip. She'd almost lost control of her emotions while they danced, which could have been disastrous. Truth be told, she probably shouldn't have even danced with him, much less kissed him again.

Mistakes. One after another after another. She'd decided on the drive home last night that it'd be better for her to break her own heart by walking away from him than to wait for him to do it by walking away from her. She wasn't sure she'd survive another goodbye from Mitch.

"No. I have to get home. Sorry."

His eyes darkened. The smile dropped off his mouth. "I want you to stay." Used to getting what he wanted when he wanted it, the frown on his face revealed his frustration at being told no. But tonight, that was the answer, like it or not.

She'd promised herself one memorable night with Mitch and she'd had last night to make her memories. Each time they parted, she left a part of her behind. She couldn't keep doing that.

She shook her head. "I can't."

"Can't? Or won't?" He leaned over her, his warm breath touching her face with each word. "I saw the look in your eyes when we kissed. Felt you shiver at my touch. You want me as much as I want you. What are you not telling me? Did you lie to me?"

Her breath hitched. Did he know about Adam? Had someone inadvertently mentioned her son? Mitch could do the math. He'd know, or at least suspect, that Adam could be his son.

"Lie? About what?" Her voice shook.

"Is there another man in your life? Are you still in love with your ex-husband?"

She almost laughed in relief. Another man. Oh yeah, she had another man and he was waiting for her at home...with his babysitter.

Her guilty conscience demanded to be spilled. Her gut roiled in remorse. The day might come when she explained her actions, however, that day was not tonight.

"No, I didn't lie. I'm not seeing anyone. And I told you the truth about Drake. I love him like a friend, but that's all."

"So stay." He gave her shoulders a gentle squeeze. "Last night was—"

"Was what? Incredible? Hell, yeah." She lowered her voice to avoid attracting attention of the other guests. "You want to know you'll always be the best lover I'll ever know? You are. There'll never be another one like you in my life. But I can't stay."

She spun away from him.

Tomorrow he'd be gone.

I can't watch you leave again.

She'd thought—hoped—if she gave herself last night, the memories would be enough to sustain her. Instead, she wanted more, even though she knew how it would end.

A tight band around her chest made each breath a struggle. Unwanted tears burned the back of her eyes. Her throat throbbed with heartache.

"When do you fly home?"

When he stepped up behind her the heat radiating from him blanketed her. She fought the urge to step back closer to him. He didn't even have to touch her to ignite the smoldering embers inside.

His large hand manacled her wrist, his fingers tightening, preventing her from walking away.

"Soon," he said in answer to her question about his leaving. He turned her to face him. "I can't stay. I wish I could stay longer but I have to get back."

She gave a hollow laugh in a vain attempt to cover her resentment at being left again. "Of course you do. Your family needs you. Your cows need you."

The tears that'd been burning at the back of her eyes began to collect in the corners. Opening her eyes wide, she tried to stop the waterworks before they got out of control. "I'm sorry. I'm being rude." She forced a chuckle. "My mother would be appalled."

She swallowed around the lump in her throat and

forced the tears in her eyes to dry. Turning to face the only man she'd ever loved, she held out her hand, praying he'd make this easy. "Goodbye, Mitch Landry. It was great seeing you again. Have a nice life."

Of course the concepts of *easy* and *Mitch Landry* hadn't ever gone together. He stared at her hand as though she'd offered him a dead cat. "So now we exchange handshakes? After last night, you offer me your hand?" He sneered. "I don't think so." Grabbing her extended hand, he jerked her against him. "You know you'd rather have a kiss than a handshake."

The touch of his lips to her mouth ignited internal fireworks. She grasped his shoulders for balance and held on. In answer to the stroke of his tongue along the seam of her lips, she opened her mouth, welcomed him inside. Their tongues met, wrapped around each other. Both tongues twisted and moved, struggling to taste as much as possible.

The kiss was deep and wet and oh-my-God sensual. He pulled her flush against him, growing long and hard against her abdomen. She felt herself growing soft and damp for him, dying to press harder against his arousal. She wanted this...Mitch and her...together...making love.

Stop it.

She had to walk away. If she didn't—and right now —she was afraid she'd beg him to stay. Knowing she had to be convincing, had to make him believe she was done with him, she shoved him away. She wiped her mouth with the back of her hand, a deliberate insult. "I offered my hand, not my mouth."

A cocky, self-assured look flashed across his face. "You didn't mean it. You wanted me last night. You wanted me during our dance. You want me now."

She ground her teeth in frustration. He was right, but that still didn't erase her irritation at his arrogance. "Believe what you want. You always do. Go home. Let me get back to my life. I've finally gotten it where I want it." She forced her feet into motion and made two steps before he grabbed her arm. She jerked to a stop.

"Liar," Mitch growled. "Your life can't be complete. You know we belong together. Didn't last night teach you anything? I was wrong six years ago. I've made mistakes. I know that. But can't you forgive me? Give us another shot? I...I still care about you."

Desperation held her body rigid, while inside her heart broke. Years of tears and regret filled her. She yanked her arm free from his rough hand. "We can't go back, Mitch. Too much time has passed. There are things I've done, things you'd never understand. You'd never forgive me. It's too late."

He frowned. "It's never too late. Come home with me. Give me a month or even two weeks to convince you to give us another try."

"I can't. I'm sorry. You'll always hold a special place in my heart. I'll always love you, Mitch, but I just can't."

Olivia spun around and hurried through the lobby, racing to get to the safety of her car before everyone saw her meltdown. The foyer shimmered through her tear-filled eyes. She wasn't going to make it to the privacy of her car before the waterworks started.

Sprinting across the lobby, her ankle went one way and the rest of her went the other. Through her eyes, everything seemed to all happen in slow motion. The world shifted sideways. She threw out her arms, scrambling to find something to grab, something to stop her fall, but there was nothing around her but air. She hit the hard tile floor with a thud.

THE SOUND OF STAMPEDING CATTLE WAS A WHISPER compared to the pounding in Mitch's head. What could Olivia have possibly done she believed was unforgivable? Nothing was unforgivable, except maybe cattle rustling. You don't take what another man owns.

Damn women. All of them.

He watched Olivia's delectable backside as she dashed from the reception, her pale blonde hair flying behind her, her tight dress hugging the luscious curves of her bottom.

Damn woman.

He started after her. All he needed was two weeks. She said she loved him. Surely she could give them two weeks to rediscover a life together.

He picked up his pace, his long stride quickly covering the distance between them. He planned to intercept her before she could get to her car and lock him out of her life. Six years ago, he'd let go too easily. This time he'd fight for what he wanted.

He made it to the lobby in time to see the heel of her shoe snap. Her ankle twisted in an awkward position. She threw her arms up in the air for balance but there was nothing to stop her fall. He was close enough to hear the thud of her head when it hit the hard marble.

His heart shuttered, skipped a beat, and charged into overdrive.

"Oh God," he shouted. "Olivia."

He joined others from the hotel as they gathered around her.

"Call an ambulance," someone shouted.

"Is she alive?"

"Who is it?"

"Someone with the wedding party."

Mitch ignored the questions, dropping to the floor beside Olivia. Her left ankle was turned in an unnatural angle. He wasn't a doctor, but it looked broken to him. "Don't touch her," he yelled. He gently swept her hair from her face and leaned close. Her eyes were shut, but she was breathing.

"Olivia. Olivia, open your eyes," he demanded.

She groaned and opened one eye. "Shit, that hurt."

He watched the mother of the bride pushed her way through the crowd of milling onlookers. "Move. Move. I'm a doctor. Damn it. Move." She shoved a bellman over. "Make sure an ambulance has been called."

Dr. Miller squatted beside him. "What happened?"

"She's alive," he said. Relief coursed through his veins.

"That's always good news," Dr. Miller snapped. "What happened?"

Heat infused Mitch's face. He wasn't responsible for this, so why did he feel so guilty?

"The heel of her shoe broke," he said, gesturing with a nod toward a spiked heel. "Threw her off balance and she fell." He shuddered. "I heard her head hit the floor."

Olivia groaned again. "I can talk for myself."

The sound of her voice—although weak—made him take a deep breath in relief that she was conscious and alert. But concern still gnawed at his gut. The position of her ankle and knee didn't look normal.

Dr. Miller checked Olivia's head while speaking to her. "Hey, Olivia. It's Teresa Miller."

"Hi, Dr. Miller." Olivia gave a tortured laugh. "Damn high-heel shoes."

Olivia lifted her head off the floor and began to sit up.

"Don't move too much until I get a look at you." Dr. Miller applied gentle pressure to Olivia's shoulders to lower her back to the marble floor. "Good. Where do you hurt?"

"Head. Back. Ankle," Olivia said, flinching with each word.

"Okay. Hold on. An ambulance should be here soon."

"Adam," she said through gritted teeth. "Have to call him."

"I will, as soon as we know what's going on with you."

"Did I break it? My ankle, I mean." Frowning, Olivia shut her eyes again.

"I don't know. Your foot is at an odd angle. It's already starting to swell and turn purple. Maybe, if you're lucky, it's just a bad sprain."

Mitch's lips tightened. Adam again. Olivia was involved with someone…this Adam person. So that's the unforgivable thing she was talking about. She'd lied to him about being involved with someone. Well, that and the fact she'd lied when she said she still loved him.

Women did that…lied about being in love. Women used the phrase "I love you" to justify having sex with a guy. He wondered if that's what Olivia had done…last night and tonight. The thought stabbed like an arrow in his gut.

Mitch stood, looked down at Olivia's ashen face twisted in pain. He couldn't leave her until he knew she'd be okay. Adam or no Adam, he cared for this woman. Whether she still cared about him or not didn't matter. He wouldn't leave her alone when she needed him.

"Okay, Olivia. I'll go with you to the hospital.

Without tests, I can't be sure what you've done to your ankle. Okay?" Dr. Miller patted her shoulder.

"Okay."

Mitch nodded. "Yeah, probably a good idea."

The shrill scream of a siren interrupted whatever else Dr. Miller was going to say. An ambulance wheeled into the drive, stopping directly in front of the door. Two paramedics jumped out, snatching lockboxes of drugs and supplies from the van.

After stabilizing her neck in case of an injury, an inflatable cast was place on the ankle to stabilize it for transport. They started an IV and attached a bag of fluid. Finally, Olivia was loaded into the ambulance.

Mitch grabbed the doctor's arm as she climbed in the ambulance with Olivia. "Which hospital?" He held Olivia's small black clutch in his hand.

"Baylor Medical Center." She reached for Olivia's purse. "There's nothing you can do. I'll make sure she's okay."

He gave a terse nod before the ambulance door slammed in his face.

OH GOD, SHE HURT...EVERYWHERE. SHE OPENED HER eyes then slammed them shut again when one look into the ceiling lights above her drove sharp daggers of pain into her head. Her body rocked as the gurney swayed with the ambulance's movements. Voices carried on conversations around her. A male voice she recognized as one of the EMT's. Then Teresa Miller's voice.

Olivia opened her eyes and groaned. "You think this ambulance is really necessary?"

Teresa smoothed a hand across Olivia's brow. "Yes, I

do. Besides," she leaned closer, "isn't it exciting with the siren going?"

Both women chuckled, followed by a moan from Olivia. "Don't make me laugh. It hurts my head."

"Mitch said he saw you hit your head."

"Mitch?" Her heart raced at the mention of his name. "Is he here?" She frowned and even that small action hurt. "Where are we going, anyway?"

"No, Mitch isn't here in the ambulance. We're headed to Baylor to get you checked out. Mitch said you hit your head pretty hard. Can you see my finger?"

Olivia concentrated on Teresa's finger—no, her two fingers held in a V. "I see a V for victory."

Teresa smiled. "Good. I don't think you've done any permanent damage, but we won't know for sure until I get some tests."

"I need to call my son's babysitter. She's expecting me home."

"As soon as we get to the hospital and get you settled, I'll have someone call her. Okay?"

"Okay." Olivia shut her eyes. The movement of the ambulance was making her nauseous.

All movement came to a sudden stop. If only the rolling nausea would have also.

The rear ambulance doors flew open.

Lord, don't let my ankle be broken.

And please, Lord. Don't let Mitch show up at the hospital.

Chapter Five

"Can't you drive faster?" Mitch snapped. He met the limo driver's eyes in the rearview mirror and saw the man flinch.

"I'll try, sir." The limo whipped around two cars and sped past a third.

"Better," Mitch growled. He looked at his watch. Damn. Olivia's ambulance had pulled out from Grayson Mansion over thirty minutes ago. He leaned forward. "How much further?"

"About five minutes, barring any other delays."

He settled against the seatback and forced himself to relax. Since Dr. Miller went with her, at least Olivia wasn't alone.

Would Olivia have called this Adam person? Would he finally get to meet Adam and see for himself how serious this relationship was? And if she was serious about this guy, why hadn't Adam been with her all weekend? Why had she been with Mitch Friday night? Was Adam the reason she rushed away on Friday? Could it be that Adam was just out of town and not available to be Olivia's date for the wedding?

But he knew Olivia too well to believe she could be with him on Friday night, and at the same time be in a serious relationship with another man. She was not the kind of woman to lead a man on or be dishonest. Whoever Adam was, there was no way Olivia was serious about him other than as a friend.

The limo stopped and the driver stepped out. Not waiting for the driver to come around the car, Mitch flung open the rear door, leapt from the car, tossed what was probably excessive money at the driver, and sprinted into the emergency department.

"Wait for me," he yelled over his shoulder, taking for granted the driver would do as told.

"I'm trying to find Olivia Montgomery Gentry," he said to the clerk at the admissions desk. His gut roiled when he said Gentry. Her marriage—although over—still pissed him off.

"Are you family?"

He narrowed his eyes. "Why? Does that matter?" Assuming it was, he added, "Yes, I'm her fiancé."

The clerk gave a disinterested nod. "Have a seat," she said, pointing to a group of plastic chairs. "I'll find someone to talk to you."

The muscles in his cheeks flexed in agitation. He didn't like not being directed promptly to Olivia.

Instead, he paced like a wild stallion in a corral. He knew arguing with a low-level clerk would do no good. He glanced at the wall clock and marked the time. He didn't wait long before deciding that if someone hadn't come out in five minutes, he was going looking for Olivia himself.

Four minutes later, Dr. Miller walked into the waiting

area, a smile on her face. "They're doing X-rays right now, but I don't think she's got a concussion. She'll have a nasty bump on her head, but she'll be fine."

"Can I see her?" Mitch asked.

"As soon as the tech gets done taking pictures, I'll come get you. Sit down, for heaven sakes. You're making the clerk nervous."

Mitch tapped his foot and huffed. "T'ain't likely," he growled, but did as he was told.

Time moved slower than molasses in December. Mitch paced, sat, watched a cattle report on CNBC, paced a couple of more miles around the waiting room, read a six-month-old Ladies Home Journal before— finally—Dr. Miller came to escort him to Olivia. He checked his watch. He'd been waiting for twenty minutes...the longest twenty minutes of his life.

Olivia was lying in a bed, a white wrinkled hospital sheet covering the lower half of her body. Her face was pale, but seeing her calmed his churning stomach. For the first time in the last hour, his chest eased enough to allow a deep breath. When she'd been on that floor, not speaking, her eyes closed, he'd known beyond a shadow of a doubt the feelings he'd had for her were still there... as strong as ever. He loved her, now and always. What- ever it took, he would win her back. He could fix what- ever had to be fixed.

She opened her eyes. "Mitch. What are you doing here?" Her voice was weak, almost a whisper.

His long stride carried him to her bedside in two steps. "I wanted to make sure you'd be okay."

He reached for her hand but she jerked it out of his reach.

The curtain opened and a tall man dressed in hospital scrubs walked in and smiled at Olivia. "Hello. I'm Dr. Gowen, the orthopedist on call this evening. I have good news and bad news. The good news is your ankle isn't broken. The bad news is your ankle has a pretty bad sprain. Plus the MRI shows a small tear in the meniscus of the knee."

"I tore the cartilage in my knee? Isn't that serious? Do I need surgery?" After years of owning a gym and working with athletes, she knew what a torn cartilage was.

Mitch squeezed her shoulder. She suspected he meant the squeeze to be supportive, but instead she found herself growing irritated...with his uninvited presence and unwanted touch.

She needed to get home and get back to her life...her normal life. A life where it was just Adam and her. Her safe, uncomplicated life.

Dr. Gowen pointed to an anatomical picture on the wall, drawing her attention away from Mitch's presence. "See this area where the round part of your knee meets the indented areas of the shin bone?"

Olivia nodded as Mitch leaned closer to the drawing to study what the doctor was demonstrating.

Dr. Gowen traced his finger along the outer edge of the joint. "Your menisci are the areas of tough cartilage right here and here. When you fell, you twisted your knee and caused a small tear right here." He pointed to the inside of her knee. "It's not bad. I don't think you'll need surgery. We'll keep an eye on it and see how you do, but you'll need to avoid any weight bearing on that leg for a while. Ice, rest, some light pain meds should do the trick. After a couple of days, acetaminophen should take care of the pain. Do you have a pair of crutches?" When she shook her head, he added, "I'll order a set of crutches before you leave today."

"Doctor," Mitch interrupted. "Should she have a private nurse? We can hire one."

Olivia glared at Mitch for a moment then made a deliberate turn of her head away from him. "Ignore him, Dr. Gowen. You were saying?"

Mitch chuckled and squeezed her shoulder again.

She flinched. As much as she'd love to boot Mitch out, she didn't want to make a scene in front of Emily's mother. Dr. Miller had been wonderful to come with her in the ambulance. The last thing Olivia wanted to do was cause her any embarrassment at the hospital where she worked.

"You don't have to have a knee brace but some patients find one helps to stabilize the knee as you recover."

"Get her one," Mitch ordered.

Olivia didn't look at him. She smiled at Dr. Gowen. "Excuse Mitch. Apparently he's easily excitable. Now, the knee brace...what do you think I should do?" Her knee and ankle throbbed in time to the pounding in her head and Mitch was driving her crazy. She was amazed she could speak through her clenched teeth.

Dr. Gowen returned her smile and patted her shoulder. What was it with the men in this room wanting to pat her shoulder?

"I'd advise a knee wrap for a couple of days, three at the most, and a set of crutches. You won't need them for long, maybe a week or two. I'd like to see you back in my office then. If your knee is continuing to give you problems when you walk, we'll consider either using a cane for a couple of more weeks, or maybe scoping the knee.

For now, there's no emergency. Let's give it some time. Okay?"

"Thank you, Doctor," Mitch said. "Is she good to go as soon as we get the crutches and knee brace?"

Dr. Gowen looked at Teresa Miller who'd been standing at the head of the bed. "The bump on her head? That's your department."

Dr. Miller shook her head. "Films look fine. She's oriented and talking. She'll have a nasty knot for a few days and maybe a headache tonight, but she's cleared to leave."

"Excuse me?" Olivia said, her voice laced with exasperation. "I'm still here. You don't need to talk around me."

Dr. Gowen laughed. "Of course. Your fiancé had been so worried."

"My fiancé?" She frowned. "And who—"

"Shh, Livie. No jokes on the doctors. We don't want them to think you've lost your memory from that bump," Mitch said. He leaned over and planted a kiss on her forehead, then looked at the doctor. "I'll make sure she'll have everything she'll need to get better."

"Fine, fine," Dr. Gowen replied. "Once the ankle and knee wraps are in place, I'll send in a nurse with discharge instructions and a prescription for a light pain med you can fill on the way home. You probably only need it for a couple of days. From the description of your fall, you're one lucky lady," he said, stepping to the curtain. "Good luck...to you both."

Dr. Miller hugged her. "Since Mitch's here, I'm going to run along too. I'll have to scold Emily for not sharing the good news about you and Mitch's engagement. Now, don't thank me," she said when Olivia opened her mouth to speak. "I'm glad I was there."

After both doctors had left and Mitch and Olivia were alone, she glared at him. "What are you doing here? And why does everyone think we're engaged? Go home, Mitch. Please."

He shook his head. "I'm not leaving." He cleared his throat, his tan complexion paling. "And everyone believes we're engaged because that's what I told them."

"Why would you do that?" she asked with a gasp.

"Your family lives an hour away. Your best friend's on the way to Hawaii for her honeymoon. I didn't want you to be alone. The admitting clerk wasn't going to let me come back, so…" He shrugged and gave her his never-fail killer smile. "I was a little creative when describing our friendship."

Friendship. She pressed her head into the pillow and shut her eyes. "It's time for you to go home, Mitch."

He leaned close. "I don't have to leave yet. I care about you, Livie. Let me help." His warm breath brushed across her face as he spoke.

I care about you. His words marched through her head. *Maybe you did, Mitch, but not enough. Not enough.*

"You're swept up in all the emotion of the weekend. I'll be fine. Really." Olivia opened her eyes and rolled her head to look at him. The movement sent a sharp pain lancing through her head. She grimaced. "This isn't your problem. I'm not your responsibility. Don't worry about me. You can go home with a clear conscience."

"I am not swept up in the weekend. And of course I'll worry about you. You're all alone. How will you get around?"

Olivia shut her eyes again in frustration. Hard-headed cowboy. "I'm not alone. Good Lord, Mitch. I have friends, family who can come to town. Heck, I can go to my parents' house if I need to. I have lots of options. Besides, I've only bummed up a knee and ankle. It's not like I broke a leg. Get out of here. Go back to your life and let me get back to mine."

"No."

"Damn it. Go away."

"Mrs. Gentry?"

Olivia saw Mitch curled his fingers into fists when the nurse called her Mrs. Gentry.

A pretty young nurse rolled a cart through the curtain. "This is Joe Greeson, our ortho tech," she said with a nod toward the man who followed her into the room. "He'll be showing you how to put on and take off wraps."

"Ma'am," Joe said with a polite nod. "If you have any questions as I go along, just ask."

Olivia nodded and immediately regretted the movement. "Okay."

"And," the nurse continued, "these are the instructions for caring for your ankle." She handed Olivia a piece of paper. "In a nutshell, it says rest, stay off your feet, use the ankle wrap for support and crutches to keep any weight off that ankle until you can bear weight without pain. Also, put an ice pack on it through tonight. It's important to give your leg time to heal. Okay?"

"Got it," Olivia said.

She glanced toward Mitch. He'd moved to the foot of her bed to watch the technician apply the stretchy wrap to her ankle and a thicker beige wrap around her knee. She'd applied a million of these wraps on herself as well as her clients. She probably could have wrapped her own ankle and knee, but moving her head to look down rattled her brains, so she assumed the role of good patient and let the tech do all the work.

Mitch's gaze met hers and held. Suddenly, the room

seemed to be too small, too warm, too claustrophobic. She struggled with each breath, as if she were sucking air through a thin straw. If she was going to pass out from lack of oxygen, was there a better place than a hospital emergency room?

"You're probably going to want to contact your work and let them know you won't be in for a couple of days. Do you have someone to help you?" The nurse's question jerked Olivia's attention away from Mitch and her ability to breathe improved.

"She does," Mitch said, answering for her.

Olivia rolled her eyes, worsening her headache and dizziness. Bad idea. "I've got plenty of help. Maybe more than I want," she said pointedly at Mitch.

The tech finished with the wraps and picked a pair of crutches off the bottom shelf of the rolling cart. "You know how to use these?"

"Yes."

"Okay. Good luck."

The nurse handed Olivia a couple of pain pills followed by a form to sign. "For insurance," she explained.

"Wait here and I'll be back with a wheelchair," the nurse said when the pills had been swallowed and the appropriate papers signed.

And then, too soon, she and Mitch were alone again.

"Mitch, hand me the phone and let me call someone to give me a ride home."

"Don't be ridiculous. I have a limo waiting. I already told you, I'm not leaving you alone to fend for yourself. As soon as I know you have someone to help you, you can kick me out. I don't have to fly home immediately. Besides," he said with a wink and a blinding smile, "I bet all the cute girls have been claimed at the reception anyway."

"Argh. You're as stubborn as one of your bulls. You're giving me a headache."

"So quit making a big deal out of a simple car ride and let's get out of here."

Because the doctors weren't sure of the extent of her injuries when she and Nancy had spoken, Olivia had thought it would be best if Nancy took Adam to her house for the night. Since she didn't have to worry about a meeting between Mitch and Adam, and since she did need a ride home, and since the pain pills had kicked in and sedated her rational mind she said, "A limo, huh?"

"A mile long."

"Is there a bar in the back?"

He chuckled. "Even if there were, no mixing alcohol with those pain pills. Plus, you're already slurring your words. I don't think you need any booze."

She gave a loud, dramatic sigh. "Fine. You can give me a ride home, but only because I'm high and not in my right mind. Oh, and because I've always wanted to ride in a limo like a movie star." She gave the beauty-queen-parade wave.

He laughed. "Fine, Ms. Movie Star. Let's get your movie-star butt into a wheelchair and get out of here. I hate hospitals."

The nurse returned with a wheelchair. After pushing it close to the bed, she and Mitch helped Olivia move from the bed to the chair.

Mitch grabbed the handles. "Thanks. I've got it." He began wheeling Olivia toward the exit. Double glass doors slid open with a whoosh as they approached. As soon as they'd rolled outside, a car engine fired up and a black, stretch limousine pulled up to the curb. The driver jumped out and hurried to the rear door. Swinging it open he said, "Do you need help, sir?"

"I've got it. Thanks."

An orderly engaged the chair's brakes. Olivia rose slowly from the chair, holding on to Mitch's arm for support.

"Easy," he said. "Take it slow."

Olivia gingerly lowered herself onto the leather seat then swung both legs inside. "Ha. Told you I didn't need help."

Mitch's lips twitched, as though suppressing a smile. "So you did."

He handed off the chair to the orderly, closed her door, and walked around to the other side. Olivia saw him hand a piece of paper to the driver before sliding onto the seat next to her.

"What'd you give him?"

"Who?"

"The driver. That piece of paper."

"It's a prescription for your pain killers. Is there a pharmacy you use? We should probably fill it before we get to your house."

"Okay." She rested her head on the back of the seat and shut her eyes.

"Olivia?"

She jumped. "What?"

"You fell asleep. I need to tell the driver where to get your prescription filled. And since I don't have your address, you need to tell me that too."

She lifted her nose in the air. "And whose fault is it that you don't have my address? You never asked for it." At least that's what she thought she said.

He leaned closer. "What did you say?"

"Nothing. My address is 1974 George Avenue. We'll

pass a drug store on the way to my house. Anderson's. Stop there."

After Mitch had passed along the information to the driver, he settled back onto the seat and slipped his arm around Olivia's shoulders. He pushed her head down on his shoulder. "Rest. I'll wake you up when we get to your house."

"I don't need to...sleep."

"Livie. Wake up. We're at your house."

"What?" She lifted her head from his shoulder and squinted through the dark window pane. "Where are we?"

"Your house. You fell asleep."

Straightening up on the seat, she drew in a deep breath. She shoved her hair off her face. "Right. My house."

The driver opened the rear door and she scooted to the edge of the seat, preparing to stand. Woozy from the pain pill, she swayed.

"Wait a minute." Mitch scrambled out the other door and hurried around the car. He stood next to the car door, holding out his hand. "Can I help?"

"No, no. I need to do this myself."

He nodded and pulled back his hand, but remained close.

She put the rubber-tipped ends of the crutches on the street. Then she slowly moved both legs out the door and placed her right foot on the concrete. Using the crutches for balance, she rose slowly out of the car. She gasped in pain and staggered. Mitch caught her and swept her up into his arms, allowing the crutches to crash onto the sidewalk.

Olivia opened her mouth to complain she didn't need him to carry her, but even with the pain medication, her whole leg throbbed. So she shut her mouth, wrapped her arms around his neck, gave herself permission to enjoy the feel of his muscular arms under her knees, his rough fingers pressed into the flesh on her legs. Gave herself permission to enjoy the feeling of security when he pulled her snuggly against his hard chest.

Tonight would be the last time. She flicked her eyes shut, concentrated to store the memory of the width of his shoulders, the way his hair tickled her nose, the aroma that was uniquely Mitch Landry. There'd never been another man for her, and she knew there'd never be another like him in her life.

"Where's your key?" he asked, jarring her out of thoughts.

She unclasped her clutch. "Here."

He took the ring of keys and unlocked her door. Once through, he stepped into her unlit living room and stopped. "Where's your bedroom? Upstairs?"

Even though the question wasn't in any way suggestive, Olivia felt a flutter of sexual awareness. Followed by panic that he might go upstairs.

"No. Not upstairs. Turn left. There are two bedrooms. Mine is on the right." Her thick-tongued voice was slurred and whispery. She cleared her throat. "My bedroom's on the right. Thanks for the ride, Mitch." She sighed. "In the limo." *And in your arms.*

He looked into her eyes for moment, then kissed the tip of her nose. "Anytime. You're a whole lot lighter than those calves I wrestle."

She giggled. "Thanks…I think."

He set her gently on the yellow duvet covering. The satiny material was cool against legs that had been heated in his arms.

"I'll be right back. I'll go get your crutches from the sidewalk and pay the driver."

After he left, Olivia stood, wincing as soon as her left foot barely brushed the floor. Using the bed for support, she hopped around the bed until she could reach her dresser. She transferred support to the solid piece of furniture, standing on one foot while she searched through the top drawer for a pair of pajamas.

"What are you doing?"

The unexpected shout jettisoned adrenaline through her bloodstream. She screamed and lost her balance. She was on her way to the floor for the second time tonight when Mitch snatched her back into his arms.

"I said, what the hell are you doing?" he asked through gritted teeth. "I leave you for one minute and you can't do what the doctors told you?"

She leaned into his chest, her heart racing. "You scared me to death. Don't do that."

He hugged her tight. "I scared you? You don't know what scared is until you see someone you care about hit her head on a marble tile."

Someone you care about… She wanted to believe him. Wished things could be different. Her throat became so clogged with emotion she couldn't find the words to speak.

"Now," he said, placing her back on the bed. "What was so important that you had to get up?"

She pushed her hair off her face. "I was trying to get to my pajamas."

"And that couldn't wait until I got back?"

She sighed. Reality time. "It could, yes. But you won't always be here to get things for me. I have to learn to do for myself without hurting my foot again. And before you say anything, don't. You have to go home to the Lazy L. I know how hard my family worked to keep everything going on our place, so I know you can't be gone long."

He crossed his arms across his chest as a look of determination covered his face. "I have an idea. Why don't you shut up for once and let someone help?"

There was no use swimming upstream. As much as she hated to admit it, she did need a little help right now. Even worse, she didn't want him to leave…not yet. She had some time before Adam came home. Her secret was safe. An hour delay before Mitch left wouldn't affect that one way or the other.

A smile twitched at the corners of her mouth. Flopping back on her pillows, she crossed her arms. "Fine then, slave. Bring me a dozen peeled grapes. You can hand feed them to me."

He chuckled. "I don't know about that. How about some comfortable pajamas instead?"

"That's a good idea too. Top drawer on the left. Look for the blue set."

He opened the drawer and she said a silent prayer of thanks she'd done her laundry before the wedding. Mitch pulled out a short red see-through teddy and turned toward her, holding it up in front of his body.

"What about this?"

She lifted herself on her elbows to see what he'd pulled from the drawer and giggled. "It doesn't do a thing for your figure. And the color's all wrong for you."

He gave an exaggerated sigh, refolded the teddy, and pulled out a blue satin top and matching tap pants. Waggling his eyebrows he whistled. "Not bad, Ms. Livie. Not bad at all. Those are definitely your color."

"Give me those," she said, pretending to be embarrassed.

He tossed the set on the bed. "Lean up and I'll unzip this purple monstrosity."

"It's not purple. It's eggplant."

He rolled his eyes. "Right. Lean forward."

She did, and he unzipped the dress.

"Can you wiggle it up to your waist? Then I can pull it over your head."

This time, she rolled her eyes. "I am not giving you a free peep show."

Grinning, he pulled his wallet from his jacket pocket. "Will a hundred dollars buy me a private show?"

She threw a pillow at him. "Get out of here. I can do this."

He held up his hands in mock surrender. "I'm being all caring and professional here and all I get is criticism."

She yawned. The stress and drugs combined to make it almost impossible to stay awake. "I appreciate all you've done for me. Coming to the hospital. Giving me a ride home. Helping me get settled. But you don't have to stay. I'm home. In bed. Almost in my pajamas. I'll call my mom to drive in from their place. She'll be here within an hour or so. Besides, I think I'll be asleep pretty soon. Now turn around. I want to get out of this eggplant...I mean, dress."

He turned and she wiggled the dress over her head. The satiny material slipped over her head with a quiet swoosh. After unfastening her strapless bra, she tossed both across the room to a chair. Her brand-new thigh-high stockings, with their rips, snags and runs, had been left in a trash can in the emergency room.

"Mitch?"

"Yes?" he answered without turning around.

"I think I made a mistake with my pajama selection." She covered herself with the satin blue top.

He turned. "You want that red teddy now?"

She smiled, too tired and too drugged to laugh. "Ha. Ha. I need a gown. I think I'd be more comfortable."

"Same drawer?"

"Yes, but you'll have to dig a little deeper, near the bottom. I don't wear gowns much."

"For my money," he muttered, "you don't need to wear anything at all."

This time he bypassed the teddies. She suspected he'd seen a few lace bras and thongs, but when he finally pulled something from the drawer, it was her short, white cotton gown.

"This one?" he asked, holding the gown up.

"Perfect."

He tossed the cottony-soft material to her. "Toss me your top and I'll put it back in the drawer."

"Thanks," she said, or rather, slurred. She pitched the pajama top, too exhausted and medicated to care what he might or might not see.

As soon as she had the gown settled around her, thick waves of exhaustion overwhelmed her. Heavy weights pulled at her eyelids, making it almost impossible for her to hold them open any longer.

"Have to sleep."

Mitch pulled the duvet from under her. After her brief time spent on scratchy hospital sheets, she gave a silent thank you for high-thread-count cotton sheets and fabric softener before she settled into her own sheets.

"Remember," she said on a yawn. "You need to leave now." Her eyes now at half-mast, she took one last look at the most handsome man she'd ever seen and wanted to cry…not from the pounding in the head or the throbbing in her leg, but for what might have been.

Chapter Six

M itch slipped a hanger into Olivia's discarded dress and hung it inside her closet. Picking up the picture of a newborn baby off her dresser, he studied the face. The baby looked familiar, but since it was probably a niece or nephew, it wasn't surprising the baby held a resemblance to Olivia. He smiled as he remembered seeing numerous other framed pictures in her darkened living room. She was obviously crazy about the kid. One day, she would be the best mother, and if he had anything to say about it, he'd be the father. All it would take was a little wooing and convincing on his part and she'd be back in his arms where she belonged.

After pulling one of the overstuffed reading chairs to the side of her bed, he sat and studied her face pale against the white pillowcase. Stroking a finger down her soft cheek, he questioned every decision he'd ever made that had excluded this incredible woman from his life.

Could he ever tire of looking at her? He didn't think so.

Would he ever stop loving her? No. Never.

He did love her. He'd loved her six years ago, but he'd been honest when he'd said he wasn't ready for marriage. Every time he remembered their fight, how he'd walked away, he hated himself more. Though everyone was entitled to youthful mistakes, and he'd made a couple of doozies. Leaving Olivia and marrying his late brother's pregnant fiancée topped his list of regrets.

He'd been right. He hadn't been mature enough for marriage…to anyone, especially not to Joanna St. Claire. She was too society-conscious for him. She'd have been the ideal wife for his brother, James, the gentleman rancher. As a working rancher's wife, she struggled.

Strands of Olivia's blonde hair fanned across her pillow. He caught a few in his hand, allowing the silky texture to slip between his fingers.

So many mistakes. So much lost time.

At the time, he'd believed he'd made the right decision when he'd left Olivia in Dallas and encouraged her to date around. He was five years older and a heck of a lot more experienced than Olivia.

He'd worried that her professed love for him was based on his being her first lover, that she was confusing lust for love. The last thing he wanted to do was take her hundreds of miles away from her family to his isolated ranch and have her regret the decision. He'd loved her enough to give her the time she needed to be confident in their love.

Walking away. Mistake number one.

He brushed hair off Olivia's forehead and kissed her. *I'm so sorry.*

Then there was Joanna. Mistake number two.

Joanna and her parents had been like a second family, her house a second home. James, Joanna and he had been the three musketeers growing up—all for one, and one for all. When James died and Joanna told him she was pregnant with James's baby, Mitch did what he hoped James would have wanted and married her. James's child deserved to be born a Landry.

The headrest of the chair caught his head with a soft bounce as he blew out a long sigh of frustration. Joanna had tried to be a good wife. It wasn't her fault the marriage had failed. No, that distinction was all his.

The marriage had failed because he wasn't there for Joanna. He'd even been away in Montana on a cattle-buying trip when she miscarried just barely into her sixth month. Even then, she didn't fault him. For almost four years, she'd tried to be a good and loving wife, but Mitch never loved her the way a man should love his wife…the way he loved Olivia…then and now.

He suspected Joanna never loved him either and tried to make the best of a bad situation. It had always been James for her.

He leaned forward again, his forearms resting on his thighs. Olivia's breaths came slow and regular. Was it too late for them?

Olivia seemed obsessed with someone named Adam. Was her situation with *Adam* serious enough that he'd lost his chance in getting her back?

If he could just get her to come to his ranch for a month—or even a couple of weeks—he believed they could find their way back to each other. Maybe build a life together. Raise a family together. She still loved him. He was sure of it. What he wasn't sure of was what was holding her back? What had she done that she thought so unforgivable?

For half a minute, the thought flittered through his mind that with Olivia knocked out on heavy painkillers, he had the whole house to himself. He could explore, examine the pieces of her life, look for evidence of her involvement with another man.

But a room-by-room search was beneath him. Hell, even the slimy thought was beneath him. He was embarrassed that he'd even had it. He needed Olivia to trust him enough to tell him she'd moved on and was in a new relationship. Rifling through her house while she slept might give him information, but would not endear him to her.

No. Waiting for her to give him more details of her life was important.

One thing he could do while she slept was get his things from Grayson Mansion. The tux he'd worn since this morning had long since passed the expiration point.

He hated the idea of leaving Olivia alone long enough to go to the Grayson, pack his things and return. Knowing her, if she needed something she'd try to use the crutches again and possibly do more damage to her ankle or her knee or both.

One lesson life had taught him was if you were willing to pay, you could usually buy whatever you wanted.

He called Grayson and spoke with a very accommodating night manager. It might be almost midnight, but the staff at the exclusive hotel was happy to pack his luggage and forward it in a cab to his location. One phone call. Problem solved.

Fatigue hit him like a tidal wave. He yawned and checked his watch. It'd be at least an hour before his luggage arrived. Odds were Olivia wouldn't stir for a while and he really needed a shower. He couldn't imagine that she'd mind him borrowing hers.

The bathroom was exactly as he'd expected. Marble

tiled walls. Shiny floors. Spotless mirrors. Olivia's
perfume scenting the air. Fresh towels hung on chrome
bars. Make-up scattered across the counter. Mitch gave
the room a once over and decided he could get used to
sharing his space with Olivia.

The master bath at his house was unnecessarily large
and ornate. Too much so, in his opinion. More than
once, he'd thought the space large enough to accommodate a family of six. The idea of sharing his home—and
bathroom—with Olivia, making babies and building a
large family with her made the corners of his mouth
twitch with a grin.

A sense of right and peace filled him, feelings that
had long been absent from his life. He wouldn't mess it
up this time.

He stripped, then flipped the water to hot in her
shower. Stepping under the spray, he sighed with relief.
The day had been long and stressful after a night of very
little sleep, although he wasn't complaining. Being with
Olivia again was as much as he'd hoped and more than
he expected.

They were meant to be together. Now, he only had to
convince her to leave Adam and come with him, to give
them a chance to rediscover the love they'd shared.

When the water turned cool, he turned it off and
stepped out. Lifting his forearm to his nose, he sniffed.
The shampoo and soap was a little feminine for his taste,
but he smiled with the knowledge that no male grooming
products littered her shower. Obviously Adam didn't
have claim to her bathroom. And if he had anything to
say about it, Adam never would.

He slicked back his hair. Growing out his usual close-
cropped hair for the wedding had been a favor to the
groom. He couldn't wait to get home and see his barber.

After wrapping a dry towel around his waist, he moved back into the bedroom. He'd rest for a minute, then slip back into his tux pants before the taxi arrived with his clothes.

Retaking the chair beside the bed, he leaned over to check on Olivia. She gave a cute little snore. He grinned. Propping his feet on the bed, he leaned back in the chair to await the arrival of his luggage.

The loud dong-dong-dong of the doorbell startled him awake. Springing from his chair, he glanced at Olivia. She cleared her throat, rolled on her side and went back to sleep.

He shoved his legs into his tux pants at the same time calling, "Hold on. Be right there."

Olivia's groan from the bedroom had him checking the time. Three-thirty a.m. Her pain medicine should be wearing off. After tossing his luggage into a corner of her room, he got water and her pills.

"Olivia." He gently shook her shoulder. "Olivia. It's time for your meds."

Her eyes flittered open. "Mitch?"

"Yeah. It's Mitch. Here," he said, holding out the two pills in the palm of his hand. "Take these."

"Why are you still here?"

He touched her hand. "Take these pills."

She took them and washed both tablets down with the water he gave her. She laid her head back on the pillow. "You need to leave. I'm fine by myself. Used to it."

"Uh huh. I hear ya."

In a minute, her soft snore filled the quiet room. He stretched his arms out in front of him then tilted his head side-to-side to loosen the muscles. He wasn't going anywhere without Olivia. Or at least, not without a promise from her to visit him. After removing his tux pants, he slipped into bed beside her.

A DOOR SLAMMED LOUDLY. THE RATTLE OF THE pictures hanging on her walls made Olivia bolt upright in bed. The backside of a warm male body pressed up to hers...a body she'd know even in her sleep.

"Momma?" The voice of a young boy echoed from the living room. "Momma? You up?"

"What the...?" Mitch rolled, facing the direction of the noise.

"Mitch. I can explain. But for now go to my bathroom and put on some clothes. Please. And hurry."

"What—"

She pushed his shoulder, trying to move him out of her bed. Her puny shove had about the same effect as if she'd tried to move a mountain with her bare hands.

"Just go. Now. Please don't argue."

Mitch grumbled as he slipped from her bed, grabbed his luggage and sequestered himself in the bathroom. She breathed a sigh of relief.

Adam darted into the room. Her Adam. The love of her life. All three-foot four-inches of snips and snails and puppy dog tails.

He wore a white T-shirt dotted with spots of chocolate, probably ice cream, and wrinkled khaki cargo shorts decorated with splotches of spaghetti sauce. He was minus shoes.

"Momma. Nancy said you got a boo-boo. Did it bleed? Where is it? Can I see?"

Olivia's heart swelled with pride at the sight of her beloved son. "Come here, sweetheart. Momma is going to be fine. It's just a little boo-boo. Sorry. No blood and gore." She grinned.

Adam giggled.

Olivia lifted the sheet off her legs to display her wrapped ankle and knee. Hanging around the gym, Adam had seen lots of wraps and braces but never on his mother.

His little eyes widened. "Can I touch it?"

She smiled. "Sure, but be careful and don't push too hard."

His small hand barely touched the brown bandage. "Did that hurt?"

His touch didn't hurt, but her entire leg throbbed with every heartbeat.

She forced a smile. "No, not at all." She held out her arms. "Come here. Did you have fun playing with Nancy and Mark last night?"

Adam climbed into her bed and into her arms. His pointy elbows dug into a bruise on her side she didn't even realize she had. She bit her lip to keep from crying out.

Wrapping her arms around her precious child, she kissed the top of his head. "What did y'all do last night?"

He wiggled out of her arms and bounced on the mattress. "We had skettie and ice cream. Then we watched *Cars* and *The Incredibles*."

"Really? Spaghetti and ice cream, huh?" She poked his belly with her finger, getting a laugh and squirm. "I'd have never guessed. Wow, that sounds like quite an evening."

She looked at the young woman who had come with Adam. "Thank you for looking after him. I wasn't expecting to see you two so early."

"Sorry about that, Olivia. Mark got up to open the

gym at five. Adam got up too. I guess he's used to your schedule. Honestly, it took everything to keep him at my place for two hours. He charged through the house before I could grab him."

Olivia chuckled at the description of her son. "I know. Stopping him can be like stopping a runaway locomotive." She kissed the top of Adam's head again, savoring the little boy smell of sweat and youth. "I can't begin to thank you for watching him. Once I knew you'd keep him for the night, I didn't worry about him at all. He wasn't any trouble, was he?" she asked, stroking Adam's dark, wavy hair.

"No more than usual," Nancy replied with a laugh.

Adam pointed toward the corner. "Who's he?"

In her joy at seeing Adam, Olivia had forgotten Mitch.

Dressed in jeans and a button-down shirt, Mitch stood in the corner near the bathroom door. Verbally, he was quiet. However, his clenched face and balled-up fists screamed volumes.

She glanced toward him with arched eyebrows, praying he'd excuse himself and leave without making a scene.

He didn't.

Mentally, she crossed her fingers he hadn't gotten a good look at her son.

He had.

His gaze bounced between her and Adam, his face flushed, his eyes cold and flat. He didn't have to say a word. The wrath in his expression said everything.

MITCH WAS FURIOUS. AND IN SHOCK. WHEN HE'D moved to the corner, he wasn't sure who would be coming through the door. If someone had suggested Olivia's son, he'd have scoffed. To his astonishment, a miniature replica of himself stared back at him from her bed.

Last night, when they'd gotten to her house, he hadn't turned on lights. Instead he'd navigated through the entry hall into the shadowy living room and down to her bedroom with the light from the full moon. Later, he'd kept the room dark so she could rest. Of course he'd noticed the baby pictures, but he'd assumed they were pictures of a nephew. But now…

He was thankful he was leaning on the wall. His legs melted to mud at the sight of her son. He'd ridden bucking horses that'd left him less stunned.

Adam was Olivia's son, not her lover.

His son? Their son?

No, impossible. She'd never have kept their child a secret from him. She wouldn't. She couldn't.

She had.

So what was Friday night all about?

Mitch pushed off the wall and took two long strides to the bed. Holding out his hand he said, "I'm Mitch Landry."

The little boy eyed him critically then placed his small hand inside Mitch's large one. "I'm Adam Montgomery Gentry."

Mitch smiled. It wasn't his son's fault he'd been kept away. "It's nice to meet you, Adam. You should call me —" He hesitated and locked gazes with Olivia's fearstruck eyes. She knew he knew. How could he not? "You can call me Mitch. So Adam, how old are you?"

"I'm five," the boy said, holding up five fingers spread wide apart.

This child's black hair and blue eyes were straight out

of his gene pool. If a picture of five-year-old Mitch were placed side by side with a picture of Adam, he doubted his own mother could tell the difference.

Olivia hugged the boy close to her, as though Mitch would snatch him. The little boy pushed against his mother's chest to sit upright. Olivia flinched, either from fear or pain, and right now, Mitch didn't care which. He was so mad that—

He shoved his anger at the child's mother into another compartment of his mind. Compartmentalizing. It was one of his strengths. "Five. Wow. You're really getting old, huh?"

Adam—his son—nodded.

Mitch smiled through gritted teeth and decided to bide his time until he could speak with Olivia alone. No need to upset the boy…his son.

His son. Oh God. He had a son.

"Mitch is my friend," Olivia explained to Adam. "He helped me get home last night. But he lives far away and has to go home."

Mitch dropped into the overstuffed reading chair he'd pulled next to the bed last night. "No, I don't have to go home right now," he said. Was it only a few hours ago he'd sat in the exact chair and considered a future with Olivia?

"My dad lives far away too," Adam said. "Well, he's kinda my dad and—"

"Mitch doesn't need to hear your life history," Olivia said, tousling Adam's hair.

"Oh, but I'm interested," Mitch said in a tone reserved for horse thieves and cattle rustlers. "Tell me about your *kinda dad*. Where does he live?" The pounding in his head made it almost impossible to hear Adam's reply.

Adam looked at his mother, then back at Mitch. "'Oming."

"Wyoming," Olivia corrected. She smoothed his hair with her fingers. "Remember? Drake is living in Wyoming right now."

Adam huffed. "That's what I said. 'Oming." He looked at Mitch. "I don't have a real daddy, so Drake said he'd be my daddy. But I've got a bunch of uncles."

The muscles in Olivia's face buckled as she gnawed the inside of her cheek.

Mitch's jaw ached from being clenched so long and so hard. No real daddy, his ass. Adam's real daddy lived in south Texas. He rasped in a deep breath and let it out slowly, a trick he'd learned to help keep his anger in check, something he had to do for now.

He glanced toward the young woman who leaned against the doorframe observing the soap opera playing out in front of her. One sandal-covered foot rested on top of the other. "I'm Mitch Laundry." He stood and stretched his hand across the bed.

The girl stepped forward to grasp his hand. "I'm Nancy Luther. My husband and I work at Jim's Gym with Olivia."

"Nice to meet you, Nancy. Thank you for taking such good care of Adam last night. I know how worried Olivia was about him."

Olivia squinted her eyes in a threat and frowned at Mitch.

She didn't scare him. He'd faced down mad bulls and wild horses. He moved his gaze from her to Adam, his son.

Good Lord. *His son.*

He backed up until his legs hit the chair and he sat. False cheer brightened Olivia's face when her gaze moved from him to Adam. "I guess Momma was wrong. Mr. Mitch isn't leaving right now."

"What did the doctor say?" Nancy asked.

He watched in a fog as Olivia told Nancy about the emergency department visit and the doctor's recommendations. His mind continued to reverberate from the shock of realizing he had a son.

I have a son.

"So, that's about it," Olivia said, drawing his attention back to the discussion. "I'll be up and around before you know it." She hugged Adam. "Honey, Momma needs to get some rest. I bet Nancy has some fun things for you to do today. And then tonight we'll go get pancakes for dinner. Chocolate-chip pancakes. Would you like that?"

Adam's bottom lip jutted out in a pout. "I don't wanna go back to Nancy's. I want to stay here and play with my Legos."

"I know, sweetheart, but I'll see you in just a little while."

"No. I'm not going."

Adam twisted out of Olivia's embrace and accidentally bumped her leg. She grimaced. That bump must have hurt, but right now Mitch was too irate to feel sorry about her pain.

Olivia pressed her cheek to Adam's hair. "Nancy will bring you home this afternoon." She looked at the young woman leaning on the doorjamb. "About four? I'm pretty sure he has clean clothes in my office." She poked a finger into Adam's belly, making him laugh. "Make sure he takes a shower too."

"We can do that. Tell you what, big guy," Nancy said to Adam, "let's go down to Jim's Gym. You can ride the bikes and lift weights like your momma does. Then you can help me sweep the whole place. What do you think about that?"

Adam tilted his head to one side as though in deep contemplation of Nancy's suggestion, then he nodded and said, "Okay. Can I have ice cream this afternoon for helping?"

Mitch wanted to smile at Adam's oblivious manipulation of the situation, but he didn't. He was too busy doing the math in his head. Had Olivia known she was pregnant when he left Dallas? Had she known when he'd called to tell her about marrying Joanna? Known and chosen not to tell him?

Conflicting thoughts battled for control of his mind…and his emotions. The overwhelming confusion was too much to allow him the ability to perform anything more complicated than subtract five from six. He noticed his knee was shaking and leaned forward on his elbows, digging them in to quell the movement.

Olivia kissed Adam's cheek. "I think, just for tonight, you can have ice cream after your pancakes."

Pleased he'd gotten what he wanted, Adam slid from the bed. "Okay." Nancy took his hand. "Don't forget about the pancakes."

Olivia smiled. "I won't. Momma loves you."

"Okay," Adam said. "I'm ready to go now," he said to Nancy with a big grin.

"I'll talk to you later today," Olivia said to Nancy. "Thank you again for taking care of him. It's one less thing I have to worry about."

"Sure thing, Olivia. The big guy and me are going to have some fun today. Right, Adam?"

"Right," his little voice said and he began pulling Nancy from the room. "Can I sweep first?"

Olivia smiled and waved as Adam and Nancy left.

Mitch stood and stared in stunned silence at the woman he thought he'd known so well and loved so deeply.

The same woman who'd hid his son from him. Lied to him. Deceived him. Made a fool of him.

"Isn't there something you'd like to tell me, Olivia?"

Chapter Seven

S he laid her head on the pillow and shut her eyes, praying he'd leave. No way she could get that lucky.

"Olivia. You're not asleep. Goddammit, open your eyes." Fury radiated from every word.

She flinched and squeezed her eyes tight. "Go away, Mitch. I need to rest."

"Not in this lifetime, baby."

The mattress dipped and she rocked. His scent and warmth surrounded her. She peeked through slit eyelids. He was braced on his hands, leaning over her. A battalion of shivers racked her body.

"Don't try to tell me that wasn't my child who just walked out of here. Adam is my son."

What could she say? How could she explain? He'd never understand. Heck, he'd probably not believe her anyway. Besides, it was his decision to marry that had changed their lives.

When she didn't respond, he slapped his hands on the mattress. A jolt of fear shot through her. What was she going to do?

"Answer me," Mitch demanded. "I dare you to tell me that Adam isn't my son."

Olivia opened her eyes, but she couldn't find the words to speak. She slipped her hands under her thighs so he couldn't see them shaking.

If only she hadn't fallen. If only she hadn't accepted his ride home. If only she hadn't fallen asleep. If only…if only…

There was no way to change the past. There was only the reality of the present. She struggled again to find the words. She swallowed, but the knot in her throat remained firmly lodged.

Mitch jerked away from her and stood, staring down. The muscles in his cheeks flexed as his jaw tightened. "Damn it. How could you not tell me? How could you keep me from my son?"

She scooted up in bed and crossed her arms. "His name is Gentry, not Landry. Drake Gentry is the only father Adam knows, and don't you forget it. Drake. Not you."

He gave a snort of incredulity. "Surely you're not going to try to bluff your way out of this."

His expression kept changing from anger to disbelief, to disappointment, then back to anger for another cycle. She wasn't sure which bothered her the most, his anger or his disappointment in her.

Turning away from her, he paced around the room while he uttered savage cuss words under his breath. His fingers curled into fists, relaxed, then curled again. Abruptly, he picked up the water glass from last night and smashed it against the far wall. His fingers balled again into fists, then released.

"Did breaking my water glass help?"

He whirled to face her again. "I don't give a rat's ass

who you were married to at the time or whose name you wrote on that birth certificate. That boy is my flesh and blood." When she opened her mouth to reply, he said, "Don't even bother to deny it. You'd just be wasting your breath. He's my fucking clone."

Beneath her thighs, her fingernails dug into her flesh as she infused steel into her backbone and her voice. "You are not going to barge into our lives, throw your weight around and get what you want. It doesn't work that way. Adam is a great kid with a man in his life who loves him."

"In his life?" Mitch scoffed. "He doesn't even live in the same state with this 'incredible man in his life'. God, Olivia. How could you have let some other man claim my child as his own?" He raked his fingers through his hair, tugging on the roots in frustration. "Could you not have found ten minutes to call me and let me know I was going to be a father?"

Heat infused her cheeks, a touch of embarrassment mixed with a pound of resentment. "Let's see, Mitch," she said, venom dripping from every word. "I guess I could have told you when you called to explain that you were marrying your dead brother's fiancée because she was pregnant and you wanted the baby born as a Landry. Telling you then seemed a little tacky. I thought one unplanned pregnancy was enough of a burden on you." She leaned toward him, "But then I guess you could have gotten your younger brother to marry me. You know, keep it all in the family."

He slapped the back of the chair near her bed. She startled, pressing her back into the headboard.

"Damn it, Olivia. That's not funny." He paced away from her. "You should have told me."

He didn't turn around and she wondered if he was

unwilling to look her in the eye, unwilling to acknowledge his culpability in their current situation.

"When?" she yelled in frustration. "When would have been convenient? My God, Mitch, you were marrying someone else. You had already told me that you didn't want to marry me. How do you think that made me feel? Did you ever stop to think about what you were doing to me? Did you ever even think of me at all?"

He turned toward her. Sadness emanated from his eyes. "Of course I thought of you...every damn day." He resumed pacing the room then kicked the dresser before slamming the bathroom door against the wall.

"You have a mighty strange way of showing it. You never called. You never came to see me. Never made any effort at all to get in contact with me. I realize calling me while you were married would have been wrong, but you've been divorced for a while now."

He dropped into the chair furthermost from her bed. "I did call. You changed your phone number. Travis hung up on me when I called him." He exhaled loudly. "I knew when I married Joanna that I'd screwed things up with us. At the time, I thought I'd done the best I could with a bad situation. I figured you hated me. I just didn't know how much."

"I did hate you. Despised you with every cell in my body. For a long time, any time your name was mentioned, I got queasy. But that wasn't healthy for my baby. I didn't want him to grow in such hate. Then I married Drake, and you became my past. Hear what I'm saying...you are the past, Mitch. I want you to stay in my past. Neither Adam or I need you in our lives today."

He held his head in his hands. Strands of black hair hung over his fingers. His voice was eerily calm and quiet as he said, "I can't believe no one told me about Adam.

Especially your brothers, my faithful fraternity brothers. On second thought, why didn't any of them come down to the Lazy L and beat the crap out of me?"

"Travis had to almost chew his arm off to keep from calling you. Mom took Jason's truck keys on the weekend of your wedding and hid the rest. Cash was in Montana in a PBR event. Trust me. You're a dead man to my brothers." Realizing that her fingers no longer shook, she pulled her hands from under her legs and adjusted the sheet. "I'm not surprised Travis hung up on you. He never told me about the call. You have to believe me about that."

"Your marriage. Does what's-his-name think he's the father?"

She shook her head. "His name is Drake Gentry and no, he doesn't. I was five months pregnant with Adam when we married. I told Drake everything. About you. About James. Joanna St. Claire. The pregnancy. Your marriage. Drake gave me the strength and stability I needed in my life. But never, ever doubt that he loves Adam. He does. And Adam loves him. I'd never do anything to come between them. And neither will you."

"So if Drake was such a great guy, why are you divorced?"

She glared at him. "My marriage and my divorce are really none of your business. Same goes with my son." She threw out the bluff and hoped he'd bite and leave. She didn't hold out much hope.

"You can't possibly believe I'd walk away, do you? You're smarter than that, Olivia." He leaned toward her. "*My* child *is* my business. Tell me this though, is my name on the birth certificate?"

She shook her head again. "No. I told you, Adam is a Gentry, not Landry."

He slammed his fist into his hand. "That's so wrong, Olivia. I have a right to know my son and damn it to hell, he has a right to know who his real father is."

She pulled herself into an upright position and faked a confidence she didn't feel. She was exhausted and in pain, but she would not let him see any vulnerability. "It doesn't matter now. What's done's done. It's too late."

"The hell it doesn't matter. That's my child. My flesh and blood. He carries Landry blood in his veins, not Gentry, and you know it."

"Look, Adam and I are doing great. We've done without you for five years. We'll do without you for the rest of our lives. How many times can I say this? We don't need you."

He snorted. "Says the woman lying in a bed supporting a sprained ankle and a knee brace with orders to stay off it for a couple of weeks. How the hell are you going to work and take care of Adam?"

Incensed at his refusal to believe she'd built a life for herself and her son without him, her vision swam in frustration. Her mouth tightened. "You seem to forget, I have friends and family, Mitch. People who care about me. You met Nancy. She's not exactly the babysitter. While it's true she and her husband work for me, they're more than employees. We've been in negotiations for them to become my partners in Jim's Gym. Expand the personal-trainer services. Maybe move to a larger location and grow the services we offer. So my business is well covered. My mother will be here as soon as I call. My brothers would be here in a flash if Adam or I call. These are people who are here for me when I need them. People I can trust to stand by me."

"And you're saying I'm not there for you? What about the last twenty-four hours? And hell, I didn't even know about Adam. How could I have been there for you if I didn't know about my son?"

"My son. Adam is my son. You're not a part of his life. He's a little boy. Your walking into his life and announcing you're his father will just confuse him. He has Drake, his uncles and my father as male role models. They're good to him. Love him. Drake regularly sends him letters and pictures from his digs. Adam knows these men care about him. He doesn't need you screwing up his life like you did mine."

He leaned close, almost nose to nose. She had to make herself not flinch or draw away. His scent filled her nose and threatened to cloud her mind. She fought to ignore the tingle between her thighs. Fought to ignore the attraction still gnawing in her gut.

Damn him.

"Then let me ask you this…what was all that crap you spouted about still loving me? How can you profess to love me and lie to me about my son at the same time?"

"I do love you. You're the father of my child and I'll always love you for that. But I'm not in love with you. Not anymore. That died the night you broke it off with me. It was dead and buried the day you married Joanna."

He stood, his back ramrod straight. "Well, let me tell you something. You may have kept me from being his father for the first five years, but I'm damn well not walking away now. You might want to wrap your mind around the idea that I'm here to stay."

"Good Lord, Mitch. Think about Adam and not yourself for once." Her tone was pleading, and she was. *Please, please don't screw up our lives.* "He's a happy child. He loves me. He loves Drake. He thinks of Drake as his father. We've built a good life here in Dallas. He doesn't need you waltzing into his life messing with his mind. I don't need you either. I learned a long time ago how to not need you."

Mitch raked his hands through his hair then kicked a lightweight trash can, spilling its contents. "I don't care if you need me. My child needs a father…his father. Me. Not some pretend father."

She knotted the sheet in her fists. "And how in the hell do you propose to be his father? Your life is six hours away at the Lazy L. Our lives are in Dallas. Letters? Emails? Christmas and birthday presents? Fly him down for weekends? Don't be a total jerk about this, Mitch," she said on a sigh. "You'll only confuse him. He's too young to understand all this. Can't you wait until he's older? We can figure out what to do then."

She tried to sound reasonable, tried to keep her voice from quivering and alerting him to all the fear and anxiety filling her. Not for one minute did she believe he would just walk away from his child. Her only hope was to delay the inevitable, try to prepare Adam for the news…some day in the future when he was older and could handle it. Only when Adam was older could he understand the reasons behind her decision to not tell his father about him.

"I don't even know his birthday." Containing all his ire had drained every drop of his energy. He dropped back into the chair, his head drooped as his fingers threaded through his hair. "I don't even know my own son's birthday." He glared at her. "And whose fault is that?"

"August," she said in a thin voice. "August fifteen."

He scrubbed his face with his hands. "I will get to know my son, Olivia. You can't keep me from him."

She said nothing for a moment, just kept clenching and unclenching the sheet in her fist. "I wanted to involve you. You didn't want me, didn't love me. You told me in no uncertain terms that you weren't ready for marriage. You were going home and I should start seeing other guys. You left and never looked back. You found someone else. Loved someone else. Why would I have assumed you'd welcome me with a baby in my arms? I'm sure your wife wouldn't have appreciated my arrival on your doorstep with your illegitimate son."

"We'll never know, will we? You made that decision for me and for Joanna."

He spun and paced the room, occasionally pausing to slap a doorframe, or throw his head back and take deep breaths.

She couldn't imagine what he was thinking. He was upset. That much was obvious. She tried to put herself in his shoes, to see the situation from his point of view, but it was so uncomfortable she quickly gave up the exercise. Deep inside, she'd known this day would come. She'd hoped she'd be better prepared. Now she didn't know if that could have been possible.

"Mitch——" she started, but was stopped when he threw a furious look her way.

He flashed his palm toward her like a stop sign. "Don't, Olivia. Don't say another word." His breaths came in heavy huffs and sighs. "I'm almost speechless. You hated me so much that you kept my son from me?" He gave a snort of derision. "I guess I should be thankful you kept him."

"How dare you," she shouted, slapping her palms on the bed. "How dare you begin to suggest I wouldn't keep him? I love Adam. I loved you."

"Love?" He spoke the word with derision then shook

his head. "You don't know what love is. No woman who loved a man would keep his child from him."

Straightening into an upright position, her back rigid against the headboard, she pointed her finger at him. "Let me tell you what love is. Love is being pregnant and not telling the man you adore because you don't want to screw up his life with another woman. Love is making it on your own when all you want to do is crawl in the bed and die. But you can't because you have a screaming baby with colic at two in the morning and you have to open your business in two hours and you've gotten a total of three hours of sleep in the last twenty-four. But all that is okay because you love your baby. You'll do anything for him, even protect him from a man he doesn't know. A man who walked away."

"Damn it, Olivia! I didn't know!"

He paced the room like a caged lion, stopped to slam his hand against the door. In the dresser mirror she saw herself flinch. Their gazes met in the mirror. She hated that he saw that flinch. It made her look weak, and she couldn't afford to show any vulnerability right now. She had to remain strong.

Mitch whipped around and stalked to the edge of her bed. In a voice that was so calm it was frightening, he said, "Here's what's going to happen. I am taking you and Adam to my ranch for your recovery."

No! I can't spend even more time with you. I can't!

"No. I—"

He placed a work-roughened finger against her lips. She shut her eyes and stopped talking. Drawing in a breath, she forcibly calmed her racing heart.

"I said…"

She opened her eyes when he paused and met his gaze.

"I said," he repeated, "I'm taking you two to the Lazy L so I can get to know my son. It's that, or I'll call my lawyers and start child-custody proceedings. I'll do all the required tests to prove Adam is mine, but you and I both know that isn't necessary. So, unlike what you gave me, I'll give you a choice. We can all go to my ranch and play nice, or we can all meet in a courtroom. Let me warn you." He leaned in closer. His eyes were dark and his expression deadly serious. "I don't play fair when there's something I want, and I want my child. I'll use every resource I have to get him. Do you understand? My son will know his father."

She tightened her lips, refusing to be intimidated by his stand or seduced by his presence.

Her head pounded, from her shouting, his shouting, the damn tile floor at Grayson Mansion. Mitch might be rich as Croesus, but financially she could fight him. She had some money in a trust fund her grandparents had bequeathed, but she'd set that aside as a college fund for Adam. Her family had the deep pockets that could be used to fight a custody suit, though a court battle would cost more than money. Adam's parentage would be splashed across the newspapers. Mitch—or more likely his team of high-priced lawyers—would fight dirty, would accuse her of neglect or worse. No matter how stable and wonderful her son was, the lawyers could mess with Adam's mind, destroy his self-confidence.

Adam was her first and only priority. He was her life, the only thing that kept her sane. The only thing that had made her want to live after seeing wedding pictures of Mitch with his new wife, Joanna St. Claire Landry, plastered on every prominent Texas newspaper.

"I have a job, a business to run. I can't run off to

south Texas on a whim, especially for weeks at a time. Be reasonable."

He stood, stared down at her. The ire in his icy blue eyes made her shiver. "You have a small gym and a married couple to help run it. Hell, they want to buy the place. Of course they'll take care of it. I have a sixty-thousand-acre ranch and run thousands of head of cattle. Which one of us can be away from the business longer?"

His expression, which had been hard and impersonal, softened. He sat beside her on the bed and sighed, his back releasing some of its rigidity. "You be reasonable. I can't stay here waiting until you decide it's now acceptable for me to get to know my son. Whether you listed me on his birth certificate or not, I am his father. I have rights."

A tear leaked from her eye, the first of many she feared. So much for remaining strong. She nodded and drew in a deep breath. "I know, Mitch. I do. But Adam is my life. I'll do anything to protect him. I thought giving him Drake's last name was one way to shelter him from being hurt."

"You thought I would hurt him? Joanna would hurt him?"

"I didn't know. You were gone. Someone else's husband. You'd left me behind. Moved on." She laughed and wiped a tear. "I do believe my brothers would have strung you up if I'd have let them."

"Must have been a real kick in the ass to them to see how much Adam looks like me."

She smiled. "Actually, for me it was like having a piece of you with me every day. Some days, it was almost more than I could take."

"I'd have never married Joanna if you'd told me, Olivia. I'd have come to you."

She shook her head. "Maybe, but I didn't want you on those terms. I didn't want you to want me because I was pregnant. I told myself that if you'd loved me, you wouldn't be marrying another woman. I had to make a life without you for my—our—son."

He uttered a foul cuss under his breath. "My marriage wasn't what you think." He shook his head, a dark curl sliding over his brow. She battled the urge to brush it back.

"Well, I'm here now and I'm not going away, not without getting to know my son."

She rubbed her eyes and acknowledged her defeat with a nod.

"I suggest you make whatever management arrangements you need to for Jim's Gym. You and Adam are coming home with me."

She surrendered because not only did he have a valid point, but she couldn't see that he'd left her any options. A custody fight would hurt everyone. She could make Adam believe this was a vacation, some place fun to go. He loved going to his Uncle Travis's ranch, so this would be an exciting trip for him.

Now, if only she could convince herself that learning to live without Mitch after being with him all day, every day, for weeks would be a breeze.

"Mitch, I'll come and bring Adam, but don't tell him you're his father. Not yet. I want him to think we are taking a wonderful trip to visit some new horses. Visiting a new friend. He needs to get to know you."

He nodded. "I'll think about it."

"You do that. In the meantime, it'll take me a couple of days to get everything in order to be gone for while. I need to pack for both of us and that'll be slow. Why don't you go on home and we'll come down in a week or so."

He shook his head. "Not happening, babe. I'm not leaving without Adam."

She noticed that Adam was his priority. Would he even notice if she wasn't there but his son was?

"You don't trust I'll bring Adam to the Lazy L?"

"I don't know, Olivia. Once I would have trusted you to do what you say, but now I just don't know. I want Adam to come home with me."

She sighed, remembering how stubborn he could be. "Unless you're planning on driving my old car for a couple of days to get home, I'll have to get plane tickets, arrange for Nancy or Mark to open and close Jim's Gym every day. There are lots of things I need to do before we can leave."

He shook his head again. "Remember when I said I wasn't leaving immediately after the wedding? I've bought a new plane for the ranch. A company rep is flying it up today for the test flight tomorrow. If everything checks out, I'll take possession. Getting you and Adam to the Lazy L isn't a problem."

He stood and handed her a telephone. "Call whoever you need to get the ball rolling. I want you and Adam packed and ready to fly home by Tuesday at the latest. Tomorrow would be even better. I need to go out for a little while. Can you manage for an hour or so?"

"I've got a bummed up leg, not a broken back. I'll be fine. As I told you last night, I'm used to doing for myself."

He left, then popped his head back around the doorframe. "In case you were wondering, I'm not moving to a hotel. I'll be staying here until we leave."

The door banged as he stormed from her house. Her life, her perfect life, would never be the same. God only knew what the future held.

The house was so quiet she could have heard a feather land on the carpet. No air conditioner cutting on and off. No refrigerator humming. No laughing squeal of a little boy. The only sound was her heart pounding in her ears like a bass drum.

She'd never meant to hurt Mitch, or her son. Guilt ate at the lining of her stomach. At the time, she'd done what she'd thought best for everyone. Okay, no use crying over spilt milk. Done's done and all that.

She lifted the receiver from the phone Mitch had set on her mattress and dialed a familiar number. "Hi, Mom," she said as soon as the phone was answered. "I need a little help here."

Once she'd finished talking to her mother, she called Drake, and then her lawyer.

As Mitch closed Olivia's front door the line, "Honey. I'm home," sprang to mind. With the old Olivia, he'd have yelled that and she'd have thrown herself into his arms. Now he figured she'd throw something at his head. He dropped her car keys on the entry table.

"Hello, Mitchell."

He turned toward the voice, raising his gaze to the top of the stairs.

"Hello, Jackie."

Olivia's mother lifted two suitcases. "Give me hand, will you?"

Mitch met Jackie Montgomery halfway down the

stairs and took both luggage pieces. The weight
suggested they were packed but neither was very heavy.

"Adam's clothes," she explained as they made their
way down the stairs.

Mitch glanced at his watch. Four p.m. "Is he
home yet?"

Jackie shook her head. "Not yet. Olivia asked Nancy
to keep him until I could pick him up. I'm heading over
in a couple of minutes."

Mitch set the luggage by the door. "Where's Olivia?"

"In her room. She was on the phone a couple of
minutes ago. She's probably avoiding me."

Mitch lifted an eyebrow. "Now why would your
daughter be avoiding you, Jackie?"

Jackie leaned against the entry hall table. "Probably
because of what I said. The same thing I'm going to tell
you." She laid her hand on his chest. "Right now, *you* are
not important." She pointed toward Olivia's closed
bedroom door. "*Olivia* is not important." She picked up a
framed picture. "The only person who matters right now
is my grandson. I will not let the two of you tear him
apart." She held up her hand to stop him from speaking.
"I know you feel Olivia was wrong in not telling you
about Adam six years ago when she first discovered she
was pregnant. It was not a decision she came to lightly.
Trust me. She suffered. I suffered with her. She's my
child. I know she's not perfect, but at the time she felt she
was doing the best thing for all concerned."

Mitch scoffed.

"Mitch, try to put yourself in her place. You had just
lost your brother. You'd gotten married and were starting
a new life with someone else."

"That's bull and you know it."

Jackie shook her head. "You hurt her, Mitch. No

doubt about it. She was crushed when you broke off with her and devastated when she heard about your marriage. But I honestly believe she thought she was doing the right thing. That doesn't matter now. It's old news. You two have to find a way to work together, move forward. I'll tell you both the same thing, park your emotions at the door and do what is best for your child." She touched his chest again. "Listen with your heart and—" she bopped the side of his head with her fingertips "—not this hard head."

He smiled for the first time. "Hard head, huh?"

Jackie chuckled. "Between my daughter, three sons and my husband, I know hard heads. Okay, I've gotta scoot and pick up Adam. You and Olivia bring the tension level between you down." She kissed his cheek. "I'm not sorry you found out about Adam. I'm sorry how it happened, but Adam is a great kid. He'll have you in the palm of his hand in no time."

Mitch figured she was right...about everything.

As soon as the front door closed behind Jackie, the door to Olivia's bedroom swung open. She stuck out her head and looked around. "Is she gone?"

"Yep."

"Whew. Only so much mothering I can take in a compressed time period." She hobbled out of the bedroom, her crutches firmly planted under her arms, her injured leg not touching the floor. "You get the lecture?"

"The lecture?"

"Yeah. You know, how *we*—me and you—aren't the important ones here. How we have to get along for Adam. That lecture."

"Got it."

She nodded. "I figured as much." She swung the

crutches forward and moved toward the kitchen. "What time do you want to leave tomorrow?" she tossed over her shoulder. "I see Mom's got Adam ready to go."

"Mid-morning would be good." He followed her to the kitchen. "You packed?"

She shrugged. "Pretty much." She lifted a carafe of coffee from the warmer. "Want a cup?"

He nodded. "Sure, but I can get it." As he neared, scents of soap, minty shampoo and light perfume battled with the aroma of freshly brewed coffee. He inhaled deeply. "Smells good," he said, not positive if he was talking about the coffee, her, or both. "Why don't you grab a barstool and I'll hand you a cup."

"Sounds good." She hobbled to the counter and slid onto a stool.

"You still take it with milk?"

She sighed. "I know I shouldn't…all those extra calories, but yeah. There is creamer in the fridge. Cups are directly above the coffee pot."

He opened the cabinet door, pulled down two large mugs, then pushed the door shut with his elbow. After pouring two coffees, he sat hers down in front of her, then retrieved the cream. He watched as she gave her cup a liberal dose of milk.

Holding out his cup, he said, "Black. The way coffee is supposed to be drunk." He took a sip and his eyes opened wide. "Wow. That's some kind of strong coffee."

Olivia laughed. "I know. Mom's used to making coffee for Dad and the ranch hands, and you know how cowboys like their coffee."

"Hot, black and strong enough to stand without cup support."

She leaned forward and clinked her cup against his. "Exactly."

She tilted her head toward her cup. "That's why I use the cream. Sometimes at their house, I fill my cup with half coffee and half water."

Mitch slipped onto a stool beside her and gathered his thoughts. After a couple of minutes of quiet, he turned toward her. "Why the sudden change? When I left, I was sure you would call your brothers to bring a rope. When I get back, you're almost friendly." His eyes narrowed. "What are you trying to pull?"

She took a sip of coffee. "The next couple of weeks are going to be hard enough without fighting with you the whole time. We've agreed we're not in love. There never will be anything between us again. So, for the sake of my son, I'm doing the best I can to get along with you. That's all that's going on. Okay?"

He stared at her, trying to read the expression on her face. She seemed sincere, but her calm exterior was making him antsy.

"Okay. I've thought a lot about what you said earlier. Regardless of what you think of me, I'd never do anything to hurt a member of my family. I don't want to upset Adam or do anything that could damage my relationship with him before it even has time to begin. I won't say anything to him...not yet. I want him to get to know me. But the day will come when Adam will know everything. I hope he can forgive us both."

She nodded, but said nothing. Her face betrayed nothing.

He narrowed his eyes. "Don't think for one minute that I've forgiven you. I can hold a grudge when someone knees me in the balls and I have to say, you're the queen of ball racking. Right now, I'm not sure how I feel about you."

What a lie. He knew exactly how he felt. He loved

her…and hated her. How could those two emotions be so closely related?

"Same here."

Thank goodness cowboys don't cry, because her words shredded his aching heart. He fought back the only way he knew how…with words as caustic as hers.

"I'm glad you're not in love with me. No, not glad… more like relieved, because I could never have feelings for someone I couldn't trust, and frankly, Olivia, you've shown you are not to be trusted. So no love lost between us. I'll do what I can to make your stay at the Lazy L restful but that's about it."

"You stay out of my way and I'll stay out of yours. Deal?" She held out her hand.

"Deal."

He knew he held her hand a little too long, a little too snug. When she didn't pull it back or struggle to break the hold, he wondered, what if?

Chapter Eight

The front door of Olivia's house banged opened and little feet pounded on the hardwood floor.

"Adam Montgomery Gentry. What did I tell you about running in the house?"

Olivia smiled at the sound of her mother's voice. How many times had she heard her mother saying the same thing to her or one of her brothers?

"Sorry, Mimi. I forgot."

"I doubt it. Olivia. Where are you?"

"In the kitchen, Mom."

Adam flew into the kitchen, ran directly into Mitch's leg and staggered back. "Sorry. Hey. You're still here. I thought Momma said you were leaving."

Mitch reached down and ruffled Adam's hair. "Hey, Adam. Not gone yet."

Jackie Montgomery followed her grandson. "Hello again, Mitchell. You're still here I see."

"Yes, ma'am. Still here."

Jackie lifted one eyebrow. "Did you two get a chance to talk?"

"Yes, Mom. And guess what, Adam?" Olivia leaned over and motioned her son over to her. "Mitch has invited us to go to his ranch for a little vacation. Doesn't that sound like fun?"

Adam's eyes widened. "A ranch? Like Uncle Travis's?" He whirled toward Mitch. "You have horses? And cows? Can I have my own horse? Uncle Travis is going to give me my own horse."

Mitch laughed. "I have lots of horses and cows. Not sure about that *your own horse* thing though."

Olivia gave Adam's bottom a loving swat. "Enough. Uncle Travis did not promise you a horse."

"Did to. Just ask him."

Olivia decided to let the comment pass. Knowing her brother, Travis probably had promised Adam a horse. There wasn't much her brothers wouldn't do for their nephew.

Olivia met her mother's gaze. "Thanks, Mom, for everything. Doesn't a little vacation sound just wonderful?"

"I'm sure you'll both have a great time." Jackie squatted down and held out her arms. "Come here and give your Mimi a hug before I go."

Adam raced into his grandmother's embrace. "Bye, Mimi."

Jackie kissed Adam's cheek. "Be good and mind your mother. Have fun at the ranch."

Adam's head bounced enthusiastically. "Okay."

Jackie stood and blew a fingertip kiss to Olivia. "Be good and mind your mother. Have fun at the ranch."

Olivia chuckled. "Thanks, Mom."

"Mitch, nice to see you again. Tell your mother hello."

"I will, but something tells me you'll be talking to her before I do."

Jackie grinned. "Maybe so." She turned to leave and waved over her shoulder. "Don't get up. I'll see myself out."

In a moment, the sound of a door closing reached the kitchen.

"Are we still having pancakes for dinner?"

Olivia looked down into the upturned face of her son.

"Yeah, Olivia. Are we still having pancakes for dinner?"

She looked up into Mitch's face. His eyes twinkled with mischief.

"Two against one, Momma." Adam danced around. "Pancakes win."

She glanced at the clock. Four-thirty.

"How about we go to The Pancake and Waffle Shoppe for dinner instead of cooking? Be less mess for the kitchen. That's provided Mitch will drive."

"Sure. No problem."

Adam hopped around on one foot. "Oh boy, oh boy."

Olivia pointed up the stairs. "You go change into clean clothes and wash you face and hands before we go."

"Aw, Momma. I'm clean."

"I don't think so. What's that on your shirt?"

Adam pulled the front of his T-shirt out and looked down at the yellow stain. "I don't know."

"My point exactly. Go."

Adam clattered up the stairs.

Olivia glanced back at Mitch. Amusement covered his expression. He looked at her. "He's incredible."

She smiled. "I know. Dad and my brothers have been wonderful with him. Drake too."

Mitch sobered at the mention on Drake's name, his mouth pulling tight. "Don't remind me of all I've missed the first five years of my son's life." He walked to the sink and rinsed his cup. Without turning he said, "It's not that I don't appreciate what your father and brothers have done for Adam, but I'm his father." He turned to look at her. "I want to be his father in every way."

Olivia noticed the glaring omission of Drake's name. "I understand, Mitch. I do. But you can't push this. You—"

The sound of little boy tennis shoes hitting the floor in a jump stopped her.

"We'll finish this later, when we don't have little ears."

Adam hopped into the kitchen. "I'm back. Let's go."

Mitch smiled. Heck, his face glowed with happiness. "All right, partner. But I think we need to give your mom a minute to get ready. Don't you?"

Adam rolled his eyes. "Girls."

She bit her lip to avoid laughing at his dead-on impersonation of her brother Travis.

"SEE THOSE COWS?"

Adam pressed his face against the window in the co-pilot's seat. "All those cows are yours?"

Olivia smiled at the amazement in Adam's voice.

"Mine and my parents."

Adam turned in the seat toward Mitch. "Where are your horses?"

Mitch banked the plane to the left and circled. "See that hill?" He pointed through the cockpit window.

"Which one? There's a bunch of hills."

"Very true."

Mitch had met each question from Adam—and there had been many since leaving Dallas—with a serious response, treating Adam not as a child, but as a peer. Adam's relationship with her dad and brothers had always been close. He'd never been a shy child. But he'd taken to Mitch quickly, more quickly than he'd taken to Mark at Jim's Gym. She wondered if it was because Mitch treated Adam like a friend and not a kid, or if there was some underlying genetic response a boy had to his father. If she only had a nickel for each question, she'd be a very rich woman.

"See the middle hill? The one with four trees?"

"Uh huh."

"Well, over that hill just a ways is where I live. I keep most of my horses closer to the ranch."

Olivia settled back against the seat and glanced around Mitch's new four-seater plane. It still had a new plane smell of fresh leather.

By the time Olivia had gotten all her responsibilities at Jim's Gym delegated and met with her orthopedist about traveling, they hadn't gotten off until Tuesday morning. Mitch had been missing most of Monday checking out the plane, but when he put Adam in the co-pilot's seat and placed a headset over his eyes with *Adam* painted on the left ear pod, she knew where part of his day had been spent. Tuesday morning, she'd overheard Mitch's telephone conversation with someone, at the ranch she'd assumed, telling them to prepare the guest rooms and to expect his guests to be there a month. She'd started to argue that she and Adam were only going for a couple of weeks, but in the end had decided to cross the departure bridge when she got to it. Mitch had helped Olivia into the plane and to get settled, but after that, all his attention had been on Adam.

"Put your hand on that steering wheel in front of you."

Mitch's statement made Olivia bolt up straight. Had she heard that right?

"Like this?" Adam's voice trilled with excitement.

"Yep. Just like that. Now, when I let go, you'll be flying the plane all by yourself."

"Momma! Momma! I'm driving the plane."

Olivia leaned forward into the cockpit area. "I see that."

Adam's smile stretched from ear to ear. His feet didn't come close to the plane's steering pedals, but his feet moved back and forth as though he controlled the pedals with each twitch of a foot. Olivia shifted her gaze to Mitch and saw he had a couple of fingers on the lower edge of the steering wheel out of Adam's sight.

"He's doing a great job, isn't he, *Mom*?" Mitch's jab hit home.

"He is."

"Okay, Adam, turn the wheel toward me so we're turning left."

Adam followed Mitch's instructions and the small, fixed-wing aircraft slowly turned left.

"That was excellent, Adam. You'll be flying all by yourself in no time."

"Hear that, Momma? Mitch said I could fly this plane."

"I heard that, but you probably are going to have to wait until your feet touch the pedals."

Adam looked down at his dangling feet. "Yeah," he said wistfully.

"I'll tell you what, buddy. I'll take back over, but you

can keep your hands on the wheel and practice. What do you think?"

"Okay."

Mitch made a big production moving his hands back onto the wheel and Olivia doubted Adam ever knew that Mitch had really never let go of it.

"Ready to land this bird?"

Adam giggled. "Okay."

ZEB HOBBS, MITCH'S RANCH MANGER, MET THE PLANE as soon as it touched down on the grass landing strip. She'd met Hobbs—nobody called him Zeb—quite a few times during college when she'd come home with Mitch for the weekends. He'd always been overtly friendly, welcoming her with bear hugs. This time, however, when Mitch helped her from the plane, Hobbs was restrained in his greeting. Courteous, but definitely reserved.

Hobbs tipped his hat. "Ms. Olivia." He didn't offer his hand.

"Hobbs. How nice to see you. It's been a while."

Hobbs shifted his gaze toward Adam and back. "Yes, Ma'am. 'Bout six years I'd say."

Mitch handed Olivia her crutches. "Hobbs. There's more luggage in the hole if you'd give me a hand."

Hobbs nodded and moved away.

In no way could she say Hobbs had been curt or unfriendly toward her, but she missed his previous spirited hugs.

The twenty-minute drive to Mitch's house was consumed by Adam's questions, which either Mitch or Hobbs would answer. But neither of them directed any questions or statements to her.

As they drove between the brick pillars and under an

arched Lazy L sign, Olivia's heart raced. Sweat slicked her palms. Mitch's home. She'd been to his parents' house years ago, but she didn't know what to expect of a house Mitch had selected and built. She'd been able to see the rooftop when they flew over, as well as the pool in the back, but those glimpses hadn't adequately prepared her.

They pulled into a curved drive in front of a two-story gray limestone house. An arched doorway led to a double-door front entrance. Long, paned windows glittered in the sun. A *porte-cochere* connected the first floor of the house to a garage that would house four cars if Mitch owned a car for each garage door.

Hobbs stopped the car in the circle drive and both he and Mitch exited. Mitch opened the truck's back door and Adam jumped to the ground with a loud stomp on the concrete. Hobbs held Olivia's door and even offered her a hand to assist getting out and onto her crutches.

"Hobbs, can you get one of the guys to give you a hand with the luggage? I spoke with Magda this morning, so I'm sure she has the rooms ready."

"Not a problem." Hobbs pulled a cell phone from his pocket and wandered off.

Grinning broadly, Mitch flung open both doors to his house. "Come on in."

They walked into a two-story foyer with a sweeping staircase to the left. Bright shafts of sun glinted off the hardwood floors. Colors from the crystal chandelier danced on the flooring.

"Welcome to Chez Landry."

Olivia looked up the stairs toward the female voice that had spoken. Joanna St. Claire Landry walked down the staircase, her manicured hand lightly sliding along the highly polished wood rail.

"Oh no," Mitch muttered. His face reddened. "Joanna, what are you doing here?"

"Daddy told me you were bringing home, um, guests and well, with that housekeeper you hired, I wanted to make sure everything was done right."

"You didn't need to do that. I'm sure Magda has everything under control." He cupped his hands around his mouth. "Magda."

Adam slipped his hand into Olivia's. "You're not supposed to yell in the house."

Mitch looked at him. "You're right, but let's make an exception this one time. Magda."

From the rear of the house came the disembodied reply, "Hold your horses. I'm coming."

"See, Mitch? That's what I mean. She shows you no respect all at. It's a good thing I came here today. Why, she hadn't set up one of the bedrooms upstairs for Olivia." She said Olivia as though it left a sour taste in her mouth.

A thin, tattooed, twenty-something woman with unnaturally black, spiked hair walked through the formal dining room into the foyer. She wiped her hands on a dishtowel and stored it on her shoulder.

"I'm here. I'm here. Don't yell in the house."

Mitch laughed. "Adam already scolded me."

The young woman knelt in front of Adam and held out her hand. "I'm Magda. You must be Adam."

Adam dropped his mother's hand to shake Magda's. He nodded.

She stood and faced Olivia. "You must be Olivia then."

Olivia smiled, confused as to why Mitch would hire someone so young. And attractive. And tattooed. She took the proffered hand. "Olivia Gentry."

"Magda Hobbs."

"You're married to Hobbs?"

Mitch and Magda both burst out laughing. Olivia glanced toward Joanna. She wasn't laughing. A frown darkened all her facial features.

"Sorry," Magda said and released Olivia's hand to wipe her eyes. "Lord, no, I'm not married to Hobbs. He's my father."

Olivia opened her eyes wide in surprise. "I had no idea Hobbs had ever been married."

Magda glanced down at Adam, then back to Olivia. "He hasn't. It's a long story."

The front doors opened and Hobbs entered, followed by a couple of ranch hands carrying luggage.

"This way, Hobbs," Joanna said. She started back up the stairs. "Our guests will be staying up here."

Magda looked at Olivia, tilted her head toward Joanna, then rolled her eyes.

"Joanna."

Mitch's sharp tone stopped Joanna's foot in mid-step. She set her foot down and turned. "Yes?"

Mitch shook his head. "Hobbs, take Olivia's things to the master suite."

"But, Mitch…" Joanna took a step down.

Mitch's lips pulled tight. He waved toward the crutches. "The master suite, Hobbs. Olivia can hardly climb stairs." He looked at Magda and raised a questioning eyebrow.

"I set you up in the balcony room. If Adam is okay with having his own room, I put him in the front bedroom." Magda glanced toward Olivia. "If you'd rather, I can set up a bed for Adam in the master suite."

"I don't know," Olivia said, readjusting the crutch

pads under her arms. "We can talk about it. I'm sorry, but I need to get off my feet. My ankle is throbbing."

"Of course you do. What are you thinking, Mitch?" Magda punched his arm. "The two of you come with me to the kitchen. I have iced tea, lemonade and fresh cookies. How does that sound?"

Adam grinned. "I like cookies."

Magda held out her hand. "Then c'mon. I need someone to eat these."

Adam took Magda's hand. "C'mon, Momma."

"You two go ahead. I'll be right there."

As soon as Adam and Magda were out of sight, Olivia whirled around to face Mitch and Joanna. "I don't know what little Texas two-step dance you two are playing, but Adam and I are not going to be in the middle." She held up her hand when Mitch began to speak. "The minute I'm back on my feet, we are gone, even if we have to walk off this ranch to get a ride."

When she turned to follow the path taken by Magda and Adam, Mitch touched her arm. "I'm sorry, Olivia. I wasn't expecting Joanna to be here."

"But I was just trying to help," Joanna protested. "I wanted our guests to feel welcome."

Our guests? What was going on between Mitch and his ex? He'd led Olivia to believe he and Joanna were done, over, finished. So what was Joanna doing here welcoming them into the house as though she were still mistress of the manor?

"After all," Joanna continued, "it's obvious Mitch is Adam's—"

"That's enough," Mitch barked. "Enough." He dragged his fingers through his hair. "Joanna. I'm sure you meant well, but Magda is perfectly capable of taking care of things around here."

Joanna sniffed. "Please. The girl's a drug addict."

Olivia gasped and turned. "Mitch?"

He huffed. "She's not a drug addict. You just think that because of the tats."

"Only white trash has tattoos. Why, my daddy would just die if I came home with something so tacky." Joanna stepped off the last step and walked up to Mitch. "You need a proper housekeeper. Someone who understands the needs of someone in your social status."

Mitch snorted and shook his head. "Joanna. I'm a rancher, not someone with a social status. Now, I'm sure you meant well, but we're all tired. Once Olivia and Adam get settled in, I have a million things I need to tend to." He took her arm and pulled her toward the front door. "Goodbye, Joanna."

Her back muscles were rigid. Her lips pressed tight. A fire burned in her hazel eyes. Olivia remembered that look from knowing Joanna in college. The lady was seriously irate.

Then Joanna's shoulders slumped and her bottom lip began to tremble. Unshed tears filled her eyes. She sniffed. "I'm sorry, Mitch. I really was trying to help."

Mitch stopped walking. It must have been the tears, or maybe the trembling lower lip, but whatever she'd done worked. Mitch moved his hand from her elbow and slipped his arm around her shoulders.

"I know. I'm just tired and cranky. You go shopping with your friend Helen or your mom. You'll feel better."

She kissed Mitch's cheek. "I'll talk to you later." When she hugged him, her gaze locked with Olivia's. The look on Joanna's face was anything but regret. There was a sly smile on her lips to go with the defiance in her eyes. It was another expression Olivia remembered from their sorority days…Joanna's victory expression. As Joanna broke the hug, her appearance reassumed the sorrowful eyes and trembling lip. She lifted her hand in a half-wave. "Bye, Olivia."

Before Olivia could respond, Joanna shut the door behind her. Olivia shook her head. The woman hadn't changed a bit since they'd been sorority sisters. What Joanna wanted, Joanna took, no matter who got stepped on in the process. And now, it seemed Joanna wanted Mitch back.

Olivia turned in the direction Magda had taken Adam. She followed the aroma of hot chocolate-chip cookies and found her way to the kitchen.

The gleam from all the stainless steel and granite countertops was blinding. Adam sat on a barstool, a glass of milk in his right hand and a chocolate-chip cookie in the other. Magda was leaning with her elbows on the countertop, engrossed in Adam's story of driving Mitch's plane all by himself on the way down.

"Wow, Adam. That's really something. I don't think Mitch has ever let anyone else fly his plane." Magda took a cookie off the plate and took a bite. "He must really like you."

"Uh huh." Cookie crumbles dropped from Adam's stuffed mouth.

Olivia hobbled into the room. "Excuse me? Do we talk with food in our mouth?"

Adam swallowed. "No, ma'am."

Magda grinned. She ruffled Adam's hair and stood. "Can I get you something, Olivia? Iced Tea? Coffee? Lemonade?"

"Coffee, if it's already made. I don't want to put you out."

"Grab a stool. Coffee's hot. How do you take it?"

"A little milk, please." Olivia bit into a cookie and moaned. "These are wonderful, Magda. What's your secret recipe?"

Magda set a cup of coffee down. "The back of the chocolate-chips package. I think you're probably just hungry."

"I don't know about that. Adam and I are cookie experts, aren't we?"

Adam nodded enthusiastically.

He reached for another cookie, but Olivia slid the plate out of his reach. "You've probably had your fair share."

"*Momma.* Magda. Tell her I didn't have that many."

Magda began storing the extra cookies in a plastic bag. "Sorry, partner. I don't get between a guy and his mother. But tell you what…" She pulled out a small sandwich plastic bag. "I'll store some 'specially for you. Then when your mom says you can have more, you'll have your own stash. How's that?"

His face lit up. "All right."

Olivia finished her coffee and glanced at the clock on the stove. "Magda? Would you please show Adam and me to where I'll be staying? With all the rushing around and the travel down, I'm beat. I think an afternoon nap is just what the doctor ordered for both of us."

"Not me," Adam declared emphatically. "I'm not tired and I'm too old for a nap."

Olivia sighed. Had they not just had this discussion? "Tell you what, pal. You go lie down with me. If you're still awake after thirty minutes, we'll get back up. Deal?"

Adam pasted a stubborn look on his face and crossed his arms. "I'll go, but I won't fall asleep and you can't make me."

Olivia noticed Magda sucking in her bottom lip, restraining a smile tickling the edges of her mouth.

"Okay. Fair enough." Olivia stood. "Whenever you're ready to lead the way, Magda."

Magda sealed the cookie packages and slipped them into the cabinet. "This way." She started back toward the dining room and entry hall.

"C'mon, Adam." Olivia balanced herself on her crutches. "Don't argue with me."

Adam slid off his stool with a loud thud on the hardwood floor. "I'm coming, but I'm not going to sleep."

After going back through the formal dining room, a formal living room and down a short hallway, Magda pushed open a set of double doors. The three of them stepped into a coffered-ceiling entryway, the master bedroom to their right overlooking the pool and the master bath to their left. The hardwood flooring continued into the master bedroom but stopped at the master bath, where brown marble with gold swirls began.

After Olivia thumped into the master suite entry hall, she realized the master suite encompassed the entire end of the house.

"Wow." She turned her head to look around. "Big."

"It is. You ought to have to clean it." Magda laughed. "The master bedroom is this way." She hiked a thumb over her shoulder. "You've obviously figured out the bathroom is the other way."

Olivia and Adam followed Magda to the bedroom. The spacious room had a coordinated, designer feel. A yellow duvet covered a massive bed with tall, thick posts and handcrafted headboard and footboard bearing the Lazy L brand. The bed dominated the room. Mahogany bedside tables, mirror dresser and highboy glistened from diffused lighting. The Lazy L brand was repeated in the thick multi-colored rug. Olivia's luggage rested unopened on the bed.

"Don't worry about unpacking your bags." Magda lifted the suitcases off the bed and set them by the dresser. "I'll help you with that when you wake up."

"Where's my stuff?" Adam turned in a full circle examining the room.

"Upstairs. You have your own bedroom up there, remember?"

"Oh yeah." He looked at Olivia. "Can I go up there for my nap?"

Olivia smiled. "I don't think so. Not today. For now, stay here with me."

Adam's grin fell in disappointment, but she knew her son. Out of her sight and he'd talk his way out of an afternoon nap. By early evening, he'd be one cranky little boy.

"Fine, but I'm not going to sleep."

"Right," said Olivia.

Magda pulled back the yellow silk comforter, exposing pale yellow sheets. Olivia was tall enough to sit on the edge, but no way could Adam reach the mattress without help.

"Here. Let me help." Magda lifted Adam. When his feet were dangling, she untied his tennis shoes and slipped them off.

"Thanks, Magda." Olivia slipped off her shoes and let them drop to the floor. "Okay, Adam. Scoot over to the other side of the bed."

He bounced across the bed on his bottom. He looked over his shoulder at Olivia. "I'm not tired."

"I know. Lay down just for thirty minutes, then we'll

get up." Olivia's head hit the soft pillow with a puff. "Thanks, Magda. Lay down, Adam."

Adam lay down and shut his eyes. Magda closed the curtains over the doors leading outside, then flipped off the light. The bedroom door clicked softly behind her.

AFTER CONVINCING JOANNA THAT HE WASN'T ANGRY with her—when in reality he was quite put out—and assuring her that he understood she was just trying to help, Mitch headed off to the barn. Hobbs kept an office there. Even though Mitch had offered him much better office accommodations, Hobbs always said staying in the barn kept him close to what was going on. Plus, Mitch suspected Hobbs enjoyed the smell of leather and horses as much as Mitch did.

"Hobbs."

"I'm in the office," came the muffled reply.

Hobbs had taken the door off the office a few years ago and had it cut in half, converting the once solid door into a makeshift Dutch door. The upper unit stood open while the lower unit was closed. This was as close as Hobbs would ever come to an open-door policy.

Mitch leaned on the edge of the lower door unit's sill. "How's that new calf doing?"

Hobbs looked up from the spreadsheet on his desk. "The one born right before you left?"

Mitch frowned. "Is there another new calf?"

Hobbs shrugged. "Nope."

"Then, yeah. That calf."

"Doing fine. Kept him and his momma here for a couple of days. Wanted to make sure both of them were okay after that rough delivery. Sent them down yesterday with the other calves and moms."

"You got them in Lee's Pasture or have you moved them yet to Black's Ranch?"

As the Lazy L had grown and bought up surrounding acreage, Mitch and his hands had never bothered to rename the lands. It just seemed easier to keep calling them what they always had. So Lee's Pasture had been bought from Chuck Lee. Black's Ranch had been owned by Russell Black.

"Right now, they're still in Lee's. Figured I'd wait until you got back to move 'em to Black's." Hobbs pulled a sheet of paper from his desk. He always had the current cattle-rotation list handy.

Mitch didn't do grain-fed cattle. He believed cattle raised in the field on grasses produced better tasting and more tender beef. To keep the herd adequately supplied, he and Hobbs followed a field-rotation schedule that kept the cattle moving from area to area, providing fresh grass while allowing the previous field time to replenish. Moving cattle on a regular basis was time consuming and labor intensive, but all the extra work had paid off. The Lazy L produced the highest quality beef in the state.

"Let's move them tomorrow. I'd like to get them a little closer. With the drought, the ocelots in the area will be hungry and thirsty. It'd be safer for our calves and the ocelots. I'd hate to have to shoot one of those fellers."

"Right. What time you want to head out in the morning?"

Before Mitch could answer, the radio on the desk squawked. "Hobbs."

Hobbs keyed the mike. "Yeah. Hobbs here."

"We've got a cow down."

"Damn it," Hobbs muttered. "Where?"

"Section 320."

"Ocelot?"

"Maybe. I'm thinking wild hogs though. She's torn up pretty good."

"Okay, let's get the rest of the cattle moved out of that section and into...hold on a sec." He pulled out his rotation schedule and glanced at Mitch. "Move 'em to Lakeland area?"

Mitch nodded. "That should work. Have the guys haul the carcass as far away from the rest of the cattle as possible."

Hobbs keyed the mike. "I'll be heading down your way shortly. Look around for any other lost cattle. Be there in about thirty."

Mitch stood. "Give me ten to change clothes and I'll head down there with you."

Hobbs stood then shoved his chair under his desk. "You don't have to come along. You got better things to do than clean up a dead cow."

"Today, I think I'd rather deal with a dead cow than women."

Hobbs snorted. "I feel that way every day."

Mitch jogged back to the house. As was his habit, he let himself into the master suite entry hall using the French doors leading to his private deck. Since Joanna had moved out and vacated one of the walk-in closets, Magda had separated his clothes. His rough work clothes and boots were in the smaller closet adjacent to the master bedroom. His dress clothes had been moved to the larger walk-in closet adjacent to the master bath. Personally, he had no preference which closet was his, or if his work clothes shared space with his nicer things, but if the segregation of his work duds made Magda happy, then fine with him.

On reflex, he glanced into his bedroom as he passed.

Olivia was asleep in his bed, a sight he'd never thought he'd see. One long slender leg curled outside the sheet covering the rest of her. His body tightened at the picture.

Then a little head popped up beside her. Adam grinned and waved.

Mitch waved back and crooked his finger in a come-here motion.

Adam checked his mother, slid from the bed and hurried across the floor, his sock-covered feet gliding silently on the wood flooring.

"Hey, buddy. What cha doing?" Mitch whispered.

"Taking a nap, but I'm not sleepy. I told Momma that, but she made me lay down anyway." He motioned to Mitch to come closer. "I think she made me take a nap because she was sleepy."

Mitch bit the inside of his lip to keep from laughing. Smart kid.

"What are you doing?" Adam asked.

"I'm changing my clothes and…" Mitch paused. Would telling a five-year-old about a dead cow scare him? He tried to remember about himself at that age. Would he have been scared or grossed out by a dead cow? Probably not. In fact, he'd have loved it, blood, guts and all. He made his mind up. "Remember Hobbs who drove us to the house?"

Adam nodded.

"Well, he and I are going down to Section 320. I have a, well, something killed a cow. The ranch hands are moving the rest of the cattle to another field for grazing tomorrow. Hobbs and I are going to drag the dead cow farther away and let the wild animals have it."

Adam's eyes lit up. "A dead cow. Cool. Can I come?"

Mitch hesitated. He glanced toward Olivia. Still

asleep. Would she mind if he took Adam? But then, wasn't that why he'd insisted she bring Adam to the Lazy L, so he could get to know his son? Mitch didn't spend a lot of time hanging around the house, so if he wanted to spend time with his son, the boy would have to come out with him. Hell, truth be told, this place was way too fancy. He'd tried to tell Joanna they didn't need anything like this, but she had really loved the plans. Guilt at not being with her when she'd miscarried James's child had driven him to giving her carte blanche when it came to spending his money. She'd made a dent in his bank account, but he'd figured that if building this damn house would help with her post-pregnancy depression, then at least he'd been there for her this time. But now he was stuck with the palace, as his parents called it.

"Let's go find Magda. I want her to know where you are in case your mom wakes up and looks for you. Okay?"

Adam's grin lit up his face. His eyes sparkled with excitement.

Mitch remembered feeling that way when his dad took him along on ranch chores, especially ones his mother thought too disgusting. Those were always his favorite. And a dead, chewed-up cow would have been the ideal chore for him and his dad.

They found Magda reading a magazine on the covered patio overlooking the swimming pool and adjacent whirlpool. She looked over her shoulder as Mitch and Adam walked through the French door. She frowned at Adam. "What are you doing up? I thought you were down for a nap."

Adam crossed his arms over his puffed-out chest. "I'm too old for a nap. And I'm not sleepy."

"I see." Magda laid her magazine on the glass-top

table in front of her and picked up her iced tea. She took a sip. "So what am I going to do with you the rest of the afternoon?" She checked her watch. "I have a load of towels coming out of the dryer in ten minutes. You want to help me fold them?"

He shook his head. "Me and Mitch are gonna move a dead cow."

"Really?" She stood and motioned for both guys to follow her in the house. "Adam, I left a couple of cookies on the counter for you. You want them?"

"Yes, ma'am." He took off for the kitchen in a run.

"You're taking Adam with you to take care of a cow carcass?" Magda slugged Mitch's arm. "Are you nuts?"

He rubbed the spot where she'd hit him. "He'll love it. I did when I was his age."

"Yes, but you grew up here. He's a city kid and—" She broke off as Adam came back into the living room carrying a cookie in each hand. "Here, Mitch. I brought you one."

Mitch took the cookie. "Thanks, pal." He ate the cookie in one bite. "Magda thinks you'd rather stay here and help her."

Adam shook his head vigorously. "No. I want to go with you."

Mitch smiled. He wanted Adam with him. He wanted to show Adam the ranch and all the cattle and horses and… He laughed to himself. How sad. He was trying to impress a five-year-old boy. But this just wasn't any boy. This was his son.

"Okay. You need to get some shoes on."

Adam hurried from the room.

"If Olivia wakes up, let her know Adam is with me, okay?"

Magda snorted. "When Olivia finds out you've taken her son to see a dead cow, that cow may not be the only dead thing around here tonight."

He shrugged. "I'll handle Olivia."

Chapter Nine

O livia paced the kitchen. Thump of the crutches, stomp of her good foot. Thump. Stomp.

"I can't believe he took Adam to see a dead cow. What was he thinking?"

Magda stopped kneading the bread dough and turned to look at Olivia. "Probably thinking he wanted to show Adam the ranch." She went back to work on the dough. "Adam wanted to go, so Mitch took him. Besides, do you know a little boy who wouldn't want to go out with the guys rather than take a nap?"

"I know, I know. It's just that—"

The sound of running feet broke Olivia's concentration.

"Momma?" Adam's voice echoed in the living room.

Olivia released a sigh of relief.

"Back here, Adam. The kitchen."

Adam's tennis shoes squeaked on the tile as he skid to a stop in front of her. "Momma. Guess what I did?"

Olivia motioned for him to follow her to the breakfast nook where she could sit down. "Now, tell me what you did."

"I helped Mitch drag a dead cow down a hill. We're going to let all the wild animals eat it. Mitch said it wouldn't be any good anymore for people. Mitch said it would feed lots of different animals."

Olivia brushed Adam's sweaty hair off his flushed face. "Did he?"

"Uh huh. And Mitch said I was a lot of help."

"That you were, buddy. Lots of help."

Olivia glanced from Adam's glowing smile to Mitch's grin. Her heart stuttered. It was as though she were looking at Adam thirty years from now.

"Yeah," Adam said, pulling her attention back to him. "Mitch said that I really needed some cowboy boots like all the other cowboys have." He held up one foot and looked at it disgustedly. "Tennis shoes are not right."

"Well, you have some boots, remember? You left them at Uncle Travis's house."

"Well, I need some here too. Mitch said cowboys don't wear tennis shoes."

"I see." Olivia bit the inside of her bottom lip to keep from smiling.

"Yeah. And I need cowboy pants too."

"Cowboy pants?" She glanced toward Mitch, who'd continued standing in the kitchen doorway watching her and Adam. "Umm, what are cowboy pants?"

Mitch turned around and pointed to his butt. Too busy admiring the shape and firmness of Mitch's rear, she missed the name of the brand.

When he turned back around, she cleared her throat. "Ah'hm. I couldn't read it from here."

"Wrangler," Mitch said.

"Yeah," Adam said. "I need real cowboy pants. Not

these sissy shorts."

Olivia glared at Mitch. "Sissy shorts?"

He shrugged and held up two hands. "I didn't say it. Talk to Hobbs."

Magda snorted.

"You don't have sissy shorts. These are a perfectly good pair of khaki shorts."

"And I need some chapstick to cover my legs."

Mitch laughed. "I think you mean chaps."

Adam looked toward Mitch. "That's what I said. Chapstick." He turned toward his mother again. "Mitch said that I need to protect my legs when I ride a horse tomorrow."

"Excuse me?" Olivia snapped her gaze toward Mitch. "Horseback riding?" This time he gave her a sheepish grin and shrugged.

"Mitch and me are moving some cows tomorrow morning. He needs my help."

"Really? I'm not sure that's such a good idea, honey." A little seed of fear sprouted in her gut. She wasn't ready to ride again. And if Adam went, then…

Her little boy was too young to ride a horse on a cattle round-up, except he had ridden before with her brother, but Travis wasn't Mitch. Her brother knew how to protect her child. She continued to glare in Mitch's direction. "Mitch, I think as his mother this is something you should have discussed with me."

Mitch strode toward them then draped his arm around Adam's shoulders. "Hobbs mentioned moving cattle first thing in the morning and this cowboy volunteered to help. I told him we needed all the help we could get."

"Mitch, I don't think—"

Adam whirled toward her, dislodging Mitch's arm.

"Momma. I have to help. Mitch needs me. He said so."

Mitch crossed his arms and watched the mother-son interaction with a hint of a grin.

"Oh, Adam. I'm sure Mitch can do this without your help."

Adam crossed his arms in a defiant stance. She had to admit he was his father's clone in looks and actions.

"Mitch said I could help and I want to."

She pulled Adam close and hugged his stiff body. "I know, buddy, but tomorrow Mitch won't be in his truck. Right, Mitch? You'll be on horseback?"

"Right."

"So, you see——"

Adam pushed away from her embrace. "I know how to ride." Frustration tinted Adam's voice. "Uncle Travis always lets me ride Patches at his ranch."

Olivia sighed. Her brother strikes again. Patches was a Shetland pony that had to be older than dirt and wouldn't move faster than a slow walk, not exactly the same as a cutting horse working cattle. She opened her mouth but Mitch cut her off.

"He'll ride with me, Olivia. He'll be fine." When she lifted her head to argue, he shook his head. "Trust me. Nothing will happen."

"Yeah, Momma. Nothing will happen."

Olivia decided to try a different tactic to dissuade Adam. Actually more like a bribe than persuasion. "What about cowboy pants and cowboy boots? Wouldn't you rather wait until you get those?"

Adam hopped from one foot to the other. "Nope. Don't have to. Gettin' 'em tonight."

Olivia glanced at Mitch. "What is he talking about?"

Mitch's face turned red. "Well, um, you see…"

"Hello? Where is everyone?" a female voice called

from the front door. "Mitch?"

Olivia's brow furrowed into a deep frown of disapproval. She knew that voice.

Mitch at least had the dignity to look embarrassed. "In the kitchen, Joanna."

"Hey, Adam." Magda walked over to the threesome at the table. "Can you give me a hand for a minute?" She put her hand on Adam's shoulder and turned him toward the laundry room. "I need to get something and I need a strong guy to help."

"Sure." Adam looked at Olivia. "I need to help Magda, okay?"

"Of course."

Magda took Adam's hand and led him from the kitchen.

Olivia waited until Adam was gone to light into Mitch. "Did you ask your ex-wife to buy clothes for my son? How dare you? I can buy him whatever he needs. I don't need you or—"

"There y'all are." Joanna flounced into the breakfast nook, shopping bags hanging from her wrists. "Look who I ran into today."

Mitch's mother followed Joanna into the kitchen. "Hi, Olivia. Mitch." She came to the table and hugged Olivia. "It's so good to see you again, Olivia." She scrunched up her face when she eyed Olivia's wrapped ankle. "Heard about the ankle and knee. How are you doing?"

"Hi, Sylvia." Olivia returned the hug. Olivia was sincerely glad to see Mitch's mother. She had always been warm and kind to Olivia. "I'm healing much faster than the doctor predicted. I'm sure I'll be up and back home very soon."

"Lookie here," Joanna crowed, drawing all attention

to her. She was almost bouncing on her toes in excitement. Her face glowed with glee as she poured out four pairs of small jeans from one sack. The second held small cowboy shirts with snap openings and six pairs of white socks. From the last, two shoeboxes plopped onto the table. "Thank you, Sylvia, for asking me to help shopping for your…Adam. He is darling. Why, you must be thrilled that he looks so much—"

"Like his mother," Sylvia interjected.

While wanting to hug Sylvia for cutting Joanna off, Olivia had to restrain herself from clunking Joanna over the head with her crutch. She ground her teeth. How dare they? She could believe Mitch would fall for Joanna's act, but Sylvia too?

"Get this…this…*stuff* out of here before Adam sees it." Olivia began scooping the clothes back into sacks. "I can provide for my son just fine."

"What's your problem, Olivia?" Joanna flipped her hair over her shoulder. "It's obvious Mitch is Adam's father. He has every right to buy something for Adam if he wants to."

Olivia uttered a vile curse under her breath, which apparently didn't work as Joanna was still breathing.

"Joanna. That's enough," Sylvia said.

Joanna's mouth closed, her lips pulling tight across her teeth.

"Olivia." Sylvia squeezed Olivia's shoulder. "Joanna didn't buy any of this. I did. Don't blame Mitch. It was my idea. If you want to be mad at someone, it's me."

Being angry with Sylvia wasn't possible. Mitch's mother had been a tower of strength for her. Supportive. Loving. Accepting. Olivia felt her anger tide ebbing.

"I could never be mad at you, Sylvia." She eyed the boot boxes and clothes again. "You did this?"

"Guilty as charged, I'm afraid."

"Right, so don't get all huffy with me." Joanna tossed her hair around again and tried to appear the injured party.

"Joanna, dear, I promised your mother you would only drop me off and then you'd be on your way. Something about dinner plans."

"Oh, that's right. Daddy and Mummy are hosting a small dinner party at the club for some of Daddy's clients." She tapped her forehead gently. "I have to go." She turned and said over her shoulder, "Mitch, be a dear and walk me out."

As soon as Joanna and Mitch left the room, Sylvia rolled her eyes. "I do not understand what either of my boys saw in that girl."

Olivia stifled a grin. "Where's your car?"

Sylvia pulled out a chair and sat. "It was making a strange noise and I left it at the dealership to have it checked out. I ran into Joanna at the mall and she insisted on driving me around." She sighed. "I should have gotten a rental car like I'd planned." She leaned over and patted Olivia's hand. "You know, dear, that I would never do anything to upset you. I talked to Mitch today and he told me you were here with your son. Of course, your mother had already called, but I didn't tell him. When he mentioned getting Adam some boots, well, I guess I just went a little overboard."

Olivia smiled. "You have always spoiled him."

Sylvia shrugged. "What can I say? You're right. Plus —" Her eyes sparkled with excitement. "I believe one of those boot boxes might be in your size."

Olivia pulled the Lucchese box toward her. "You shouldn't have done this, Sylvia. These are much too expensive."

"Pfft. My money. I can do what I want with it."

Olivia pulled out a pair of leather black and brown cowboy boots with a hand-tooled design. "Oh, Sylvia. They're beautiful." She leaned over, removed her tennis shoe, and slipped on the right boot. Straightening out her leg, she rotated her foot side to side to get the full effect of boot on her foot. "I should make you take these back."

"But you won't."

Olivia studied the boot for a minute and smiled. "Nope. I'm keeping them."

"And they are meant to be used for riding, not just wearing around the house."

The smile dropped from Olivia's face.

"Olivia, it's time to get back on the horse, so to speak. It was a freak accident."

"Maybe, but—"

"Hey! Women! There're hungry cowboys in the house," Mitch growled as he came back into the kitchen, Adam riding on his shoulders. "Feed us."

"Yeah, feed us," Adam echoed then howled with laughter.

"If you hungry cowboys would get out of the way, I'll get dinner finished," Magda said, pushing past Mitch and Adam.

Adam giggled. When his gaze fell on Mitch's mother, his face lit up like the sun. "Nana SuSu," he cried. He wiggled to get off Mitch's shoulders. As soon as his feet hit the floor, he ran over to Mitch's mother and wrapped his arms around her knees.

"Hey, Adam." Sylvia bent and kissed his cheek. "Look how big you're getting."

"I know." Adam's chest puffed out. "Hey, did you know I'm gonna ride a horse tomorrow with Mitch?"

"Look what she brought you today, Adam. What do you say?" Olivia prompted.

Adam eyes opened wide and his mouth stretched into a wide grin. "Cowboy boots! Thanks, Nana SuSu." He hopped around on one foot. "Mitch! Mitch! Look!"

"I see," Mitch said. "Isn't Nana SuSu just full of surprises?"

"You know Nana SuSu?" Adam asked.

Olivia turned Adam toward her. "You know how you're my little boy?" Adam nodded. "Well, Mitch is Nana SuSu's little boy."

"Mitch's momma?"

"Right."

Adam seemed to think about this, then said, "Okay. Now can I try on my boots?"

Mitch's stance was rigid and defiant. His face bloomed into a blotchy red mask. Anger radiated like heat from his body. The only person in the room who didn't seem to notice was Adam, whose interest was focused totally on his boots, and for that, Olivia gave a silent thanks.

Sylvia looked at Olivia with a deer-in-the-headlights expression. She gave an almost imperceptible shrug before turning her gaze toward Mitch. "Well, I'd better get going. Mitch, dear, I need to borrow your extra truck. I'll have Dad run it back tomorrow. Okay?"

Mitch turned his head but not his body toward his mother. "Fine. No, wait. Better yet, why don't I drive you home? Apparently, it's been too long since we've had a nice long talk."

She gave a nervous laugh. "No, no. You have house-guests. I'll just run along." She smiled. "I'm assuming your keys are still hanging on the key rack by the garage door, right?"

"That's right, Mrs. L. The keys are there," Magda said over her shoulder as she slid a roast out of the oven.

"Stay for dinner, Nana SuSu," Mitch said, his tone conveying more a demand than a request.

"I can't, dear. You know how your father is about his dinner. Plus, it's your dad's poker night. Our time to host, so I'd better run and get the house ready for cigar smoke." She hugged Adam and gave him another cheek kiss. "Be good. I'll talk to you later, Olivia."

"Okay. Later." Olivia was helping Adam put on his new boots. "Tell Nana SuSu thank you for your boots and clothes."

Adam stomped his feet, imitating a cowboy knocking mud off his boots. "Thanks, Nana SuSu."

Sylvia Landry waved over her shoulder as she hurried from the room.

"Dinner's ready," Magda announced. "Hey Adam, give me a hand and carry these napkins to the table."

Adam galloped across the kitchen, the hard soles of his boots clacking on the tile.

"I have some work to do," Mitch said. "I'll grab something later. Right now, I seem to have lost my appetite."

He left the room in the same direction his mother had just taken.

"Don't worry," Magda said to Olivia as she placed the sliced roast beef on the table. "He'll come around."

Olivia smiled. "I'm not worried." Adam handed her an empty plate. "As long as my little guy is fine, I'm fine. We're a team, right, Adam?"

"Right."

MITCH STORMED AFTER HIS MOTHER...OR RATHER

Nana SuSu. His mother knew about Adam. Had known about Adam. Had met his son and never told him. Nausea roiled through his gut. His left eye twitched with the headache building behind it.

He reached the garage as his mother was lowering the garage door. He slammed his fist on the automatic opener on the wall to stop then reverse the door.

"Come back here," he yelled.

His mother waved as she pulled away.

"Coward."

Several hours and many shots of bourbon later, Mitch headed out of his temporary bedroom onto a balcony overlooking the covered patio, pool and whirlpool at the rear of his house. The night air was crisp and relatively mosquito-free for a change. Killer heat and the millions of bugs that drove sane people indoors were still a couple of months away. Sage and pine scented the air. He drew in a deep breath and stretched his neck, working the tension out. Spring had always been his favorite time of the year. This year, the season had delivered its fair share of surprises, and right now he wasn't sure how he felt about them.

He took the chair closest to the balcony railing, set his most recent drink on the table and lit up a cigar. It'd been quite a while since he'd smoked one, but dammit, he needed something to do with his hands besides wrap them around Olivia's neck...or her waist...or her hips as he drove inside her.

He blew out a long stream of smoke. Apathy toward Olivia had never been his problem. From the day they'd met in college, he'd wanted her. How was it possible he could love a woman so much, crave her touch to the point it was painful, and at the same time wish he'd never met her?

No, that wasn't true. He'd wanted her in college and damn if he didn't still want her now. His desire for her hadn't abated in the least.

The inky sky was alight with stars, the occasional plane and a firefly or two. There was barely a breeze in the air. He settled back in the chair to think about Adam and Olivia and the stunning realization that his mother knew about Adam, and apparently had for some time.

Of course, if his mother knew, his father did, too. As far as he knew, there were no secrets between his parents. What astonished him was that his parents had been able to keep Adam a secret, which also made him furious. How dare they all decide that he didn't need to know about his son.

But you married someone else, his subconscious rumbled. Was it possible, even in the slightest, that they thought they were doing the right thing for him? Did everyone believe Joanna would be so unforgiving that if she'd learned of Adam, she'd have taken it out on the child?

He had to admit that he wasn't sure he would have married Joanna if he'd known about Olivia's pregnancy. He probably would have asked Olivia to marry him, but it would have been for all the wrong reasons. If he and Olivia had wed, it would have been a marriage founded on a pregnancy, not a union rooted in the concept that they couldn't live without each other. That's what he wanted…a marriage rooted in devotion and love rather than obligation.

The pain from that insight tore at his gut. His head dropped to the back of the chair. Six years ago, he'd been so full of himself. Sure he was going to set the world on fire. Then with James's death, Joanna's pregnancy, their marriage and her subsequent miscarriage, his whole life had changed. Nothing had turned out quite as he'd envisioned.

He couldn't change the past. If he could, James would still be alive, married to Joanna, and running the Lazy L with Mitch and their dad.

His past—what he'd experienced and all that he'd learned—had made him the man he'd become. Without it, without the loss of his brother and the nephew Joanna had been carrying, he might not appreciate what he had under his roof right now. He had a son. Best of all, he had a son by the woman he loved.

He and Olivia had both made mistakes. The challenge would be putting those mistakes behind them and building a life together. If he could just get her to see things his way.

And if he could get past the anger that tended to flare whenever he thought of the years he'd missed with Adam.

The crickets and fireflies seemed to have called it a night and maybe he should too. He stubbed out the cigar, ready to hit the sack, but before he could stand, the soft click of a door latch beneath him snagged his attention. Leaning forward in his chair, he saw Olivia slowly making her way down the patio stairs off his bedroom toward the pool. It was late. What was she up to?

He remained glued in his chair, waiting to see why she was up and outside so late. He watched as she glanced around before dropping her robe at the top of the stairs leading into the pool. Silvery moonlight shimmered on her naked body. He sucked in a quiet breath. Seeing her could still steal the breath from his lungs. Seeing her naked body drove him insane. His balls tightened. The zipper of his loose shorts pulled snuggly across his hardening cock. He readjusted himself but never took his eyes off the sight below.

Olivia dropped her crutches on the concrete by the pool stairs. Using the handrail to support her weight, she hopped down each step until she touched the bottom of the pool. After shoving off, she began swimming laps. When she got to the far end, she flipped and returned. She was using more arms than legs to pull herself through the water, although he could see her exercising her injured ankle and knee. After ten laps, she stopped in the deep end and treaded water. When she checked her surroundings again, Mitch made sure he was deep in the shadows.

She swam back to the steps and hobbled out, again giving him a delicious view of her toned shape. He smiled. Who needed bourbon when her effect on him was more intoxicating than alcohol?

He'd expected her to collect her robe and head back into the house. Instead, she tossed the robe around her shoulders and made her way over to the whirlpool. She tapped the power button with the end of one crutch. Water gurgled from the jets and swirled in the deep tub. As she had at the pool stairs, she dropped her robe and crutches and hopped on her good leg into the whirlpool. She sat on one of the benches and leaned against the tub's wall, her head falling back to rest on the lip. From this distance, he couldn't hear her sigh as she sank into the hot bubbles, but he had a good imagination. Her shoulders slumped as she relaxed and allowed herself to float amid the bubbling water. After a couple of minutes of inertia, she swished her injured leg in the whirlpool's turbulence. Was this some type of exercise designed to hasten healing? Was she using the water's force as a counterforce to her muscular motions? He had no idea if this would help or not, but his hardening cock took notice of her shapely limbs as they drew figure eights in sexy, sinuous movements.

He leaned forward, not that a change in position would improve his view. As it was, he had a straight shot of the scene below. When she made her way closer to the pounding whirlpool jets his mind began tossing out lewd suggestions of how firm shots of water could be used to pleasure her. A burning ache to touch her, to make love to her tortured him.

That's it. He quietly stood and made his way to bed… but only after a long cold shower.

GROWING UP ON A RANCH IN HOT SOUTH TEXAS required waking before the sun to work the cattle. Mitch rarely needed an alarm. He greeted most mornings ready to hit the ground running. But this morning, the harsh buzz of the alarm was as welcome as drought.

By the light of the moon, Mitch buttoned his jeans and found a clean shirt for the day. After stomping his feet into his battered work boots, he headed downstairs praying Magda had remembered to set the timer on the coffee pot. Most mornings, coffee and maybe a bowl of cold cereal was all he had before heading out. As soon as he reached the bottom step, the aroma of freshly brewed coffee and hot biscuits filled his nose. Bless her. Thank goodness he'd had the sense to hire Magda over Joanna's loud and prolonged protest.

"Hey, Mitch. I'm already to go. See?" Adam sat at the bar, a bowl of half-eaten oatmeal in front of him. As he spoke, he held up his left foot to show off a cowboy boot.

"Morning, buddy. I see that."

Olivia stood at the stove, one crutch under her right arm. Looking over her shoulder, she said, "Adam. Finish your breakfast if you want to go with Mitch."

Adam shoved a heaping spoon of oatmeal into his mouth. When he grinned at Mitch, oatmeal coated his teeth. Mitch ruffled Adam's hair as he passed on the way to the coffee pot.

"Thanks," he said, pulling a mug from the cabinet. "Magda doesn't always remember to set the coffee timer."

"No problem. Since I had to get up with Adam anyway, I went ahead and made biscuits and sausage. I didn't know if you ate before you worked, or came home later in the morning."

Mitch pried open a hot, fluffy biscuit, enjoying the steam and aroma. "Magda isn't much of a morning person, so if I get breakfast, it's usually something cold and on the run. This is a treat. Thanks."

He noticed Olivia wore jeans and a shiny pair of unscuffed boots. "You going with us this morning?"

She glanced at Adam, then back to Mitch. "I am. I thought maybe Adam could ride with me. I know you have work to do and he'll just be in the way."

"No. I want to ride with a real cowboy," Adam cried.

"Adam—"

"No, Momma. Please. Mitch promised."

Olivia sighed and opened her mouth to respond.

"I did promise," Mitch said as he slid a sausage patty into a steaming biscuit. "Besides, I have plenty of hands this morning. He won't be in the way."

She turned so her back was to her son. "Mitch," she whispered. "Adam is so young. You're not used to little boys. We can follow in the truck, or in the Rhino ATV."

The whole time she spoke, she nervously turned her

coffee mug on the counter. He heard a surprising fear in her voice. Olivia had been a speed demon, a daring barrel rider, but everything in her manner reflected the nervousness of an inexperienced rider. What was making her so antsy? It couldn't be about him taking Adam on a horse. She knew he'd been riding since before his feet could touch the stirrups. Did she honestly think he couldn't protect Adam? The idea infuriated him.

"What's the problem?" He spoke a low tone so Adam couldn't overhear. "I grew up on a horse. My son needs to be able to ride too." Then in a harsher tone he added, "Do you think I'd let anything happened to him? Don't be ridiculous. He'll be fine."

Olivia chewed on her bottom lip. "I really wish you had spoken with me before promising him he could go with you this morning."

"Why? So you could have said no?"

"Hey. What are y'all whispering about?"

Olivia smiled at her son. "Just grown-up stuff. You wouldn't be interested."

Adam huffed. "You always say that when you don't want to tell me something. You know I'm almost six."

"Not hardly." Olivia tossed a look at Mitch. "You better make sure he comes back in one piece. And don't think you're going without me."

"Fine. Come along. I've got a spunky, little mare you'll love." When her face paled at the mention of the lively mare, he added, "I thought you'd like that."

She shook her head. "I've already called down to the barn this morning and spoken with Hobbs. He said he knew just the horse to give me."

"Yeah," Adam said with a mouth full of oatmeal. "She said she wanted something old and slow."

"Don't talk with your mouth full," Olivia said.

Chapter Ten

✤

Mitch pulled a beat-up, mud-covered Ford F-350 around to the front of the house and stopped. Olivia and Adam climbed into the front seat, her jeans catching on the tears in the seat repaired with strips of duct tape. Looking around the truck, she laughed. "You didn't have to pull out the fancy truck just for us."

Mitch grinned and put the vehicle in first gear. "Anything to impress you guys."

Adam bounced on the seat. "How far, huh? How far?"

Mitch shifted into second. "Not far."

"I'm a little surprised you built the house so far from the barn."

Mitch frowned. "Joanna wasn't much of a horse woman. Said the smell of horses made her ill."

"Hmm. Well, to each their own, I guess." Olivia turned to look out the window. "You have a beautiful place, Mitch."

"Thanks. I've enjoyed being home again."

He stopped in front of a large red barn. Cowboys in

jeans, dirty boots and sweat-stained hats milled around waiting to get the day started.

The thought of being on a horse after so many years made Olivia's heart claw up into her throat. She locked her fingers together to quell the shakes. It wasn't falling off a horse that unnerved her. Heck, she'd been bucked lots of times growing up. But every time she looked at Adam, she thanked God he'd lived after such a premature birth. Riding so far into her pregnancy had been foolhardy and rash and made her realize that Adam had to come first. She couldn't risk another fall and possible long-term injury, or even death, once she'd become a mother.

But she should have known this day would come. This is what happens when you let a cowboy father your baby. The baby will grow up wanting to ride horses, and have a father who'll encourage it.

Hobbs led a gray mare from the stable. Given the flea-bitten color and swayback, this old gal had some age on her. Olivia caught Hobbs's gaze and gave him a smile and nod. The mare was exactly what she needed. Slow enough to give her time to adjust again to the back of a horse and fast enough—she hoped—to keep up with Mitch and Adam.

Mitch wheeled the rattle-trap truck off to the side before hopping from the driver's seat. Adam climbed over and out the driver's door right behind Mitch. Once Olivia unclasped her fingers to reach for the door handle, she noticed the shake had returned. Taking a deep, steadying breath, she opened her door and stepped out, balancing on her crutches. Man, she hated these things. The sooner she could walk—even hobble—she was tossing them in the closet.

"Hobbs. Why did you saddle Lady Belle?" Mitch

walked over to the gray mare and stroked her nose. "Hey, girl. Did mean ol' Hobbs wake you up too early?"

"She's for Ms. Gentry," Hobbs said. "She asked me for a gentle mare, and there's none more gentle than Lady B."

Olivia hobbled over as quickly as she could before Mitch could tell Hobbs to saddle a different horse. "She's perfect," Olivia said. She slid her fingers down the mare's velvety nose. "I don't think I ever get tired of this. I love how soft their hair feels." She pulled an apple from her pocket. "I brought you something, girl. We're going to be buddies, right?"

"I have much better horses, Olivia. Bigger. Faster. More like what you're used to."

Olivia's gut roiled at the idea of a different horse. Had she not learned how quickly things change? How quickly life can end? The thought of her beloved horse Alice Cooper after their devastating accident caused a hitch in her breath. If she lived to a hundred, she'd never forget the look in the mare's eyes right before Travis put her down.

"Olivia? Are you okay?" You're as white as a sheet."

Olivia licked her lips and pushed the threatening nausea back down. "I'm fine. I don't want a different horse, do I, girl?" Olivia moved the apple to the palm of her hand.

Lady Belle's lips pulled back and her teeth clamped around the red apple.

Olivia laughed and rubbed the horse's nose. "Very ladylike."

A look of confusion flashed across Mitch's face before he shrugged. "Fine. You can ride any horse you want in the stables."

Olivia noticed Adam was glued to Mitch's side. Probably thought if he stayed close to Mitch she wouldn't have the chance to make Adam ride with her.

"C'mon kiddo. Let's go get our horse," Mitch said.

"Yeah. I want a fast one. And a big one." The grin that popped onto Adam's face was so broad and so bright there was no way she could change her mind, but the thought of Adam on a fast horse whipped the acid in her stomach into a froth. She swallowed against the fear climbing into her throat to join her heart.

Mitch picked up Adam and sat him on a fence rail before turning his back. "Hop on."

Adam climbed on Mitch's back and wrapped his legs around Mitch's waist. Olivia watched as they walked toward the barn, Adam chattering like an over-caffeinated magpie. Mitch's head nodded as he listened.

Olivia patted Lady Belle's neck. "Okay, girl. Let's check your saddle."

The western-style saddle sat securely on the horse blanket. A single cinch strap was wrapped around Lady Belle's belly. The belt appeared snug around the horse. It might have been almost six years since she'd ridden, but she remembered all the puffing up tricks. Usually she would gently knee Lady Belle's gut to make her exhale so the strap could be cinched tight. But on crutches, that would be impossible.

Before she could ask for help, a squeal that could only belong to her son drew her attention and stole her breath. She turned to see Mitch leading an enormous beast from the stable. Adam sat high in the saddle of the mahogany-color steed that had to be at least sixteen hands. The idea of Adam falling from such a height practically stopped Olivia's heart.

Fringe flopped from a pair of miniature leather chaps that had magically appeared on her son's legs. Adam's hands squeezed the saddle's horn. The boy's face shone like someone had thrown a spotlight on him. When he saw Olivia, he loosened one hand enough to wave.

"Momma. Look at me. I'm riding all by myself."

Olivia gulped again. Nervous fear swelled in her throat. Forcing a smile on her frozen lips, she said, "I see you, honey. Hold on with both of your hands, okay?"

Mitch led the large animal toward her. While the horse seemed calm and placid as it neared her, Olivia had to force herself to hold her ground, force herself to project a calm exterior.

"He's a natural," Mitch said. "Must be in the genes."

Adam looked at his denim clad legs. "Yep. It's my new jeans."

Mitch laughed. "Hobbs. Everyone ready to head out?"

"All except your guest."

Mitch looked at Olivia, then at her crutches before arching an eyebrow. "Problem?"

Olivia ran her hand under Lady Belle's stomach band. "I need this tightened. I was trying to figure out how to do that. On crutches it's a little tough."

Mitch pursed his lips. "A little tough?" he repeated. "How about a little impossible?" He tossed the reins of his cutting horse to one of the cowboys. "Hold this." Mitch stepped up beside Olivia. "Scoot over," he said, then turned toward the horse, leaving Olivia staring at his denim-covered bottom. She might not want to admit it, but the man looked good in jeans. Then the memory of how good he looked all over flashed through her mind and she felt her flush as it rushed up her neck and onto her cheeks.

Her fascination with his shape only intensified when he bent his leg to tap his knee against Lady Belle's gut to force her to exhale. That action moved the muscles in his rear in such a delectable fashion it had Olivia licking her lips. When he jerked the strap through the rigging ring, securing the saddle tight on the horse's back, the muscles in his forearm twitched and flexed, reminding her of how strong Mitch was. Reminded her of the time he held her against a shower wall while making love.

"There," Mitch said, stepping back to admire his work. He looked at Olivia. "Are you okay? You look a little flushed."

"I'm fine. Just excited to get going," she lied.

"Have you thought about how you're going to get on Lady Belle?"

She gritted her teeth. He knew she was going to need some help. Her lips pressed together as she thought of how to answer him.

"I've got an idea." He picked her up and sat her in the saddle. Her crutches fell to the ground. He picked them up, walked over to his truck and tossed them into the passenger's seat. "Now, let's get gone. Daylight's burning."

She wanted to be incensed at how he manhandled her into the saddle, but the feel of his strong, hot hands around her waist, the bunching of the muscles in his arms as he'd lifted her, woke a swarm of butterflies in her stomach. Of course, that fluttering could be fear of being on the back of a horse. Or it could be because she was supposed to be sitting with her leg propped up and not riding a horse. But Dr. Gowen would just have to cut her some slack today. No way was Adam going without her nearby.

Olivia checked her watch. Daylight burning, indeed. It was just now six a.m.

Mitch threw himself into the western saddle behind

Adam. Gathering the reins in his right hand, he wrapped his left arm around Adam and pulled him snug.

"Grab the horn and hold on," he instructed Adam.

Adam wrapped all ten fingers around the saddle's knob. "I'm ready. Let's go."

Hobbs rode out first with the rest of the cowboys close behind at a trot. Mitch wheeled his horse toward the other riders and followed at a somewhat slower pace. Olivia was left in the yard. She clicked her tongue and tapped the heels of her boots against Lady Belle's side. The horse began to move at a pace appropriate to a snail —perfect as far as Olivia was concerned.

Lady Belle's broad body between her legs felt as familiar and comfortable as a worn pair of jeans. She'd missed the feel of having a thousand pounds of horse-flesh under her control. She leaned forward and patted the old horse's neck. "Good girl. You're exactly what I needed today." And she was. Olivia hadn't realized how much she'd missed riding until now.

But as good as it felt to be on a horse's back, she couldn't help but flashback on that awful day six years ago. Given her advanced pregnancy, she had no business riding Alice Cooper, but she'd spent so many years on a horse, and on her personal mare specifically, riding was like breathing.

The day had started out well. The sun was full and bright, but the typical sweltering Texas temperatures hadn't yet arrived. The grass had just begun to turn green. Tiny leaves were pushing their way out of tree limbs. She and new husband, Drake, were spending the weekend with her parents. She'd awakened that morning rested but restless. The Dallas Herald newspaper arrived on her parents' doorstep delivering a two-page spread on the society wedding of Mitch Landry to Joanna St.

Claire. Although she'd known of the wedding plans from
Mitch's own mouth, the reality of the situation spelled
out for her in color pictures and detailed descriptions
sent her fleeing to where she always found her comfort…
riding and her beloved Alice Cooper. AC greeted her
with a toss of her head and a loud neigh, seemingly as
restless as Olivia herself.

So far, her pregnancy had been unremarkable. No
hint of any problems other than some light spotting early
in the first trimester, but her doctors had assured her
there was nothing to worry about. As she'd stroked AC's
nose and neck, Olivia told herself that between being a
new mother, a new wife and running her gym business,
her opportunities for riding would be few and far
between. She wasn't due to deliver for another ten weeks.
She needed the peace and comfort that riding always
gave her.

After saddling her racer, Olivia had used a small
ladder to help propel her onto the horse's back. At a little
over seven months pregnant, swinging into the saddle
using a stirrup was out of the question. Nudging Alice
Cooper forward with her knees and a click of her
tongue, they'd charged from the barn into the open
pasture. Her pregnant belly poked over the saddle's
horn, making the ride uncomfortable at times, but the
sheer joy and mental high she got from being out in fresh
air—and as far away from the newspaper reports of
Mitch's wedding as she could get—offset any minor
physical discomfort.

About forty minutes after she'd ridden out, she
turned into a pasture Travis had added to his holdings.
She'd never been on that piece of land and should have
been more cautious, but she'd finally lost a battle with
her emotions and tears filled her eyes. Blurry-eyed, she

failed to see the uneven ground and numerous holes. She kicked AC into a gallop, sending them both charging across the unfamiliar landscape. Five minutes into the run, AC's front leg dropped into a deep hole, causing the horse to stumble and tossing Olivia over the horse's head and onto her swollen abdomen. Alice Cooper screamed in pain. Olivia looked on in horror as her beloved mare tried to stand on a broken front leg. The rest of the day was pretty much a blur. The phone call to Drake. The ambulance arriving to transport her to the hospital. The pain in AC's eyes just before Travis was forced to put her down.

Her breath skipped at the memory. A blanket of guilt settled over heart.

"Hey, pokey. Get a move on," Mitch called over his shoulder.

"Yeah, pokey," Adam parroted.

Olivia's vision focused on her son's shinning face. She pushed her lips up into a smile. "What'd you call me?"

Adam threw his head back against Mitch's chest and giggled hysterically.

"Everything okay with Lady Belle?" Mitch asked as he circled back into the barnyard. "She not the spunkiest mare I own, but usually she's faster than this."

Olivia shook her head. "No, no. Everything's fine. I was just thinking."

Adam looked over his shoulder at Mitch. "She thinks a lot."

Giving Adam a very serious look, Mitch nodded. "I see." He looked at Olivia. "Do try to keep up with the rest of us. I realize you haven't ridden in this pasture before, but I don't have time to keep circling back to check on you."

Heat climbed into Olivia's cheeks. She nodded. With

that, Mitch turned his horse and cantered toward the rear of the herd of slow-moving cattle.

The sound of hooves beating on dirt reached her ears just before Sylvia Landry rode up beside her.

"Good morning, Olivia."

Olivia smiled at the older woman. "Morning, Sylvia. I see you're up with us early birds this morning."

The older woman shook her head with a chuckle. "Robert loves getting out there with his sons to move the cattle so I told him I'd ride over this morning."

Olivia looked around. "I didn't see Caleb. Is he home from college?"

"No. I don't know what I was thinking. It's just Mitch out there."

Olivia knew Sylvia was remembering the days with her husband working alongside James and Mitch before James's death. The two women began walking their horses side by side.

"I would have liked to see Caleb. It's been a long time."

"Yes, it has." The older woman paced her horse to match Olivia's speed. "It's good to see you on a horse again, dear. You doing okay?"

Olivia nodded then drew in a shaky breath. "So far, so good. I admit my heart's racing just a tad." She patted Lady Belle's neck. "But I'm being well taken care of this morning."

"Lady Belle is a good horse. You pick her?"

"Nope. Hobbs."

Sylvia nodded. "Good choice."

They rode in silence for a moment, both of them ignoring the elephant in the room, so to speak.

Finally, Sylvia sighed. "Okay, you haven't volunteered

any information, so I guess I have to ask. What happened after I left last night?"

"Nothing. Mitch locked himself in his study and we didn't see him the rest of the night. I figured he'd called y'all."

She snorted. "Oh yeah, he called. Must have left ten different messages but…" Sylvia caught Olivia's gaze. "This isn't our story to tell him. You have to be the one to explain about the accident and Adam's birth. Robert and I can't keep avoiding our son."

Mitch's whistle drew her eyes toward him. A calf had decided to make a run for it. Mitch signaled and one of the ranch hands broke off and raced after the small black calf. Within moments, the cowboy had the little guy rounded up and reunited with his bawling mother. If she'd had any remaining questions about allowing Adam to come along today to move cattle, they were answered by the whoop and grin on his face right now. She couldn't hear the conversation, but Adam appeared to be talking non-stop to Mitch, who didn't show the least bit of annoyance, more like the patience of Job.

Olivia drew in the smell of horseflesh, dirt and cattle. The combination of scents took her back to her earlier life of rodeos, barrel racing and cowboys. Until today, she hadn't missed those days, but a wave of nostalgia swept through her and elicited a loud sigh. She looked back at Sylvia. "I'm sorry you got caught in the middle of this mess." She shook her head. "My mother should never have called you that night. But since we were all convinced Adam wouldn't make it to morning, she thought you should meet him. She meant well, but it sure has put you in a rough situation with Mitch. I've always been bothered by that."

"I thank God every day that not only did Adam live,

but that you've allowed us to be a part of his life. I agree this is a bad situation all around. But talk to Mitch. You two have got to figure out how you're going to make this shared parenthood work."

The idea of sharing her son with Mitch made Olivia feel slightly queasy. She swallowed against the rising nausea and nodded. "I will. Soon. I promise."

THREE DAYS OF EARLY MORNINGS AND HARD RANCH work had finally taken their toll on her son.

"Adam. Sit up and eat your dinner," Olivia said as an exhausted Adam slumped in his chair.

Getting him to bed each night had been easy. Keeping him awake for dinner and baths was the challenge. But still, she couldn't remember ever seeing Adam so happy. He mimicked Mitch in dress, attitude and stand.

Last night at supper, he'd complained when he'd been given milk to drink while Mitch drank tea. Mitch had stood, poured his tea in the sink and refilled his glass with milk. Olivia's heart had softened at Mitch's action. So far, nothing she'd said or done had softened Mitch toward her. Around their son, Mitch smiled and chatted, putting on a good front, but outside Adam's presence, Mitch hadn't spoken to Olivia.

The tension between them was palpable. Olivia knew she couldn't let this go on. Time had come to open up the can of worms known as their past.

Adam propped his elbow on the table and his head in his hand, holding his face a scant few inches from plate. "I am sitting up."

His little-boy whine screamed overtiredness. Olivia wondered if she'd be able to keep him awake long enough to take a bath. His eyes slid shut. His head swayed dangerously close to his mashed potatoes.

"I think he's done, Magda."

Magda ruffled his hair. "Long day, huh?"

Adam yawned and opened his eyes. "Me and Mitch worked hard today. He said I was the best help he'd ever had."

"You sure were," Mitch said. "You're gonna be the best cowboy on the ranch pretty soon."

Magda smiled at the child. "I bet you were loads of help." She picked up his dishes and carried them to the sink.

"I think it's bath time for you," Olivia said, pushing her plate away. "You smell like that little calf that tried to make a getaway the other day."

Adam giggled. "Do not."

Olivia struggled to her feet, slipping the crutches under her arms. "Oh yeah, you do," she said with a laugh. "I'm going to herd you into the bath like that cowboy herded that calf."

Adam stood but dragged his feet leaving the table.

"What's wrong?"

"I don't want to take a bath anymore. Cowboys take showers, not baths."

"Is that so? Says who?"

"Hobbs."

Magda laughed. "Good ol' Hobbs strikes again."

Olivia brushed a lock of sweaty hair off Adam's face. "Well, I think Hobbs is wrong. Remember that movie we watched last month? That cowboy took a bath. Remember?"

Adam squinted as he thought. "Yeah." He yawned again. "Do you, Mitch?"

Mitch smiled. "Sure I do, buddy." He leaned over

and made a big production out of sniffing Adam's head. "And your mom's right. You do smell a little like a cow."

Adam laughed.

Olivia pointed a crutch toward the door. "Okay, cowboy. Let's go." Before she'd taken a step, her phone began playing the theme from Jurassic Park.

"Drake," Adam yelled. "Let me talk to him. I wanna tell him about riding a horse today."

She hesitated answering the phone. Her gaze met Mitch's across the table. His expression hardened. Before she could stop him, Adam snatched her phone off the table.

"'Ello? Drake? It's Adam." Adam laughed at something Drake said. "I miss you too. But guess what? Mitch says I'm the best cowboy he's ever had. Uh huh." He listened "Uh huh. Uh huh. Okay." He held the phone out to Olivia. "He wants to talk to you."

She took the phone. "Hi, Drake. Can I call you back? I was just getting ready to give Adam a bath."

"I'll do it." Mitch shoved his chair back and stood.

"Hold on a sec." She covered the receiver. "You don't have to. I can call him back."

Adam looked with an anxious expression from his mother to Mitch. The last thing Olivia wanted was for Adam to pick up on the tension between Mitch and her. She forced her hunched shoulders down into a relaxed position and smiled at her son. "I—"

"Olivia. I can bathe him. In fact—" he picked up Adam and threw him over his shoulder like a sack of potatoes, "—us guys have to stick together. Right, buddy?"

Adam giggled and wiggled around until he could see Olivia. "Yeah, Momma. Us guys are stickin' together."

"Okay, but make sure he washes behind his ears."

"Ears?" Mitch said as he walked out the room. "What ears?"

Adam howled with laughter.

Olivia shook her head. "I'm back, Drake. How's the dig going?"

Chapter Eleven

I n the six days since he'd discovered he had a child, Mitch also discovered his son was well-adjusted, funny and inquisitive. Nothing escaped Adam's attention. Many times he reminded Mitch of his younger brother, Caleb.

But if Mitch had had any residual question about Adam being his son—and he really didn't—tonight's bath sealed the deal. As he had lifted Adam into the tub, he'd noticed a brown birthmark on the back of Adam's right thigh—the same one Mitch had, the same one Mitch's dad had.

Mitch had always thought he understood how strong the pull of love could be. Now, as he stood at Adam's bedside watching him sleep, he realized he'd never had a clue. His heart felt ten sizes larger than it'd been just a week ago.

An overwhelming urge to protect his son from all the hurts in the world filled every crevice of his soul like sand between rocks. There was nothing he wouldn't do, wouldn't get for his son. Nothing.

That he'd missed so many years of Adam's life, missed the major milestones like walking and first words, infuriated Mitch. Combined with the undeniable fact that his parents not only knew about Adam but had had a relationship with their grandson shot his blood pressure into orbit. Attempts to talk to either of his parents about their part in Olivia's deception always returned the same response... *Talk to Olivia.* While he knew they were right and he did need to talk with Olivia, he had to wait until his fury at her duplicity had lessened.

So tonight would be the night for their talk, even if he had to break into his own bedroom. First, he needed to get out of his wet clothes and take his own shower, but his feet were glued in place. Pulling his damp shirt away from his chest, he chuckled. How was he to know that a bathtub of water, plastic cups and a five-year-old boy added up to splashes and sloshes of water over the tub's rim?

The scent of lavender alerted him to Olivia's presence seconds before she made her way quietly to his side. "Thanks for giving him his bath." She touched a wet spot on his shirt. Her finger burnt like a lit match. "What happened?"

He shrugged.

She chuckled. "Let me guess. Too much water in the tub and a set of cups." She nudged his shoulder. "Amateur."

The word made the lost years with his son a painful reality that drilled a burning hole through his gut. He struck without thinking. "Whose fault is that?"

The smile fell from her face as a mask of regret took its place. "I know. I'm sorry," she whispered, then stepped around him to the bed. "He's my life." She looked over her shoulder. "I love him more than words can describe. I did what I thought best at the time. Can you understand that?"

He looked at his son, then back at Olivia. "Yeah. I get it."

After tucking the covers snuggly around Adam, she leaned over and kissed his forehead. She glanced at Mitch. "I think it's time we talked...about Adam, Joanna, everything."

"Way past time, I'd say."

Her cheek muscles tightened. She was probably gritting her teeth. Well, let her. He'd worn his almost down to nubs.

"Your office?"

He tilted his head toward the door and she followed him into the hall, pulling Adam's door behind her until a slight opening was left.

"I'm not thrilled that he's up here and I'm downstairs, but I have to admit he seems to be doing fine."

Mitch shot a pointed look at the stairs and back to Olivia. "Like you could have gone up and down those stairs multiple times a day, which does beg the question, how did you get up here tonight?"

"Not easily. Hopped up each step."

"Not smart, Olivia," he said with a shake of his head. "But since you're already up here, c'mon. We can sit on the deck outside the guest room." He opened the door to his temporary bedroom. "Unless you're afraid to walk through a bedroom with me."

"Don't be ridiculous. I can restrain myself from throwing you on the bed."

He grinned at the vision she described. He couldn't help it. As mad as he was about her keeping Adam from him, he still loved being with her.

OLIVIA SWUNG AROUND ON HER CRUTCHES AND MADE her way into his room. His scent filled the room, assaulted her senses as she entered. She paused. The room was spotless. Bed still made. No clothes thrown away. No boots lying around.

"Nice room. Very neat."

"Thanks, but tell Magda. She's a gem. Not sure what I'd do without her."

Olivia wondered if Hobbs had it in the back of his mind to marry his daughter off to Mitch. Wouldn't that put a dent in Joanna's plans to get Mitch back?

She sighed. Good thing she wasn't entering a horse in that race. Once she was back on her feet, she'd be hightailing it back to Dallas as fast as her credit card could book airfare and be glad to be gone, done with her infatuation with Mitch, and her roiling gut, and her jealousy, and—

Liar.

"I assume we're heading out those?" She pointed one crutch toward a pair of French doors.

"Yeah, but can you give ten minutes? I want to finish what Adam started." When she frowned in confusion, he pulled his wet shirt away from his chest again. "A quick shower, then I'll join you. Okay?"

"Sure. Whatever." She opened one of the doors, hobbled through and shut it. The last thing she wanted to see was a naked Mitch.

She touched the tip of her nose to see if it was growing. A naked Mitch would be the number one item on any woman's must-do list…including hers.

The night air was warm, but not yet filled with the typical south Texas humidity. Soft mooing in the distance accompanied the closer croaking of tree frogs. A light breeze twisted her skirt around her thighs. She drew in a deep breath of the mesquite-scented air and released it slowly, forcing tension from her neck and back. The throbbing muscles in her legs and arms confirmed she'd been too long off a horse to hop back on without twinges and aches. But she was fine with those. It was the twinges and aches in her heart that threatened to wring her dry.

Toward the far end of the concrete terrace, Mitch—or more likely Magda—had set up a table and chairs. She headed there, the plan being to get off her leg and give it a rest. As she dropped into a chair with a sigh, she glanced over her right shoulder. Below her the Olympic-sized pool glistened in the moonlight. Heat flushed her cheeks as she thought about her nightly swims and whirlpool therapy. If she'd known someone could have seen her…

"There you are," Mitch said, pushing the door shut with his heel. He held up a bottle and two shot glasses. "Crown Royal Reserve."

"You remembered."

He snorted a chuckle. "How could anyone forget that you made a mini-skirt out of all our empty Crown Royal sacks?"

She smiled at the memory of Mitch's fraternity Spring Fling. "Hey!" she said indigently. "I looked hot in that skirt."

He set the bottle and glasses on the table. "No kidding. I couldn't keep my eyes off your legs that night." He chuckled. "Hell, I thought I was going to have to kill a few frat brothers who couldn't take their eyes off you either." He cracked the top of the unopened bottle and poured a couple of shots. "Salute."

Olivia took the second glass, tapped his and drank. "Oh man. That was excellent. Another."

He arched an eyebrow but said nothing as he refilled

her glass. After she downed the second shot and pointed for a third, he said, "Liquid courage, Livie?"

She rolled the shot glass between the palms of her hands. "Maybe." She drank the shot, collected her crutches and stood.

"Where are you going?"

"I'm not leaving, it's just…" She walked a couple of paces away. "This is hard, Mitch." She glanced at him. Nervous waves lapped at the sides of her stomach. She wiped sweaty palms on her shorts and grasped the handles on her crutches. "Let me talk, okay? No interruptions."

He leaned back in his chair and nodded.

She sighed and paced the best she could with a sprained ankle, twisted knee and crutches.

"I didn't know I was pregnant when you left. When I missed my period, I didn't give it a lot of thought. I'd been stressed over our split. Plus, I'd never been very regular, so I wrote it off as normal. By the time I'd missed the third month, I'd been having nausea for a couple of weeks." She laughed mirthlessly. "I was sure I had the flu." She gazed over at him. "Denial is an incredibly persuasive state." Lust curled inside her gut. She looked away because, damn it, he still looked so good to her.

And she wished he didn't.

Life would be much easier if she could keep him—and her feelings—in the past. And that might be possible if she wasn't so attracted to him. All the more reason the sooner she got away, the better it'd be. She'd never survive being rejected by him again.

She made her way to the low concrete wall around the terrace and braced herself on the edge. "I went to the doctor expecting her to give me something to get me through flu season. When she asked if I could be pregnant, my first response was no, of course not. Then I remembered our last night together and I knew. I had all the symptoms. Nausea. Missed periods. Sore breasts." She shook her head. "And I had a reasonable explanation for each of them. Flu. Menstrual irregularity. Overexertion during my workouts."

She paused, trying to find the right words to explain what she did and why. This was hard...as hard as she'd feared. When Mitch didn't say anything, she sneaked a peek to make sure he was still awake. Icy blue eyes bore into her. A familiar bolt of desire rattled through her, just as it had the first time she'd laid eyes on him. If only she'd had a third hand capable of carrying her liquid courage—as Mitch called it—with her as she paced.

Knowing she had to continue, she swallowed the lump in the throat and broke his gaze's grip to look down at the pool again. "When my doctor told me I was pregnant, you cannot believe how happy I was. I was having your baby. I couldn't imagine anything more wonderful in the world. And even though you'd told me you didn't want to get married or have kids, I was sure that you'd be thrilled when I told you. I'm pretty sure my feet didn't touch the pavement as I walked to my car."

She paced to the other side of the deck, not venturing a glance at him this time because this next part of her story was going to be difficult enough without seeing the damning in his eyes. "I started to call you immediately, but it'd been three months since we'd talked and I wasn't sure how to tell you." A hollow laugh bubbled up her throat. "Hi, Mitch. I know we haven't talked in a while and you told me to date other guys, but guess what? You're going to be a father." Each breath was like sucking a thick milkshake through a thin straw. Lightheadedness made her vision swim, but she welcomed the dreamlike feeling. Standing on Mitch's deck with their son asleep across the hall didn't feel real either.

"I wrote practice scripts. I planned elaborate ways to tell you. Skywriting. Singing telegrams. Quiet candlelit dinners. Once the euphoria faded and reality set in, I realized I had no idea how you might take the news. I decided the best way to do this would be to tell you in person. I'd planned to come to the ranch over a weekend. Then James died and everything changed. I didn't want to add to your stress, and since waiting a week or so wouldn't make a difference I decided to wait until things settled down." She walked a few paces along the retaining wall. "Of course, I couldn't come to his funeral. There was no way I could see you and not tell you, so I put it off another week. A month had passed before I got the nerve again to call you but you called me instead." She squeezed the wooden railing, trying to stem the flow of tears building in her eyes. "My hands shook so violently when I heard your voice. I'd missed you so much. Had prayed for you to call. Finally, you had. I could barely hold the phone to my ear. My mind went wild with all my practiced speeches."

She went back to the table, pointed a finger at her glass. He filled it without a word. She drank it and paced away again. "But before I could tell you my news, you told me yours. Joanna was pregnant with James's child…" Her voice hitched. Clearing her throat, she continued, "You were marrying her so the baby would be a Landry, and well, I don't know how I held it together. I knew the three of you had been inseparable growing up. I knew, or I thought, you loved her like a sister, but then this. I was…"

The memory of the phone conversation gutted her again. She massaged her abdomen, unable to reach the pain deep inside. The patio lights beneath her blurred in her teary eyes, then a tear rolled down her cheek. "I didn't know what to do. There was no way to make things right." She swiped at the tear and sniffed back the rest before turning toward him. She hoped he hadn't noticed. "What I did know was that I'd never heard that much stress and sadness in your voice. I couldn't imagine losing one of my brothers. It'd kill me." She turned her back to him. "You'd made your plans. And whether right or wrong, I loved you too much to toss another bomb into your life. So I didn't. You asked me to let you go. I let you go. It was the hardest thing I've ever done."

She walked back to her chair and sat, letting her crutches drop to the deck. "So there you have it. That's the story."

She drew back as he leaned toward her. "Not quite all the story. How did my parents come to meet Adam and what kind of threat did you use to keep them from telling me, because I know they wouldn't have done that on their own. And Drake? How does he fit into the picture?"

She flinched at hostility in his voice and the fact he'd nailed the situation with his parents. She had threatened them…sort of.

She dragged her fingers through her hair. "Drake." All the air left her lungs in a long exhalation. "Drake and Travis met in first grade. As far back as I can remember, Drake was hanging around our house, riding the horses, helping with the ranch chores. Somewhere around the age of eight or nine, Mom found cuts on Drake's and Travis's wrists." She smiled at the memory. "They'd decided to become blood brothers. Mom washed and bandaged both their arms but I don't think they did much more than scratch the surface. Anyway, Drake sort of became brother number four, until he went off to college. When he came back, he was different. More serious, or at least more serious about me. We went out a couple of times, but it wasn't long after the third date that I met you."

She looked at Mitch and tilted her head to one side with a one-shoulder shrug. "And that's all she wrote when it came to other men. You were it for me."

She scooted forward in her chair and clasped her hands between her knees, her forearms resting on her thighs. "Drake didn't give up completely, but he didn't push me either. A few days after you called with your wedding plans, Drake asked me to marry him." She blew out a long breath. "When you got married, he was there for me. He held me when I cried. Rubbed my shoulders when I couldn't sleep. Even went to childbirth classes. I needed his strength and love to survive. He gave it and never asked for anything in return except to be my husband and help raise my child."

Pausing, she stared at the space between her feet and her gaze traced the stone pattern in the flooring. She thought about the nightly calls from Drake asking if he could come get her and Adam, asking her to marry him again, promising her anything she wanted if they could put their family together again.

Her eyes misted over as she came to the next chapter of her story. She told him about the ill-fated ride on

Alice Cooper, her fall and about Travis having to put
AC down.

"Apparently, when I hit the ground, the jarring
caused the placenta to start detaching. Or maybe it was
already a problem. I don't know. The doctors told me the
fall wouldn't have caused the problem, but I think they
were just trying to make me feel less guilty. Anyway,
Adam came early…weeks early. He had lots of problems. Breathing. Jaundice. Feeding. The doctors didn't
think he'd live. Without telling me, my mother called
your mother. She thought your mother should get to see
her first grandchild before he died."

Olivia straightened, then leaned on the arm of her
chair, propping her chin in her hand. "I wish she hadn't.
I know Mom meant well, but her call put your parents in
an awful situation. When Adam turned the corner and
the doctors became optimistic about his progress, your
mother begged me to tell you, but you were married.
Joanna had recently miscarried her pregnancy. Your
whole family was still in shock over James's death and
then the loss of his child. I didn't know how you and
Joanna were getting along but the last thing either of you
needed was another emotional blow." She closed her
eyes, remembering all her fears, her threats to his
parents. "I told your parents that if they told you, I'd
never let them see Adam. Threatened to move somewhere else and not tell them where I was." Tears leaked
down her cheeks. "God, I was awful. Even though I was
married to Drake, I was insane with jealousy over your
marriage. Baby hormones ran amok through my body.

"I know your parents might have sued under Texas
law for visitation rights, but since I'd named Drake as the
father, the odds they would win were slim. They weren't
happy with my decision, but thank goodness you have

great parents. I believe they thought I'd change my mind, and I almost did a couple of times. Since Joanna had just miscarried, I knew I couldn't tell you then. It would have been a crappy thing to do to her…and you. Then your marriage started floundering, and I didn't want to be responsible if you divorced. When you did finally divorce, I thought you'd contact me. I didn't want you to want me because of Adam, so I waited for you to call, but you never did."

She finally met his gaze. "So that's it. The whole story."

Mitch poured both of them shots of bourbon. He downed his in one gulp. "Why did you marry Drake? You claim you loved me, so how could you marry another man knowing you were carrying my child?"

"How could you have married another woman when you had claimed to love me just a few months before?" She held up her hand when he started to speak. "I did— do love Drake." She looked at Mitch. "Maybe I didn't love him enough. I don't know. He loved me, and at that time in my life I needed to be loved. He understood I didn't love him like he loved me, but he was okay with that." She gave a rueful smile. "Said he loved me enough for both of us. He is such a good man. Kind. Consider- ate. He adored Adam…and me. He deserved more than I could give him. When we divorced, I pleaded with him to find someone better than me. He let me divorce him but he stayed in my life, in Adam's life."

Mitch drummed his fingers on the arm of his chair. "So he just calls in every single night to check in?"

Heat rose in Olivia's cheeks. "Not exactly. I called him before we left Dallas. I knew he'd be worried if he couldn't reach me. Plus, I wanted to tell him about the accident and about seeing you again. He knew it wouldn't take you long to figure out Adam was your son. He called because…" She looked away, searching for the right words. Turning back to face him, she said, "He gave me the divorce because I asked him to, but he never wanted it. Tonight, he called to tell me that he's giving up his job in Wyoming and taking a teaching position at SMU. He's moving back to Dallas to be with me and Adam. He wants us to try again. He asked me to marry him."

Even in the inky darkness, Olivia could see Mitch's face harden. "I see. What did you tell him? I hope you told him to take a flying leap off a cliff."

When she didn't say anything Mitch grabbed her wrist. "You told him yes?" His voice was low, almost threatening. "If you think I'm going to let another man raise my son——"

She jerked her arm away and rubbed her wrist. "Stop it. You don't have any right to tell me who I can and cannot marry, but no, I didn't say yes. I told him I'd think about it."

"Why? Why marry him again? You don't love him."

"Because of you."

"Me?" His voice vibrated in anger. "What do I have to do with this?"

"I've listened to you. I've heard what you've said and you're right. Adam needs a full-time dad. My brothers are wonderful with him and Dad is the best grandfather in the world, but you're right, okay? Adam needs a male role model in his life on a permanent basis, not on weekends or holidays. You made your point. I've heard you loud and clear."

"Are you even listening to yourself? I didn't say Adam needed *any* father. I said he needed *his* father. Hey, here's an idea. You marry me and move here. No need for Drake to rearrange his life."

"God. Could you be more arrogant?" She struggled to her feet. Her racing blood rushed the intoxicating bourbon from her gut, to her blood, to her head. Pain and disappointment squeezed her heart. She'd fantasized about Mitch asking her to marry, how he'd do it, what she'd say, but never had her daydreams included a royal decree to marry and move.

But then, how pitiful was she that if he'd said anything about loving her, she'd have done just that. Uprooted her son, sold her business and moved in with a man whose eyes were black with fury right now.

"Where are you going? Sit back down," he ordered. "We're not through talking."

She whirled around with the most dignity she could muster while balanced on crutches and glared at him. "I'm through." Her voice was gritty and harsh. "Through with this talk. This house. And you."

She wobbled slightly from the effects of the Crown Royal before getting her crutch-walking rhythm under control. The sound of a chair slamming against the railing made her flinch. In a second, Mitch grabbed her forearm.

"Wait just a minute. We had a deal. You stay here until you can walk without those crutches. I'll get to spend some time getting to know my son. You've had almost six years. I need more than six days."

She jerked away, losing her balance and falling forward. The stone flooring rushed toward her face. At the last moment, Mitch wrapped his arm around her waist, stopping her short of planting her face in his terrace. He stood her upright and held on until she got her footing.

"Thanks, but that doesn't change anything. I wasn't sure what answer I would give Drake to his marriage proposals, but thank you for helping me make up my mind." She moved as quickly as she could toward the door.

"What the hell does that mean?" he shouted.

"You figure it out."

Chapter Twelve

R*emarry Drake.* When would she stop shooting off
her mouth? She wasn't planning on remarrying
Drake. She did care about him—loved him even—but
how fair would it be to either of them when what she felt
for him was maybe a tenth of what she felt for Mitch. If
only her feeling quotient for each man were reversed.

Olivia closed the door to the deck and made her way
through Mitch's temporary bedroom. At the end of his
bed, she stopped, closed her eyes and allowed the woodsy
scent of his cologne to fill her nose. An odd combination
of despair and desire swept through her. She drew in one
final deep breath and left his room. A quick check on
Adam found him asleep and blissfully unaware of the
tension and harsh words that'd filled the air moments
ago.

At the top of the stairs, Olivia paused to plan how to
get to the bottom without sliding down each step on her
behind. After pulling the right crutch from under her
arm, she let it slide down the stairs. Grabbing hold of the
handrail, she bent her leg ready to hop down to the first

step. As she hopped up, both legs were swept off the carpet, her thighs resting on Mitch's muscular forearms. He pulled her tight against his chest.

The remaining crutch slipped to the stairs and duplicated its twin's slide.

"What are you doing?"

"Quiet. You'll wake Adam."

She placed the palms of her hands against his chest and pushed. "Put me down, Mitch." His expressionless face appeared chiseled from granite, but the pounding of his heart beneath her hands told the real story. This was more than helping a disabled woman down a flight of stairs.

He took the staircase as if she weighed nothing. At the bottom, his azure eyes locked onto hers. He pressed his forehead against hers. Ragged, warm breaths puffed on her face.

"Don't marry Drake."

She licked her lips. "Mitch—"

"No. Don't say anything." He kissed her, working his lips to the corner of her mouth, along her cheek, up to her ear. "Don't marry him, Livie." He ran the tip of his tongue along the rim of her ear. "Don't marry him."

Her heart swelled until it filled her entire chest. Lust zinged through her blood as a set of shivers rolled down her spine. Her breath hitched. "Mitch…" She caught his face in her hands and kissed him. When his tongue ran along her lips, she opened her mouth. He thrust into her mouth, tasting and stroking everywhere. She groaned as the ache between her thighs grew.

Mitch walked forward until Olivia's back slammed into a wall. He ate hungrily at her mouth, giving her deep kisses designed to inflame. They worked because she was sure she would explode into flames any moment.

"Wrap your legs around me," he said against her lips.

She did. He shoved her skirt up to her waist and pressed the hard ridge of flesh behind his zipper into her sweet spot. A moan from deep inside rolled up her throat and out. He shoved her panties off to one side and thrust a finger into her.

"Oh, God. Mitch," she gasped. "I—"

"Don't speak. You want this as much as I do."

Want was too weak a word for what she was feeling. Overwhelming desire. Craving need. Undeniable love. She licked his neck, then around the rim of his ear.

"I want this. I want you," was all she said, but that was enough. He pulled at the elastic lace of her panties until it broke and then thrust a second firm broad finger into her. The strong fingers of his other hand massaged her bottom, the callused tips rough against her soft flesh.

"Unzip me."

He didn't have to ask. Her hands had already found their way to his jeans. She unfastened them and slipped her hand in. Her fingers wrapped around his thick length, her thumb sliding over the moisture at the tip.

"Damn it. I'm sorry, babe, but I don't have a condom."

"I don't care," she said against his neck. "Just keep doing what you're doing. I'm about to come just with your fingers."

A deep-throated chuckle turned into a deep-chested groan. "Really?" His thumb fondled the sensitive jewel of her sex. Her hips moved in time to his strokes and she found herself perched on the edge of release.

"Now, Mitch, now."

He withdrew his fingers and thrust them in again and again, all the time his thumb continuing to massage her swollen nub. This time, she couldn't wait. Her body quivered with the shocks and aftershocks of the waves of her climax as it rolled through her. As Mitch watched her come, he said with a groan, "I won't allow you to marry Drake."

Olivia's legs snaked down his thighs until her toes touched the floor. Her skirt slid back into place. "Excuse me? You won't allow me? This isn't feudal England and you aren't lord and master." She pushed him, but she might as well be pushing the wall for as far as she could move him. "Move, damn it."

"Wait. You're driving me crazy, woman. That's not what I meant." After wrapping his arms around her, he pulled her close. "That's not what I meant," he whispered into her ear. "Not what I meant. I…you…we…"

"Well, you've got all the pronouns covered."

She felt his lips move into a smile against her cheek. "You've got a smart mouth, woman."

"You like my mouth."

"That I do." He leaned back until their gazes met. "Give me some time. Give us some time. Please. Don't give up on us. I'm…I'm working through my…"

"Anger?" she supplied.

"In a way, yes. I understand why you kept me from learning about Adam. But understanding isn't…"

"Forgiveness."

"That wasn't the word I was looking for, but yeah, it'll work. I'm trying, Livie."

She nodded. "Can you hand me my crutches? It's late and I need to get to bed."

"Nope. Can't do that."

"And why not?"

Sweeping her back into his arms, he said with a grin. "'Cause this is way more fun."

He carried her to his bed in the master suite and didn't leave.

BEFORE DAWN, MITCH'S INTERNAL ALARM RATTLED him awake. A warm leg lay across his groin. A hot female body pressed snuggly to his side. For a brief second, confusion clouded his mind before memories of last night's lovemaking flooded back. Gently, he slipped from under Olivia's leg. As much as he hated to leave her, he needed to get moving if he wanted any coffee before his workday began.

Standing, he looked down on Olivia. Her blonde hair spread over his pillow. The top sheet twisted around her legs. Her arms were wrapped around his pillow as though holding a lover. Memories filled his mind and he couldn't suppress the smile that broke on his face. She belonged in his bed. She belonged in his life. He'd waited a long time to find his way back to her.

His mom was right. It's never too late to love. And never too late to forgive and find happiness.

THEY SETTLED INTO A SEMI-ROUTINE OVER THE NEXT eight days. Every morning, the three of them would breakfast together before Mitch left for work somewhere on the ranch, more days than not he took Adam with him. The days that Mitch took Adam on a job that required riding a horse, Olivia would ride Lady Belle along the same route the cowboys were working. But she rode now for the sheer pleasure of it, an emotion she'd believed she'd never feel again. Unknowingly, Mitch had given her two of the most important things in her life…

Adam six years ago and now her rediscovered love of riding.

She'd quit worrying about Adam under Mitch's supervision. Mitch had a seemingly bottomless supply of patience with their son, never losing his temper or even raising his voice. No question from Adam was too insignificant or too inconvenient. Adam blossomed with Mitch in ways Olivia had never observed in his interactions with her family or with Drake. While Olivia was thrilled with Adam's growing fondness for his biological father, she worried about the day she and Adam would go home to Dallas…and they would go home. So far nothing had happened that would change that.

Most nights, Mitch made it back to the house for dinner, although she realized he went back to work afterwards. As familiar with ranch life as she was, Olivia was sure he was finishing tasks he couldn't get done during the day because of the time spent with Adam. Mitch's dedication touched something deep in Olivia's soul and produced feelings about him she'd never experienced. She'd loved Mitch for a long time, and now that love grew deeper and richer each day—and night—she stayed.

At night, after dinner, after Adam's bath and bedtime, long after she had gone to bed, Mitch would come to her and stay with her until morning. Those nights were everything she'd ever wished for.

On Sundays, Mitch took Olivia and Adam to his parents' house for the post-church lunch, a tradition that went back a generation to Sylvia's mother-in-law, who believed Sundays were for families. When Sylvia married Robert Landry, she'd continued the tradition with her sons. After James's death, Mitch and his brother, Caleb, rarely missed those Sunday lunches. Olivia looked forward to those dinners…the laughter, the stories, the look of sheer adoration on Adam's face when he looked at Mitch.

The second Sunday Olivia and Adam accompanied Mitch to his parents' house, Olivia stepped into the kitchen to give his mother a hand finishing up lunch.

"Hi, Sylvia. What can I do to help?"

Sylvia looked over her shoulder. "Check the biscuits in the oven, if you would. I think they're about done."

Olivia grabbed a pair of hot mitts and opened the oven. "Mitch said he'd had a talk with you and Robert last week about Adam." She pulled a pan of hot, golden biscuits from the oven and set it on a trivet to cool. She leaned against the counter. "He didn't say, but I got the impression the talk went okay. Am I right?"

Sylvia brushed a loose curl off her damp forehead. "As well as I could have hoped. You are probably aware that he was here very late the night we talked."

Olivia nodded.

"He wasn't happy with either of us. But now that he's met Adam and fallen so completely in love with the boy, he has a better understanding. He is crazy about his son, you know?"

Olivia laughed softly. "The feeling is mutual. Lately, everything out of Adam's mouth starts with Mitch said."

Sylvia's smile was a little sad. "I remember when Caleb was just learning to talk. Everything was either James said or Mitch told me." She sighed and turned back to the mashed potatoes she was beating. "I'm glad Mitch is excited about being part of Adam's life and doesn't hold any grudges against us."

Olivia nodded and began slipping pats of butter inside each steaming biscuit.

Mitch's feelings came as no shock, and she'd lost a

couple of nights sleep trying to figure out how to make this work for Adam and for her. Adam was too young to understand the complexities of the adult world, but on the other hand, he was old enough to understand that Mitch loved him. Was Adam old enough to also understand that Mitch was more than a friend? More than his mother's friend?

When the time was right, would he understand that Mitch was his father? Would Adam be happy to know that?

Olivia didn't have a clue when or how to broach the subject with Adam. Every day she watched for a sign that today was the day, but as yet, nothing had convinced her to tell Adam that Mitch was his father.

Adam's affection for Mitch appeared to double daily. If Mitch told him something, Adam took it as gospel. The hero worship in Adam's eyes was evident with each glance toward Mitch. While she was glad Adam was getting to know his father, Olivia couldn't be sure of a lifetime with Mitch...not yet.

Olivia loved Mitch. She was sure about that and was overjoyed he seemed to reciprocate her feelings, even if he'd never found the words to tell her. Of course, she never mentioned love to him either, trying to let her actions speak for her. Didn't every poet say that actions spoke louder than words? If that was true, then she was screaming her feelings loud and clear. But was it enough to uproot Adam from Dallas, leaving her family and her business behind? Those would require major adjustments in her life. She wasn't sure she was ready to make that commitment yet. This visit to Mitch's ranch was beginning to build her trust in their future, but time would tell.

Mitch's interactions with Adam had been heartening to watch. He was patient, answering any question, no matter how simple or complicated. He was protective, holding Adam tightly against him on horseback. He was caring, offering to help with nightly baths and story times whenever he'd finished work for the day. Olivia knew how exhausting ranch life was. Bathing a five-year-old and putting him to bed could be an ordeal, but Mitch never complained and never demurred. His love for Adam was evident with every act. No words were necessary when his actions spoke so loudly.

"Olivia."

Olivia jerked to attention and looked about Sylvia's kitchen and met Mitch's gaze. "What? Sorry. I was just thinking."

Mitch grinned and put his arm around her. "Those biscuits ain't gonna serve themselves."

Olivia answered his laugh with a playful push at his arm. "Har. Har." She picked up the plate of hot bread she'd mindlessly moved from pan to plate. "Move it, buddy. I'm starving."

He laughed and followed her into the dining room.

ON THE THURSDAY AFTER SHE AND ADAM HAD BEEN AT the Lazy L for three weeks, Sylvia Landry called and invited all of them over for an old-fashioned cookout the next night. Friday afternoon, Adam was bouncing off the wall, thrilled to be seeing Nana SuSu and Papa Rob.

The table near the pool had been already set for dinner when the trio arrived. While Robert Landry grilled hamburgers, Mitch, Caleb and Adam played water tag. Olivia wasn't sure who was having the best time as Mitch and Caleb both appeared to have regressed to age five, slapping the water, dunking each other and making Adam burst into gales of laughter.

"Y'all come eat." Sylvia set a platter of hot French fries on the table. "I don't want everything to get cold."

"Yes, Ma'am," came the reply from the pool.

Olivia caught Adam the minute he stepped out and wrapped him in a towel. Robert tossed towels to his sons.

"You two are getting dressed before we eat, right?" Robert asked as he piled the cooked burgers onto a large platter.

"C'mon, Adam. I brought you some dry clothes," Olivia said, starting back toward the house.

Adam didn't follow as she'd expected.

"Adam. C'mon."

"Is Mitch changing clothes?" Adam asked, his gaze on Mitch.

Mitch stopped rubbing the towel through his hair and tied it around his waist. "Let's eat beach style. Wet bathing suits and towels."

"Yeah, Momma," Adam said. "Beach style. I wanna eat beach style too."

Caleb tied his towel the same fashion as Mitch. "Yeah, Momma," he joked. "Beach style"

Olivia threw up her hands in surrender. "Fine, as long as it's okay with Nana SuSu."

Sylvia sat a pitcher of iced tea on the table. "Who am I to spoil the fun?"

"Yay!" Adam cried and rushed over to Mitch. "Sit by me, okay?"

"Sure, buddy."

Mitch and Adam took the seats across the table from Olivia and Caleb, with Sylvia and Robert filling end chairs. After Robert said grace, bowls and platters of bread, meat and French fries made their way up and down the table.

Olivia kept her eye on Adam, making sure he didn't get distracted and forget to eat. Under Mitch's watchful eye, Adam cleaned his plate in record time, as though trying to eat at the same pace Mitch set.

"How long have the Landrys owned the Lazy L?" Olivia asked.

"Well, let's see. My great-great grandfather, Adam Landry, settled here right after the civil war. It was a wild country then." He glanced at Adam and said, "But that's a long story. Another time maybe. So, Adam, have you been having fun at the Lazy L?"

Adam nodded.

"Don't nod, Adam. Answer Papa Rob."

Adam swallowed and said, "Yep. Me and Mitch been working every day."

"I think you mean 'yes, sir'," Olivia said.

"Yes, sir," Adam said. "I help Mitch every day."

Rob Landry smiled. "So I hear."

A puzzled look crossed Adam's face. "You're Mitch's real daddy. And Caleb's daddy, right?"

"That's right."

Olivia's heart pounded in her ears. She'd never explained the relationship between Mitch and Nana SuSu and Papa Rob, but her son was putting together pieces of information. Was today the day? Was this the sign she'd been waiting for?

"Momma?" Adam said with a serious facial expression. "Do I have real daddy?"

A loud silence fell over the table. Even the tree frogs stopped their croaking to hear her answer.

Olivia stood and walked around the table. Mitch scooted his chair back and offered it to her. While her ankle and knee were making excellent healing progress, she wasn't back to normal, so she took his chair with a smile of appreciation. Plus, sitting would put her at the same eyelevel as her son. She'd never liked talking down to people and knew she needed to be at Adam's level to judge his response to her answer. She sat and Adam turned toward her.

"You have a real daddy." Olivia's voice quaked with fear. She silently prayed for strength. She drew in a deep breath. "Mitch is your real daddy."

Adam looked at Mitch standing behind Olivia, his hand resting on her shoulder. "How come he doesn't live with us?" His bottom lip began to quiver. "Didn't he like me?"

Olivia's heart broke. She swallowed against the rising tears. Instead of jumping into the conversation as she'd expected, Mitch squeezed her shoulder and remained quiet. She sighed. "He didn't know you, honey. Momma never told Mitch about you."

"Why not?"

"You remember when you and Frankie had a fight over the red fire engine at school and you didn't want to play with him anymore?"

Adam nodded.

"Well, adults get mad at each other too. Mitch and I…"

Mitch squatted alongside Olivia. "I did something that hurt your mom's feelings, Adam. Really bad. It was my fault she never told me about you."

"Is she still mad at you?"

Mitch thought about the previous night he'd shared with Olivia in the master suite and smiled. "No, I'm pretty sure she's not."

Olivia laid her hand on Mitch's knee. "I'm not mad at him anymore, honey."

Adam nodded. "Like me and Frankie?"

"Yes. Just like you and Frankie."

He thought about that for a minute. "Okay. Can I call you daddy instead of Mitch?"

Mitch's heart leapt into his throat in joy. "I'd like that very much, Adam, as long as your mother doesn't mind."

Olivia sniffed back a tear. "I think that would be great."

"Nana SuSu? You have some dessert? We're celebrating," Mitch said as he rose.

Olivia saw Sylvia wipe a tear from the corner of her eye. "I sure do, Mitch. How about apple cobbler and ice cream?"

Mitch held up his hand and Adam slapped a high five.

Chapter Thirteen

Saturday started as every other ranch morning had started since she'd been there. Olivia was up before the sun getting Adam ready to ride the range, as he called it. She wondered if Adam had picked that up from Mitch or Hobbs. There were a number of new sayings in Adam's vocabulary, but nothing she'd had to worry about...yet.

Adam had taken last night's news that Mitch was his father much better than she'd feared. Adam had been thrilled with the news, but then again, he'd been thrilled when the cobbler and ice cream was served. Without doubt, he *understood* the fact of his parentage, but didn't appear to be as worked up over it as the adults. Maybe grownups could learn a lot from kids on how to not overreact.

"Hey, Momma. Guess what?" Adam said, his mouth full of oatmeal.

"I don't know. What? And don't talk with your mouth full, honey."

He swallowed and drank some milk. "Mitch—I

mean Daddy—said I was the best cowboy he'd ever trained. And that if I…" He scrunched up his eyes as he tried to remember what Mitch had told him. "That if I played cards with him, I could have a ranch like this when I grow up."

Olivia leaned over to wipe oatmeal off his cheek. "Did he? Well, grown up is a few years off yet. Besides, I thought you wanted to own the gym."

"I could do both." His face beamed at the idea.

Mitch came to the table and sat. "Ready to ride, partner?"

Adam nodded his head vigorously. Olivia enjoyed Adam's enthusiasm when around Mitch, evident even before last night's revelation.

Mitch hadn't brought up her remarrying Drake again, but Drake had last night when he called, just as he had every night since their conversation two weeks ago. When he'd first asked her—before she and Mitch had reconnected—she'd given thought to living with Drake again and being the wife of a college professor. She'd decided that a life with Drake would probably be calm and agreeable and, maybe even a little boring.

Would that be a good life for her son? After all, nothing was more important to her than him. Her needs and desires ran a distant second.

But if she decided to stay with Mitch, was raising Adam so far from town the right move? By virtue of the distance of Mitch's ranch from the nearest grade school, Adam would be separated from other children of his own age. No neighborhood children to play with. No close friends to ride bikes with. Was it fair to Adam to uproot him from the only life he'd ever known and plop him on such an isolated ranch?

"You going today, Olivia?"

Olivia's meandering thoughts jarred back to Mitch's kitchen. Mitch and Adam stood hand-in-hand looking at her. Both wore jeans, classic snap-closed plaid cowboy shirts, and dirty boots. Adam's cowboy hat sat slightly crooked and off to one side. Her heart seized at the vision of man and son.

"What are you two cowboys doing today?" She'd been with them every day, but she needed to get away from this house and her feelings for a while. She needed some time for herself.

"Well, the guys are branding and neutering today." When she flinched, he went on. "But I need to check a fence the hands did last week, run by and pick up some dewormer, see if any of the pregnant heifers have delivered. We'll be in the truck. Plenty of room for you if you want to ride along. We'd like that, wouldn't we, partner?" He tapped the crown of Adam's hat.

"Yep. You can come if you want to, Momma."

Yep. That'd be Hobbs's influence. She stifled a grin.

Relieved Mitch wasn't taking her son to watch calves be neutered, she shook her head. "Sounds like a great plan for the day, but I need to run to town for a while. Since your mom brought back your other truck, I thought maybe I could use it today."

"Sure. You know where the keys are," Mitch said with a tilt of his head toward the laundry room.

"Can I have a word with you before you two head off?"

"Okay." Mitch squatted down. "Will you go grab us a couple of bottles of water from the refrigerator and put them in the truck?"

Adam's face beamed. "Sure, Daddy."

Olivia's breath caught. Her son had been thrilled to find out about Mitch. Getting him to bed last night when they'd gotten home from the cookout had taken reading three books—all read by *Daddy*. It was as though Adam didn't want to let Mitch out of his sight for fear he'd disappear.

Adam's boots thudded on the kitchen tile as he raced across the kitchen, flung open the refrigerator door, grabbed two bottles, slammed it and ran back. "I'll wait for you by the truck."

Mitch tapped on the crown of Adam's hat, straightening it. "Wait for me by the front door, okay?"

"Sure." Adam galloped through the door. The echo of his boot heels on the entry hall tile made Olivia smile.

"You know, I had to make him take his boots off before bed last night. He wanted to sleep in them."

Mitch smiled and stroked a finger down her cheek. "Good morning," he said, and leaned in for a kiss.

Olivia glanced around to make sure Adam was out of the room before returning his kiss. "Morning, *Daddy*."

Mitch shrugged. "Every time he calls me daddy it feels like my chest is too small for my heart. What a kid."

She laughed. "I know."

Mitch brushed a kiss across her lips. "You were gone when I woke up this morning."

"I know. I thought it would be better if Adam didn't find you and me together. Finding out you're his father is enough of a shock for now. Let's give him some time to adjust."

He pressed his lips into her hair. "Agreed. Now, what do you need? Unless it was just use of my lips, and in that case I can hang around a minute or two longer."

She laughed. "Good thing you have a ten gallon hat to fit over that huge ego." He chuckled, the sound sending desire curling through her like hot smoke. "I wanted to thank you for finding things to do with him today besides the calf neutering."

"Olivia. Honey," he said on a long sigh. "He's a five-year-old boy. Boys love stuff like that. I did when I was his age, but I've got enough hands on that job. I really do need to run these errands and I want the company of...my son."

He said the words with such affection, Olivia's throat swelled in emotion. She swallowed past the lump and fought against threatening tears.

She nodded her understanding, not trusting her voice not to crack.

"Is there anything else?" Mitch turned to leave.

"Do you know when you'll be back?"

"Nope. How long will you be in town?"

"I'm not sure, but probably most of the day."

"No problem." He took a couple of steps then came back for another quick kiss. "Don't worry about Adam. Have a good day. Get a massage. Get a manicure. Do whatever it is that women do that drive us men crazy." He winked. "I'll be checking those toes tonight," he said with a leer.

Olivia laughed. She heard Adam starting in with questions as soon as Mitch walked into the foyer. She sighed. It'd be fun to do some women stuff today.

Olivia sat and picked up her now cold coffee. She looked at the almost empty coffee pot across the kitchen, sighed and stood. It felt wonderful to be off those crutches for short steps around the house.

"I'll get it. Sit." Magda shuffled into the kitchen wearing a pair of Daisy Duke cutoff denim shorts, a tie-dyed T-shirt and house shoes. "I like my coffee fresh anyway." She poured the remaining coffee down the sink, refilled the basket with fresh grounds, the reserve with water, and pressed the start button. "There," she said with a satisfied smile.

Olivia pointed to one of the chairs at the breakfast nook table. "Sit down and keep me company."

Magda dragged back a chair and sat. "Where are the guys?"

"Mitch took Adam with him to check on a fence and run some errands."

"And you're not going."

"Right." Olivia drew her fingers through her hair. "It's a guy day."

"You know you don't have to worry about Mitch. Adam will be fine."

"I'm not worried."

"Then why the wrinkles in your forehead?"

Olivia laughed and smoothed the skin between her eyes with her fingertips. "Not enough coffee."

Magda stood. "Well, that I can solve." She took Olivia's cup to the counter, got another from the cabinet, poured two coffees and made her way back to the table. After setting Olivia's cup in front of her, Magda sipped hers and sighed. "Love the first taste of coffee in the morning. It was always like that with cigarettes too. The first drag was always the best. The rest simply fed my nicotine habit."

Olivia twisted her cup around in her hands. "I don't think I've seen you smoke since I've been here."

"You haven't. Hobbs made me quit."

Olivia smiled. "Good for him. Bad habit."

Magda shrugged. "I know, but before Hobbs no one ever cared enough to make me quit."

Olivia thought that was the saddest thing she'd ever heard. Growing up with three brothers, a mother who'd stay up late sewing a new dress that Olivia just had to have the next day and a father who'd spoiled her rotten, Olivia had always considered her life normal. Now, she realized how fortunate she'd been.

"I've never had a chance to ask. How did you end up here with Hobbs...if you don't mind me asking?"

Magda finished her coffee, went for a refill and retook her chair. "I'm sorry. I should have asked if you wanted a refill."

Olivia covered her mug with her hand. "I'm fine."

The two women sat there for a minute, the hum of the refrigerator the only sound.

"It's times like these I wish I could have a cigarette." Magda ran her finger around the rim of her coffee mug. "Mom was...well, I guess the best description would be a buckle bunny. She followed the PBR circuit. That's the Professional Bull Riders circuit."

Olivia nodded. "Right."

Magda drank some coffee then said, "I think her goal was to bed all the majors. Back then Hobbs was quite the rider. A top contender for the world championship."

When Magda took an extended pause, Olivia said, "You know, you don't have to tell me if you don't want."

Magda smiled. "It's fine. Hard to believe how much I still miss her. Anyway, Mom and Hobbs got together. He moved on to the next rodeo. Mom told him she'd follow, but she didn't. She suspected she was pregnant. Being with a professional bull rider is a hard life. She didn't want to stay on the road with a baby. I was born in Cheyenne and we stayed there until I was seven. I guess that's as long as Mom stayed anywhere. We moved to California, Las Vegas, Tulsa, then back to Eureka, California. Mom died there."

Olivia laid her hand over Magda's. "I'm so sorry. She must have been young."

"Twenty-eight. I was ten."

The horror of being alone at such a young age broke Olivia's heart. "Oh, God. How awful for you."

Magda shrugged and drank her coffee but Olivia wasn't fooled by her nonchalance.

"The state took me because no one claimed me," Magda continued. "I must have lived in ten different foster homes before I left for good."

"Left?"

"Ran away. Went out on my own." Magda got up and refilled her coffee cup. "I'm not sure what was worse...living in some of those foster homes or living on the streets." She walked back to the table. "Somewhere along the line, social services reached out to Hobbs." She sat. "Mom did something right. She listed him as my father. He was always one step behind the foster system, though. When he finally caught up with me, I'd been on the street for a couple of years, getting by the best I could."

Olivia rubbed her eyes. Not surprisingly, her finger-tips came away damp. "Drugs?"

Magda didn't reply at first. After a couple of minutes of strained silence that made Olivia questioned whether she should have asked, Magda said, "Some. I was luckier than most. I was doing some coke and a little weed, but before I got deep into the lifestyle, Hobbs showed up and dragged me back here." She smiled. "I think he pretty much forced Mitch to give me a job."

Olivia returned the smile. "I'm pretty sure Mitch does what he wants most of the time. If he didn't want to hire you, he wouldn't have, and from what I've seen he got the best end of the deal. You keep this house running like a clock."

Pink tinged Magda cheeks. "Thanks, but I had a lot

to learn when I got here. That bitch, Joanna—sorry. I shouldn't have called her that."

"Why not? She is…most of the time."

Magda snorted a laugh. "She hated me from the minute I drove onto the property. I think she's made it her life's mission to get me out of here."

"Maybe she thinks you might beat her out of getting back with Mitch."

Magda spewed coffee on the table. She swiped at the drops on her chin. "Sorry. You should warn me before you say something like that." She laughed. "Mitch isn't interested in me, and I am certainly not interested in him. He's already in love and it's not with me."

Olivia's heart lurched. "He is?"

"Oh, Olivia. You can't be that blind. The man is crazy in love with you."

She took a gulp of cold coffee in an attempt to dislodge the boulder in her throat. "Really? You think so?" Olivia felt sure he did, but he hadn't said the words.

Magda shook her head. "When you're not looking, he's watching your every move."

"Maybe he's afraid I'm going to steal the silver."

Magda snickered. "Not hardly."

"What's the deal with Joanna? Seems like every time I turn around, the woman's oozing through the door." Olivia hated hearing the jealous tone in her voice, but Joanna's frequent visits were a sore point for her.

Joanna had *dropped by* almost every night. Amazing how she just happened to be in the area when it was a good forty-five miles from town and probably an additional twenty miles to her parents' house where she was staying. She always had a pressing issue that required speaking with Mitch alone in his study. Olivia couldn't imagine what issue was so dire as to require daily runs out to the ranch, and she didn't ask. She suspected Adam and she were flies in the ointment of Joanna's plan, and that gave Olivia perverse enjoyment.

"Oh, that woman's got her hook set for him. I can't see what he sees in her. I can only hope he is smart enough to avoid her trap again, which he will with you around. Want to move in?"

Olivia leaned back in her chair and shook her head. "Sorry, Magda, but Adam and I are going home. Probably soon. My ankle is doing much better. I think I'll be off the crutches for good by the end of the week."

Magda frowned. "I'll hate to see you both go. I've loved having you here. And Adam? I think I'm in love. Hmm. Going for a younger man. Would that make me a cougar?"

Olivia laughed and stood. "You're wonderful with him. I think he's pretty much in love with you too, but I'm not ready to be your mother-in-law."

When Magda laughed, Olivia pushed her chair back under the table. "I'm heading into town for a little shopping, a manicure and some me time, unless you want to come along?"

"Thanks, but I'm not the girlie-manicure type. Now if you wanna go get a tattoo, I'm your girl."

Olivia grinned. "I'm not exactly the tattoo sort of woman, but I'll keep you in mind if I change my mind. Do you need me to pick up anything for you while I'm in town?"

"Nope. I'm good."

"Okay, then. I should be home late this afternoon."

AFTER AN HOUR-LONG MASSAGE, A SPA MANICURE AND pedicure, and two new western belts she just had to have, joy and relaxation filled Olivia. She knew she wore a smile worthy of a rodeo clown, but she couldn't help it. Today was just what the doctor ordered. Not ready to head back to the ranch, she decided if she checked on Adam and all was well, she was going to have a long lunch and enjoy not having to cut up anyone else's food but her own.

The Red Rose Cafe came up on her left. Olivia wheeled into the parking lot. Exactly the type of place she could never take her son…and exactly the type of café she wanted—quiet, calm, and good food, if the number of cars in the parking lot was any indication. She dialed Mitch's cell phone.

"Hello?"

"Hi, Mitch. It's Olivia. How's Adam?" In the background, she could hear Adam talking and cows mooing.

"He's fine. Hold on. I'll get him."

"Hullo?"

"Hi, honey. It's Momma. Are you having fun with Mitch?"

"Guess what?"

"I don't know. What?"

"I saw a baby cow come out of its momma's bottom."

Olivia squeezed the bridge of her nose with her thumb and forefinger. "Really?" This might push her birds-and-bees talk with Adam to much sooner than she'd planned.

"Yeah. It was really cool."

"Well…I'm, um, glad."

"Daddy said I could name it."

"Oh. Is it a boy or a girl cow?"

"I don't know. I'll ask. Daddy." Adam's voice

slammed into her ear. "Momma wants to know if it's a boy cow or girl cow."

When Mitch answered in his deep Texas drawl, an army of goose bumps marched down her spine. She had it bad if just the man's voice through a cell phone could evoke images of dark nights and sweaty sheets.

"Daddy says it's a boy...like me. Can I name it after me?"

Olivia packed away her erotic fantasies until later when she could actually practice them on Mitch and refocused her attention on her son. "You want to name the bull Adam?"

"Yeah."

"Fine with me if it's okay with Mitch."

"Yay!"

"Let me talk to Mitch."

"How's your day in town going?" Mitch asked.

"Awesome. I thought I'd grab a quiet late lunch before I head back to the ranch. Will that be a problem for you? I mean, if Adam's in the way I'm sure Magda would keep an eye on him for a while."

"You go enjoy yourself and don't give us guys a thought. There's nothing I have to do today that he can't come along. Besides we're having fun, right?"

"Right!" Adam yelled into the phone.

"Okay then, I'll see you guys tonight."

Olivia smiled as she tucked her phone into her purse. Her son was happy at Mitch's ranch. She was happy. Mitch seemed to be happy. Mitch hadn't asked her to marry him again since the night of their rooftop talk, but she felt sure he would. Is it possible that the foundation for a good life together was staring her in the face? Should she give serious consideration to moving to the Lazy L? Maybe it was time for her to confess to Mitch how very much she loved him. Tonight. She'd open the discussion on their future tonight. Now that she'd made that decision, she'd answered her growling stomach.

In the restaurant, she was given a booth on the far side of the room, perfect for safely stowing her crutches. While she didn't need them at home, being on her feet so much today required a little support. But her leg was getting stronger every day. To celebrate her impending recovery, she ordered iced tea and chicken Caesar salad, then she settled back to enjoy not being a mom for the next hour or so.

It was difficult to tell how many people were in The Red Rose. Separation barriers between the booths were high and solid up to criss-cross latticework near the top. The arrangement provided for visual privacy, but like any public setting, conversations tended to float over the top of the dividers.

As she'd been led to her table, she'd noticed a couple of women drinking tea who looked to be in their mid-thirties. After she was seated, she realized her table was directly beside theirs, separated only by the wooden partition. Once she'd listened in on a table of male cross-dressers discussing a recent Victoria Secret foray and learned way more than she ever wanted to know on the subject. Since then she'd tried to shut out conversations around her in public places. However, the room was small and the tables were close, making it almost impossible not to overhear the conversation at the nearest table.

"I hear his son looks just like him," said one of the women.

"Really? Then that must be one cute kid."

"Must be. Can you imagine finding out you had a five-year-old son you knew nothing about?"

Olivia's heart lurched. Were they talking about Mitch and Adam? She focused her hearing on that conversation, trying to shut out others around her.

"Well, Joanna should be here any minute and you know she'll have all the scoop."

Oh my God. They were discussing her son.

"Where is she, anyway? She's always late."

"This time she's got a good excuse. She's meeting with Mitch's lawyer."

"Why?"

"I don't have the whole story, but if I understand it correctly, she and Mitch are going to give their marriage another try. She's helping Mitch gather the information he needs to sue for custody of his son."

Olivia's heart almost stopped. The room blurred and swayed in her vision as a thick bolt of nausea shot through her. Mitch had been planning behind her back to sue for custody? She swallowed the golf ball forming in her throat.

"I swear Joanna's a saint. I don't know if I'd be willing to take on my husband's illegitimate son."

Olivia dug in her purse for twenty dollars to pay for a meal she hadn't received and couldn't have eaten if she had. She'd leaned over to retrieve her crutches when another voice stopped her dead.

"Hi, y'all. Sorry I'm late." Joanna's voice floated over the top of the wall. "You know how lawyers are. Always wanting to chat, chat, chat and run their bills up." She laughed. "But what the heck? Mitch can afford it."

Olivia sat up and leaned against the wall. There was no way to get to the entrance without Joanna seeing her.

"I was just telling Helen how impressed I am with you. I'm not sure I could take on my husband's illegitimate son."

"Well," Joanna said, the reek of self-satisfaction coloring her tone. "I'm not a saint…at least not in Mitch's bedroom. And trust me, he likes it that way."

The three women laughed. Olivia shut her eyes as her heart shattered into a million tiny pieces.

"Here ya go, honey." An older woman with "Madge" on her nametag sat Olivia's chicken Caesar salad on the table. "Can I get you anything else?"

Olivia signaled with her finger for the waitress to lean closer. "Is there a back way out of here? There is someone I don't want to run into." She slipped the twenty across the table. "I believe this will clear my bill."

The waitress pocked the money and nodded. "Follow me."

Olivia gathered her crutches, slid from the booth and made her way toward the kitchen, which fortunately had a door and was close to where she had been seated. She didn't dare look back at Joanna's table, but the women's chatter and laughter accompanied her through the kitchen door.

She made her way back to Mitch's truck as fast as she could. Before she started the engine, her forehead hit the steering wheel with a thump. How could she have been so stupid? So duped by Mitch? The conversation with Magda had circled through her head all day on a contin-uous loop. During her massage, when she was fully relaxed and the stress of the past few weeks was seeping from her, she'd made the hard decision to give her love for Mitch a chance and give Drake a definitive negative answer to his multiple marriage proposals.

She'd decided to talk with Mitch about selling her business to Mark and Nancy and moving lock, stock and barrel to the Lazy L. Adam thrived here with Mitch. Any concerns about bikes and schools for Adam had minimized in light of his relationship with his father. Walking into The Red Rose Café, she'd been confident of her future. Now?

She bumped her forehead on the truck's steering wheel. She was such a fool to consider changing her life when Mitch hadn't moved an inch to change his. Now that she thought about it, he was asking her to make all the big life-changing sacrifices, asking her to rearrange her and Adam's lives to fit into his life and what exactly had he sacrificed? Sitting up, she steeled her resolved. There was no way she would let Mitch take her son away from her. And while there was breath in her lungs, she'd never allow Joanna St. Claire to have any role in raising her child. *Never.*

There was only one way she could think of to protect Adam.

She pulled her phone from her purse and dialed a familiar number.

"Hello?" a deep, southern male voice said.

"Hi. You busy?" She sniffed back the tears.

"Olivia?"

"Yeah." Her voice cracked.

"What's wrong, sweetheart?"

Drake's soft voice calmed her racing heart, made her believe that everything would be fine. Made her believe the Joannas and Mitchs of the world didn't always win.

She took a deep breath. "Drake, I will marry you. Come get us as fast as you can."

Chapter Fourteen

The drive back to the Lazy L was difficult, what with having to see the road through teary vision. But Olivia used the time to think, to plan…and to get angry. Mitch was a low-life bastard. All Joanna's surprise drop-ins and private conversations in Mitch's office now made sense. All the puzzle pieces fit and she could see the picture clearly. While Mitch had been lulling her into a false sense of security with soft words and hot lovemaking, he'd been working behind the scenes to steal her son. He'd even fooled Magda. He'd given an award-winning performance.

Bastard.

And to think she'd begun to plan for Mitch to be in her life for the long haul. Well that wasn't going to happen.

Once she and Drake remarried, Mitch would have a much harder time persuading the courts that he should have custody and would make a better parent than Olivia. She was a wonderful mother with a secure and intelligent son, and she'd be married to a full professor at

Southern Methodist University. She and Drake would be model parents.

So what if the love she felt for Drake didn't rise to the Mitch level? Like Drake said, he loved her enough for the both of them. She would make this marriage work. For Adam's sake, she would make herself love Drake. What choice did she have? She had to protect her son and this was the only way she knew how.

U-turning on the two-lane highway, she returned to a gas station she'd passed a couple of miles back. She sat in the truck for a minute before slamming her fist on the steering wheel. *Damn it, Mitch.* Why couldn't he have given them a little more time to work things out?

Until Drake arrived, she'd not let Mitch, or anyone, know she'd discovered the legal proceedings going on behind her back. She dried her eyes, put on her poker face and stiffened her back and her resolve. To continue to pretend to feel love and trust for Mitch would take an award-winning performance of her own, but she'd do anything for her son. She stepped from the vehicle and headed into the gas station.

The ladies' room was not the best but she'd been in worse during her rodeo days. The cold water she splashed on her face helped reduce the redness and cool her swollen eyes. When she came out of the bathroom, the female clerk behind the counter gave Olivia a sympathetic nod of the head, as if she'd been there and had her heart broken too.

"Here," the clerk said, handing Olivia a cup. "Get some ice and water to go."

"Thanks."

"Whoever he is, I hope you make him sorry."

Olivia mouth quirked up on one side. "I will. I promise."

By the time she pushed the remote control for the garage door, an emotional numbness made facing Mitch possible. As she walked into the house, she heard high-pitched little-boy laughter mixed with low-pitched adult-male chuckles coming from the family room. The accompanying beeps and tweets suggested a video game contest in progress.

"Can I ask you something, Daddy?"

"Sure, buddy. What?"

"Are you really going to name that baby cow after me?"

"Absolutely. Adam's Bull. What do you think?"

"Nope. Cowboy Adam's Bull."

Mitch chuckled. The sound of his laugh could still make lust coil in her gut like a snake ready to strike, and she hated herself for letting the sound get to her.

"Cowboy Adam's Bull, huh? Yeah, I like that. We can use the initials and call him CAB for short. What do you think?"

"Yeah!"

She stood outside the door listening to Mitch teasing Adam and Adam's responding giggles. Her heart ached with the knowledge Mitch couldn't be trusted and with fear that her child could get caught in an ugly adult war of words in the future. She sighed, forced her shoulders down into a relaxed position, checked her poker-face smile and prepared to enter the room. But Adam's next question stopped her.

"Can I ask you something else?"

"Anything."

"Are you going to come home with us?"

Olivia's breath caught. She strained to hear the rest of the conversation.

"No, pal. I live here. I have to take care of CAB, but you're not going home soon."

"But I want to go home."

"You do?"

"Uh huh."

Relief flooded Olivia and she backed down the hall a couple of steps and called, "Adam? I'm back."

"Momma!" Adam rounded the corner in a run. He wore a bright grin and a new short cropped haircut. He wrapped his arms around her legs.

Brushing the palm of her hand on top of his head, she expected it to be bristly but the ends were soft and tickled like thick-pile velvet. "Wow. You got a haircut today."

"A cowboy haircut like Mitch's," Adam said, his head tilted back to look up at her.

"Hi, Olivia. Did you have a good day?" Mitch's deep voice boomed down the hall and bounced off the walls, wrapping her in the sound.

She looked down the hall. Mitch sported the same super-short cut. As much as Adam had favored Mitch before, with identical haircuts the facial similarities were striking. The effect tied Olivia's gut into a knot.

The lying smile on Mitch's face said he was glad to see her, and how she wished it were true. Her heart cried since her face couldn't. Instead, she pasted on a smile in return.

"Yes, I did." She wiggled her fingers at her son. "Aren't they lovely?"

Adam giggled. "They're pink."

Olivia gasped. "Of course they're pink. I'm a girl."

Adam looked at Mitch and rolled his eyes. "She always says that."

"Well, son, it's true. She is."

Olivia froze. *Son?* Mitch said the word with so much pride Olivia was surprised the buttons didn't pop off his shirt.

"What are you two doing?"

Adam grabbed her hand and began pulling her toward the family room. "Daddy bought me a Wii today. Come see."

"Wait, Adam. Don't pull me. I'm coming."

MITCH COULD SEE THE DISPLEASURE WRITTEN ALL over Olivia's face when Adam announced the video game, but there needed to be some games for Adam here at the ranch. Hopefully there'd be some lazy afternoons where he and Olivia could play their own games in their room while Adam was occupied with his in his room. An excellent plan, if he said so himself.

"Now, Olivia. Don't be mad," he said, following her into the living room. He noticed she was down to using only one crutch and could bear weight on her injured ankle. Since her plan was to leave as soon as she could walk, he elected not to comment on her healing progress. "Every boy needs his own video game console."

"Yeah, Momma. I need it."

"Uh huh. You need it like I a need a third arm."

Adam laughed. "You'd look silly with three arms."

Olivia gave him a stern look. "Adam Montgomery Gentry. Did you ask Mitch to buy you this? You know better."

Mitch slipped up alongside Adam and put his arm about the boy. "No, he did not. It was all my idea, right?"

Adam put his arm around Mitch's waist, which

meant Adam's arm was stretched nearly straight. "Right."

Olivia's eyes narrowed as she studied them, then met Mitch's gaze. "I'll talk to you about this later."

Mitch and Adam exchanged glances and Mitch struggled to keep a straight face.

"Yes, ma'am," Mitch said.

"Yes, ma'am," Adam echoed.

"For now, why don't you go put on your swim trunks and let's go for a swim, okay?"

"Okay!" Adam replied with loud enthusiasm. He raced from the room.

Finally alone, Mitch moved over to where Olivia stood, took her face in his hands and kissed her. He noticed immediately that she didn't return the kiss. He backed away. "What's wrong?"

"Nothing," she said on a sigh. "Just tired, I think. Plus—" she tapped the rubber tip of the crutch on the floor, "—I'm sick to death of these crutches."

Of course she was. He knew he'd never have been as patient as she'd been.

"I know, babe." He wrapped his arms around her shoulders and pulled her against him. "But you're doing better. Another couple of months here and you'll be good as new." He leaned back enough so that he could look into her eyes. "Until then, however, I don't mind picking you up and carrying you to my bed if you need me to."

She didn't laugh like he'd expected. Instead, she frowned and pushed him away.

"I don't think so. I need to get my suit on before Adam gets back. Thanks for giving me a break today. I needed a little time alone." She backed up and turned toward the door.

"No problem. In fact, it was my pleasure. Adam and I had a great time." Mitch stepped in front of her. "Olivia. Wait a minute. Are you sure everything is okay? You seem a little...quiet."

She smiled, but it was fake and he could tell. When Olivia smiled, she glowed. This phony smile darkened her face.

"No, no. Everything's fine. If you see Adam, tell him not to go into the pool until I get out there." She moved quickly toward the door. "In fact, I'd better get a move on. Thanks again for today."

Then she was gone. Mitch stood there, confused about what just happened. She was thanking him for spending the day with their son? That was crazy. She could deny it all she wanted, but he knew something had happened today to upset her. He didn't know what or who, but he'd find out and set things right.

Olivia made it to her room without breaking into tears. It was a contest which was causing the most pain... walking on her ankle without flinching or the rending of her heart into pieces. Either way, she could show no weakness to someone like Mitch, who could stoop so low as to make love with a woman all the while making plans to steal her child.

She changed into a two-piece bikini and hobbled over to the dresser. Somewhere in here Magda had stored those powerful pain pills the doctor had prescribed. She hadn't had one since the day after the accident, but if she wanted to continue making everyone think her ankle was healing quickly, she had to have something to dull the pain.

In the top drawer, she found the bottle shoved into a back corner. The directions for usage recommended one table every four to six hours as needed. She poured two pills into the palm of her hand, recapped the bottle and replaced it into its hiding place. She dry-swallowed both tablets then made her way toward the bedroom doors that led to the pool. Tomorrow, she'd get Magda to help her get everything repacked and ready for when Drake arrived.

By the time she got outside, Mitch had changed into a pair of swim trunks and was outside watching Adam paddle around in the shallow end. She'd told Mitch not to let Adam get into the pool until she got there, but Mitch had deliberately ignored her instructions. She ground her teeth and drew in a deep breath. If Mitch was successful in his parentage case, this would be what the future would look like. Her instructions to her child ignored while Mitch did whatever he wanted.

Drake couldn't get them out of here fast enough.

Mitch glanced toward Olivia and whistled. "Looking good."

At the last minute, she elected to not fight the parenting battle here and now, especially in front of Adam. The last thing she needed was him to learn to play one parent against the other.

"Thanks," she said as she made her way to a lounge chair. "Adam. Stay in the shallow end, okay?"

"Oh, *Momma*. I can swim. Watch this." He put his face into the water and kicked his legs while moving his arms. He swam toward her and grabbed the blue mosaic tile around the edge of the pool. "See?"

"I see, but—"

"I'm going in," Mitch said in a quiet voice to Olivia. "I'll make sure he's safe."

Olivia nodded.

"Cannonball," he shouted just before jumping in the pool and splashing water all over Adam and Olivia.

For the next hour, Olivia read a magazine while keeping her eye on Mitch and Adam as they played and swam. As much as she would have enjoyed the cool water on such a hot day, she didn't trust herself with the level of narcotics singing through her blood. The pain in her ankle had eased to a dull throb. But no drug could numb the pain inside her.

As it got closer to dinnertime, Magda came out and lit the gas grill.

"Mitch," Magda called. "The burgers will be ready to put on in about twenty minutes."

"Thanks, Magda." He grinned at Olivia. "Thought we'd have a cookout to go with our play day. What do you think?"

She shrugged. "Sounds great." She turned toward the house to catch Magda before she went back into the house. "Magda, do you need help?"

"Nope. Stay put."

Olivia settled back on the lounger and crossed her ankles, the hurt one on top. She could tell Adam was fading. She smiled to herself. If he made it until eight tonight, she'd be surprised.

While Mitch grilled hamburgers, Olivia changed into shorts and a shirt. Magda took Adam upstairs for a quick bath and helped him dress in shorts and a T-shirt.

Adam got his second wind and chatted non-stop through dinner, giving Olivia a blow-by-blow description of everything he'd done all day. After dinner, the three of them headed into the family room. Adam wanted to show her how good he was with darts. It took all of her effort to lose to him without him realizing she'd thrown the match.

She laughed through a hotly contested Wii bowling competition between Mitch and Adam. In the end,

Adam squeaked out the win. Mitch had thrown the game but he'd been skillful enough that Adam never suspected. Her son had danced around the room on a winner's high. Mitch had snatched Adam up and put him on his shoulders so they could both dance in celebration. As long as she lived, she'd never be able to erase the image of sheer love and joy on her son's face as he hugged his father after Mitch set him back on the floor.

By eight, Adam was getting grumpy and struggling to keep his eyes open, all the while swearing he wasn't sleepy. When Mitch suggested the guys go upstairs and read a while, Adam agreed, but Olivia knew her son. He'd be asleep ten minutes after Mitch opened the book.

The quiet in the room after they left was like bathing in warm water on a cold day. Olivia sighed and leaned back on the sofa, enjoying the solitude. Her eyes drifted shut.

The rattle of glass started her eyes open.

"Sorry," Magda said. "Thought I'd finish picking up the dishes. You okay?"

"Yeah. Just tired."

"You sure I can't talk you and the little guy into staying forever?"

Olivia smiled. "Nope." The smile fell. "Magda. Can I trust you to keep a confidence? I'm going to need some help tomorrow."

"Sure you can."

"Adam and I are leaving tomorrow or maybe the next day. Don't say a word to Mitch."

Magda dropped into a chair. "Why? What happened?"

Olivia tapped her fingernail on her leg, debating whether to confide in Magda about Joanna and the marriage and child-custody situation.

"I can see you're trying to decide what to say. Your forehead is all wrinkled and you keep stroking that diamond heart around your neck. Stop thinking so hard and tell me what's up," Magda said.

In the end, because of how Magda felt about Joanna, and because of the affection Olivia had for Magda, Olivia decided that disclosing what she'd learned today, specifically that Joanna would be moving back into the house, was the right thing to do. Olivia glanced toward the door. "Make sure Mitch isn't out there first."

Magda went to the door and looked down the hall. She turned and leaned against the doorjamb. "I'll stay here just in case. Now what's up?"

Olivia dammed back the flood of tears that threatened to spill. "Joanna and Mitch are getting remarried. They have been meeting with an attorney to sue me for custody of Adam."

"No way," Magda said, straightening. She glanced down the hall again, then back to Olivia. "There is no way he's remarrying her. He is crazy about you."

Olivia shook her head. "I wish that were true, but no. It's all been an act to keep me in the dark."

Magda mimicked Olivia's head shake. "I just can't believe it. Are you sure?"

"Heard it from Joanna herself."

"She told you?"

"Well, not exactly. I overheard a conversation between her and a couple of her friends during lunch. There's no mistake. She didn't know I was there, so there was no reason for her to lie."

Magda glanced again down the hall, then back. "Well, there goes my job. I cannot work for that woman." She sighed. "Well, damn. You're absolutely sure?"

"Yeah."

"So what are you going to do?"

"Drake will be here tomorrow to take us home. I've told Drake I'll marry him again." She lost the battle with her emotions as two large drops overflowed her lower eyelids and rolled down her face. "I don't know what else to do. I have to protect Adam…not from Mitch, from Joanna. I honestly believe that Mitch loves Adam, but I couldn't trust Joanna with my son."

Magda came over and hugged her. "I am so sorry, Olivia. Honestly. I would never have thought Mitch was so stupid."

"Don't say anything, okay?"

"Sure. I've got your back."

"Thanks." Olivia struggled to her feet. "I'm heading to bed. I'll see you in the morning." She took a couple of steps, then turned back to Magda. "I'm sorry for you too. Thank you for making Adam and me feel so welcome while we've been here."

"It's been my pleasure, Olivia. That's one fine boy you're raising."

Olivia smiled. "I'll see you in the morning."

Olivia started toward her room, hobbling but using both feet. At the last minute, she turned toward the stairs with every intention of heading Mitch off before he joined her in bed as he had for the past week. If he did, she might just strangle him while he slept.

Climbing the stairs was slow, but easier than that first night when she'd hopped up on one leg. That felt like a lifetime ago.

Mitch was leaning over Adam when Olivia entered. He brushed a soft kiss to Adam's forehead and stood. The gentleness of his action broke her heart. She had no doubt that the love Mitch had for their son was genuine.

It showed in his every action and deed. If only she hadn't discovered his true colors, she might believe his feelings for her were real. But sometimes, the truth cut like a knife…like now. She quietly gasped at the pain inside her chest.

Mitch whipped around at the sound and smiled. "Hey, babe," he whispered. "He went out like a light."

Olivia made her way to the opposite side of the bed, leaned over and kissed Adam's forehead. "Night, sweetheart." After adjusting the bedcovers, she walked back into the hall and motioned for Mitch to follow.

"I'm ready for bed too," he said with a lascivious look. "But I'm not sleepy."

When he leaned in for a kiss, she pulled back.

"Not tonight, Mitch. I've got a splitting headache and I'm exhausted." Good grief. She sounded like a bad cliché.

"I'm sorry. Want me to rub your shoulders?"

The back of her eyes burned. If only his feelings for her matched the loving tone of his voice. But they couldn't, not if he was marrying Joanna. She forced herself to face facts. He'd given an award-winning performance, totally fooling her. How much of an effort he must have exerted to make love—no, have sex —with her.

"Really, I just need to be alone."

He frowned. "Are you sure?"

She nodded. "Yeah. I'm sure." She forced a weak smile and started down the stairs before he could kiss her. She didn't think she could stand that right now.

Chapter Fifteen

When Olivia had walked away from him last night, he'd known something was definitely wrong. He hadn't known what or how to fix it. He'd gone back to his temporary room upstairs sure of one thing…he could wait until Olivia was ready to talk. For her he'd wait forever.

But he really expected to meet her in the kitchen when he walked in at five a.m. He was surprised when Magda met him with coffee. Adam was already seated at the bar, a bowl of oatmeal in front of him. He could count on one hand the number of times Magda had been up at this hour of the morning.

"Morning, champ," he said as he rubbed the fuzz on Adam's head.

"Hi, Mitch…I mean, Daddy."

"Where's your mom?"

Adam shrugged. "I don't know."

"Magda?" He shot a laser look toward his house-keeper, who seemed to be refusing to meet his gaze.

Magda picked up a cloth and wiped at a non-existent

spill on the counter. "Under the weather. Said she'd see you guys later today."

Mitch walked to Magda and spoke in a voice too quiet to reach Adam's hearing. "What the hell is going on?"

Magda shrugged. "Nothing. Olivia just wasn't feeling good and asked me to get Adam up and ready to go. If you want to know anything else, you need to ask her."

His jaw clenched. "Fine." He whirled around. "I'll be right back, buddy, then we'll hit the old dusty trail."

Adam nodded. "'K."

Mitch made the walk to his bedroom in short order. He tried the door leading to the bedroom foyer. Locked.

He knocked. No answer.

He pounded. No answer.

"Olivia. Open this door."

No answer.

"Damn it, Olivia. I have a key, you know."

In a minute, the snick of a lock broke the silence. The door opened a crack and Olivia's blotched face looked out.

"What?"

"Honey. What's wrong? Have you been crying?"

"Nothing. A headache. I told you."

"Maybe you should see a doctor, Livie."

"No, no. I'll see you at lunch."

"Are you sure? You don't look good. I can call Dad to cover for me."

Two large tears plopped off her lashes. "Don't do that. Spend the day with Adam. I'll see you both this afternoon."

"If you're sure…"

"I'm sure."

The door closed and the lock clicked. He'd let her

have today. But tonight they were going to have to talk. He'd be willing to bet the ranch that whatever was bothering her wasn't a headache.

O<small>LIVIA SAGGED AGAINST THE DOOR AND LET HER</small> tears flow. Not that she had any choice. Holding them back would take the Hoover Dam. She headed back to the bedroom and her open luggage.

Thirty minutes later a soft knock on the door was followed by, "Olivia? They're gone. What can I do to help?"

Olivia opened the door. "I think the suitcases I used for Adam's clothes are in his closet upstairs. Can you take care of packing his things for me?"

"Sure." Magda started to leave, then turned back. "Olivia? Are you sure you heard Joanna right? I mean, Mitch was obviously concerned this morning about you. I just can't believe he'd do what you think he's done."

Olivia shook her head. "It's Joanna. Somehow she has the ability to get under his skin and into his head."

"Talk to him."

Olivia shook her head again. "I can't trust him to tell me the truth. No matter what he says, I'll always wonder. I can't live like that. I'll make sure Adam and he stay in touch. I promise that."

Magda sighed. "I think you are making a huge mistake not talking to him but..." She shrugged. "I'll see to Adam's things."

"Thanks, Magda. You know you'll be welcome in my home in Dallas any time."

Magda didn't say anything as she left, but Olivia would have sworn there were tears in Magda's eyes.

It didn't take Olivia long to repack the items of

clothing she'd brought with her. Moving to the large bathroom, she made the mistake of looking into the mirror running the length on the bathroom wall. Had the date been closer to Halloween rather than Memorial Day, the rat's nest in her hair combined with the blood-shot eyes ringed with dark circles would be the ideal look for a witch's costume.

Running her fingers through the hair tangles, she sighed. There wasn't much she could do about the dark circles, except for some make-up camouflage. She tried her best, but even after brushing her hair, her teeth and slathering on what little make-up she brought, she still appeared pale and sad. But then she was sad, wasn't she? It was only fair that she looked as rough as she felt. She scooped her toiletries into a zipper bag, made her way back to her suitcase and dropped the toiletry bag in on top of her swimsuit.

She glanced around the huge and ornate room. Where she'd felt overwhelmed when she first walked in, she'd begun to feel at home. She sighed and was surprised when two large teardrops cascaded down her cheek. Swiping at her eyes with the back of her hand, she couldn't decide if her injured leg hurt more than her heart. Both areas were throbbing painfully.

"Olivia?"

"Yes, Magda?"

"I've finished with Adam's things and carried every-thing downstairs. Do you need any help with your suitcase?"

Olivia sniffed as she pulled the top of her suitcase closed and snapped it shut. "Please. I don't think I can carry this to the front door." She looked up to meet Magda's gaze. "I want to be ready when Drake gets here."

Magda walked to Olivia and embraced her. "I am so sorry."

A sad smile formed on Olivia's lips. "Me too."

After Magda carried the suitcase from the room, Olivia checked the time. She had at least a couple of hours before Drake arrived. Time enough to take one last walk through the barn, maybe give Lady Belle an apple.

When she returned to the house forty-five minutes later, Drake's hunter green Range Rover was parked in the circle drive. Her stomach quivered, making her slightly nauseous. She wasn't sure if she was more nervous about seeing Drake after precipitously accepting his marriage proposal or facing Mitch's wrath when he discovered she was leaving and taking Adam.

She pulled her lips into the best smile she could manage and opened the front door, expecting to find Drake waiting for her. Following the mummer of voices, she heard Magda giggle at something Drake said, then Drake's deep laughter floated around the corner. The fake smile on her face disappeared to be replaced by sincere one. In the time she'd been staying here, she'd never heard Magda giggle. Laugh? Sure, but a girlish flirtatious giggle? Never. This was interesting.

Stepping around the corner, she found Drake sitting at the kitchen counter, a cup of coffee at his elbow and one of Magda's fresh chocolate-chip cookies in his hand. He wore khaki shorts and a green polo, making the emerald color of his eyes deeper and richer. Tall and tanned, his blond hair lighter from days of being out in the sun, Drake looked more like a California surfer dude than a respected professor of archeology.

Magda was leaning on the counter, infatuation worthy of a teenager girl over the star quarterback in her eyes. The minute she saw Olivia, she jumped upright and began wiping the spotless counter with a dry dishtowel.

"Olivia. We were just…"

Olivia repressed the grin tugging at the corners of her mouth. Guilt was written in the flush of Magda's face. Poor Magda. She'd been sucked into the Drake vortex.

No jealousy tugged her insides at the idea of another woman flirting with her fiancé. Somehow that didn't seem right. She should mind when another woman was so obviously enamored with the man she was going to marry, shouldn't she?

Her fiancé. The word stopped her cold. Was this really what she wanted? And was the lack of jealousy due to her security in knowing Drake loved her, or because deep down she knew she didn't love him like she should…like she loved Mitch?

Damn.

She'd be a good wife to Drake. Faithful. Honest. Take her marriage vows to heart. No man before her husband. She would get over Mitch. She'd learn to love Drake. He deserved nothing less than her total commitment.

Drake stood and wrapped his arms about Olivia's waist. "Hey, lady. I was wondering if you were packing that horse Magda said you'd become so fond of."

He kissed her. His lips were dry and soft. The kiss was gentle, non-demanding and completely unromantic, at least for her. Her heart didn't race at his touch. Her palms didn't sweat at being near him. Her insides didn't melt.

Stop it, she told herself. This is what she wanted—a safe guy who'd give her a calm, safe life.

Olivia snaked her arms around his neck. "Hey, your-self." She rubbed her nose against his. "I've missed you."

He grinned. It was a nice grin. Not a heart-stopping grin like Mitch's, but still, it was a nice, safe grin.

"You too." He stepped back.

"When did you get here?"

"Probably right after you left." He smiled toward Magda. "Magda's been keeping me company."

If possible, the flush on Magda's face deepened from pink to scarlet. Her head dipped lower as she kept cleaning areas already spotless "I...I... No big deal."

"Thanks for keeping him company, Magda. In fact, I can't begin to thank you for all you've done for me and Adam."

Magda folder her towel and set it on the counter. "I left Adam's suitcases in the foyer. Why don't I make one last run through the upstairs and make sure I didn't miss anything this morning."

Olivia checked the time. "Yes, that'd probably be a good idea." Hooking her arm through Drake's, she tried to shake off her feelings of unease. This was the right decision, at least the right decision for Adam, and he was the first and foremost factor in any decisions she made. "My bags are packed and sitting by the front door. Can you get those for me? I'm afraid my ankle is swelling up and starting to give me problems."

"Sure, honey." He kissed the top of her head. "Lead the way."

"Hold on. I'll get Magda to help you." She knew she'd be no help because her knee and ankle were already protesting.

"Don't worry about it. I've got this, Olivia." He stood there with her luggage in both hands, the muscles in his arms bulging under the weight. "I don't want you to pick up anything else. You've been on that leg too much, haven't you?"

She opened her mouth to deny it, however, the stern expression on Drake's face left no doubt that denial was futile.

"Yeah. I think I did a little too much over the last couple of days." She squeezed the bulging biceps of his right arm. "Thanks, Drake. I mean it. I don't know what I would do without you."

He kissed her. Another short, sweet, all-lip kiss. "You'd have called one of your brothers to come pick you up. Of course, one of them might have killed Landry for what he's done. Come to think of it, I might have to get in a few licks on that sonofabitch before we leave."

She let the hand resting on his arm drop to her side. "Stop it." She turned her back.

"No, you stop it, Olivia." He set her luggage at the front door, grabbed her arms and turned her to face him. "Magda told me everything, something you should have done. That man is trying to get your son. Don't forget that."

"I know." She jerked her arms out of his hold. "I know," she repeated, her voice barely above audible. Her throat swelled as tears burned in her eyes. "You don't have to remind me that Mitch let me down again. If I remember correctly, that was your favorite topic while we were married."

"Honey—"

She held up her hand. "Don't. Just don't." Wiping her eyes with her shoulder, she said, "Let's get packed and be ready to go when Adam gets back." She took a couple of wobbly steps then cupped her hands around her mouth. "Magda!"

"Yes?" came the reply from upstairs.

"Can you come give Drake a hand with the bags?"

Magda bounded down the stairs. "Sure." She smiled at Drake. "I'll get Adam's bags. They have to weigh less than Olivia's."

He returned her smile. "You know it. I think she must have rocks and bricks in here."

"Hey. I'm standing right here."

They ignored her. "If I strain my back…"

Magda nodded. "I'll see that you get good medical care."

The teasing between Magda and Drake kept on as they hefted the bags and exited. Olivia followed quietly behind. The reality was she didn't feel much like joking around when her heart and her spirit were broken.

The diesel roar of Mitch's truck reached the house about thirty seconds before he turned into the circle drive. The truck rocketed to an abrupt stop behind Drake's Range Rover, halting just short of bashing Drake's legs with the bumper. Mitch's scowl was clearly visible through the dirty windshield.

Olivia flinched. She'd been dreading the next couple of minutes since she'd made that call to Drake. Nervous tension whirled in her gut. She swallowed, but the minuscule amount of saliva she had in her mouth did nothing to abate the nausea edging up her throat.

Adam jumped from the truck, his arms wide for a hug. "Drake!"

Drake slid the luggage into the SUV and caught the little boy when he launched himself into Drake's arms. "Hi, Adam." He hugged the child tightly. "I've missed you."

"Me too."

Drake leaned back until he could look eye to eye with

Adam. "Man, you have grown. What are you? Six feet tall now?"

Adam giggled. "No. See my new boots?" He lifted one leg to hold out his booted foot.

"Wow. Those are snazzy."

When the boy wiggled to get down, Drake set Adam on his feet.

"Hey, do you know Mitch too? Did you come to see his cows? Did you know I saw a cow come out of the bottom of his momma? And Mitch let me name the baby. I bet he'd let you too. Did you know Mitch is my daddy?"

The four adults stood there in an uncomfortable silence until Drake looked at Mitch. "You must be the infamous Mitch Landry."

Mitch nodded one tense nod. "And you're Drake Gentry. What are you doing here at my house, Mr. Gentry?" Mitch's voice vibrated with anger.

Drake picked up another piece of luggage and stowed it in the back of his SUV. "It's time for Olivia and Adam to get back to Dallas. I've come to get my family."

"The hell you say. You're not taking them anywhere." With his hands in fists, he took a couple of steps toward Drake. "Get the hell off my property and don't come back."

Adam divided a look between the two men. "What's wrong? Momma, why is Daddy yelling at Drake?"

Olivia went over to her son and knelt down. "Why don't you go with Magda and help her get some cookies together for our trip? Okay?"

Magda followed Olivia over. "Great idea. C'mon, Adam." She took his small hand in hers. "I'll make you some sandwiches too."

"But—"

"Go on, Adam," Mitch said. "Don't argue with your mother."

Drake balled up his fists. "You don't tell him what to do."

When tugging his hand didn't work to move Adam, Magda grabbed him up and carried him into the house. "The adults need to talk and I need some help and nobody is as good a help as you."

Adam took a final look over Magda's shoulder then shrugged. "Okay. What kind of cookies?"

The minute the door shut behind Magda and Adam, Mitch stomped up to Drake. "Get the fuck off my property or I'll call the cops."

Drake shoved his face into Mitch's personal space. "Be glad to. Just as soon as I get my family loaded up, we're out of here."

Mitch shoved Drake. "They aren't your family. And they aren't going anywhere."

Drake shoved back. "You're a sonofabitch, Landry. You know that? You don't deserve someone like Olivia. And Adam doesn't deserve a jerk like you for a father."

Mitch drew back his arm and plowed his fist into Drake's jaw. Drake staggered back but quickly responded with an upper cut to Mitch's chin.

"Stop it!" Olivia cried, stepping into the melee between the men. "Both of you stop it."

"Get out the way, Olivia. This bastard has it coming to him." Drake pushed her to the side. He snarled at Mitch. "I didn't think you could get much lower than walking out on Olivia six years ago, but damn if you haven't topped yourself with this latest stunt."

"No, Drake. Stop it. Go get Adam and let's get out of here."

The muscles in Drake's cheeks and lips tightened as

he frowned. "Fine. Do you need help getting into the car?"

"Wait a minute," Mitch yelled. "I demand to know what the hell is going on here."

Olivia tossed a glare at Mitch before turning back to Drake. "I'm fine. Just get Adam and let's get home."

As soon as the front door shut behind Drake, Mitch grabbed Olivia's arm. "Livie, what the—"

Olivia jerked her arm from his grasp. "Don't, Mitch. This time I won't play dead and let you walk all over me. I'm going home and taking *my* son. You can have your lawyer contact my lawyer." With all the dignity she could muster while limping, she stormed to the passenger door of the Range Rover and climbed in.

Chapter Sixteen

Olivia totaled the figures again, and for the third time came up with a different number. She rubbed her eyes, dismayed to find a couple of tears there. That's okay, she was just tired. And hungry after missing dinner again. And, damn it, sad and lonely. She'd been tired, hungry, sad and lonely since driving away from Mitch's ranch six weeks ago.

She glanced at her son asleep on her office sofa. She stretched out the fingers on her left hand to study her naked ring finger. Not marrying Drake had been the right decision, for her and for Drake, not that he'd been happy when she told him. But within a week of returning to Dallas, she knew she wasn't being fair to Drake. He was a wonderful man who deserved someone much better than she. He deserved a woman who would love him with every cell in her body.

This time when tears leaked down her cheeks she didn't bother to wipe them away. Instead, she let them come. A quick glance at Adam found him asleep and oblivious to her pain. And make no doubt, she was in pain. Sometimes the ache in her chest made it almost impossible to draw a breath.

"Knock. Knock."

Olivia jumped in her chair, her head snapping up and toward the door.

Travis leaned against the doorframe and tapped the face of his watch. "Don't you think it's a little late to still be at the gym?"

"It's not that late." Olivia stood and turned away from him, quickly rubbing her face with her T-shirt sleeve. "My eyes are killing me though. Thanks for dropping by to give me the time."

He guffawed. "Little sister, I'm not here to give you the time. I'm here to—"

Adam rolled over, drawing Travis and Olivia's attention.

She glared toward him then nodded her head toward the sleeping child. "Quiet, Travis. Don't wake up Adam," she whispered.

He gestured for Olivia to follow him out into the gym. She did and then walked past him into the main equipment area.

"What are you doing here?"

"I wanted to talk to you."

Travis followed so closely she imagined she could feel him breathing down her neck. "Well, I don't want to talk to you, so there. Get out. Wait. How did you get in here? I'm sure I locked the doors."

"Mark passed me a spare key."

She kicked the edge of a mat. "I'm going to fire him."

"Too late. He and Nancy are your partners now. Besides, they're worried about you. Hell, we're all worried about you."

"I'm fine. If that's all, I'll let you out. Oh, and give me that key."

"No, that's not all." Travis grabbed her shoulders and whipped her around to face him. "This isn't healthy. You're not eating. You never go home. You're keeping my nephew up here too late at night. What the hell are you thinking?"

What she wanted to say was *if I go home, I see Mitch everywhere. If I get in my bed, I'll feel him beside me. If I take a deep breath in my house, I'll smell him. If I fall asleep, I dream about him.*

What she said was, "Nothing's wrong. Now go mind your own business." She jerked from his grasp and stomped into the restaurant area of Jim's Gym to check the lock on the door. But she never got that far.

Travis wrapped his arms around her and pulled her back tight against his chest. "Oh, kitten. I know you're hurting."

He hadn't called her kitten since she was a child. The nickname drove a stake into her resistance. Her shoulders slumped and the tears flowed down her cheeks, dripping off her jaw.

"I loved him. I trusted him and…" She gulped, swallowing her tears. "How do I live without him? It hurts, Travis. It hurts so bad. What should I do?"

Travis pushed her away enough to turn her to face him. "You live. Every day you get out of bed, put one foot in front of the other and keep moving until it's time to go to sleep so you can get up and do it again another day." He kissed her forehead. "No one knows better than I do what it means to lose a loved one."

She sniffed. Of course Travis knew. Had he not lost his wife to breast cancer when she'd been only twenty-six?

"Don't you realize that I've had to face the fact that I'll never find another love like the one I had with Susan?" He whirled, took a few paces away then turned back. "Do you have any idea what I would do to have her back? Anything. I'd do anything. But here's the difference between Mitch and Susan." He stepped close enough that Olivia had to tip her head back to look into his face. "Susan's dead. Mitch isn't."

She wrapped her arms around her big brother's waist. "He might as well be."

Travis kissed the top of her head. "It's never too late when there's love. Remember that." Then he turned her toward her office and pushed. "Go get your son and let's get out of here. It's late. And Olivia?"

She looked at him.

"Don't be a brat when Mitch calls." When she arched an eyebrow, he added, "Give him time. He'll call you. Trust me."

Following her big brother's advice, she got up every morning, went to work, fed her son, worked with her clients, put one foot in front of the other and lived. Her ankle and knee healed. Her heart didn't. It ached, but she only allowed herself the luxury of tears late at night, long after Adam had gone to sleep.

Travis had been right and wrong about Mitch. He did call every day, but to talk to Adam, never to her. The day after she and Adam had arrived home, a cell phone had arrived for Adam. It was his link to Mitch. Adam was very protective of his phone, letting no one touch it but him. As much as Olivia protested that Adam was much too young, her family finally convinced her that Adam needed this connection to Mitch as much as Mitch needed the connection to Adam. Mitch had programmed in the phone numbers for his cell phone and the ranch. Adam knew how to call Mitch and how to call Magda. He told everyone that Magda was his girlfriend.

At work, noise from the ongoing construction kept her head throbbing. Mark had bought the buildings on either side of Jim's Gym. A friend of his was putting in a taekwondo studio on the left and Nancy had finally decided to make use of her physical therapy degree and opened up the other area for sports injuries, physical therapy and massages.

Over the summer, revenue had shot up. New clients were streaming through the door. Olivia should have been ecstatic. On the outside she was all smiles and laughs. She kept up a good front for her son, her business partners and her family.

Inside, she was dead.

The August heat wreaked havoc on their air conditioning bills. Olivia muttered a couple of creative suggestions about what the electric company executives could kiss of hers as she wrote the check. She ripped the check from the book and stuffed it into an envelope, then picked up the next bill. Water and sewer. Not as bad as—

"Olivia?"

Nancy's voice cut through Olivia's concentration. She glanced up. "What's up?"

"There's someone here to see you."

Nancy's voice was…strange. Sort of giggly.

Olivia bent her head in an attempt to see around Nancy's body in the doorway. "Um, okay. Do I need to come out there? Is this person coming in here?"

Nancy shook her head. "You need to come with me, I guess."

Olivia stood. "You guess? Nancy, what's going on?"

Nancy shrugged and walked toward the rear

entrance of the gym. "He said for you to meet him out here."

Olivia sighed. "Meet who? What's going on?"

Nancy held the back door open and Olivia went through. Drake stood grinning at her, his arms spread wide for a hug.

"Drake." Olivia flew into his arms. "Where have you been? I've been so worried about you." She leaned back until she could look into his eyes. "I haven't heard from you in three months. I am so sorry, Drake. You deserve better than the way I treated you."

"Don't be sorry. You did us both a huge favor. I've met someone. She's incredible. Awesome. Beautiful. Perfect. And I have you to thank."

"Me? How? Who?"

He shook his head. "I don't want to jinx it, so I'm not going to say. I just came by to thank you." He kissed her. She could have been kissing one of her brothers for all the effect it had on her. "I've got to run. But can I give you one piece of advice before I go?"

"Of course."

"Don't be bitchy when Mitch calls, and he will call. I'm sure of it." He kissed her again. "Talk to Mitch."

"But—"

"Trust me. I love you, kitten."

She smiled at the use of her brothers' pet name for her. It told her everything about Drake's feelings.

"Love you too."

On Saturday, Nancy took Adam for the day, insisting that Olivia stay away from work for the day and get some rest. As much as Olivia would have loved to argue the point, she'd not been sleeping well for the past month and was exhausted.

At ten in the morning, she awoke to the chimes of

her doorbell. Struggling off the couch where she'd fallen asleep, she staggered to the door and flung it open.

A teenage boy stood there holding a stunning floral arrangement of red roses, pink lilies, purple iris, purple aster and cymbidium orchids. "Ms. Gentry?"

"Yes?"

The boy thrust the bouquet toward her. "These are for you."

After taking the vase, she dipped her nose among the flowers and sniffed. Incredible scents filled her nose. "Thank you. Wait and I'll get you a tip."

He smiled and shook his head. "Thanks, but the tip was included. Have a nice day."

"Thanks." She shut the door and buried her nose again in the velvety petals of the roses. The aroma immediately carried her back to Grayson Mansion and the balcony off Mitch's room. She looked for a note or a card but found neither. After putting additional water in the vase, she set it on the fireplace mantle where she could enjoy looking at the blooms.

At eleven, her doorbell rang again. When she answered, it was a different floral delivery service. This time, the arrangement was two-dozen lavender roses with a dozen stems of white spray roses. As before, no tip needed. No card included.

At noon, three dozen red tulips were delivered. No card.

At one, an enormous bouquet of pink roses, pink gerbera daisies, pink lilies and pink spray roses arrived. No card.

At two, a purple hyacinth plant appeared at her door. As before, no card.

At two-fifty-five, she began to wonder what three p.m. would bring.

At three-fifteen, when nothing arrived, her spirits deflated, but then she felt quite silly to be disappointed. Hadn't she received four arrangements already? How greedy.

At three-thirty, her doorbell rang. A smile tickled her mouth. Better late than never. She opened the door, ready to see another unfamiliar floral delivery person. Instead, Mitch stood on her porch. He thrust a mammoth vase crammed full of dozens of red roses toward her.

"Hi."

Olivia took the flowers. "Hi."

"Can I come in?"

Olivia stepped back and Mitch stepped in.

"I'm assuming the rest are from you too," Olivia said. "I don't have that many admirers."

Mitch smiled, but that didn't relax the tension in his face. "Can we take a drive?"

"Look, Mitch. I love all the flowers, but—"

"Hear me out, Olivia. Give me that much."

"Why should I? You were planning to take my son away from me."

"No. I'm…" He sighed. "I'm not trying to take Adam away from you. Take a drive with me. I have something I want to show you."

When she hesitated, he added, "Please."

She set the roses on the entry hall table. "Okay, but this'd better be good."

They drove about seventy miles outside the city limits. The drive was quiet, both seemingly afraid of speaking and mucking up the tentative peace. Mitch turned onto a paved driveway and under an archway. Olivia looked around at the fields of green grass and imagined what a herd of prime cattle would look like grazing in all the tall grass stalks. Mitch followed the circle drive to the front door of a two-story white columned manor.

"Whose place is this?" she asked.

"C'mon." Mitch stepped from his truck and walked around to her door. Opening it, he extended a hand to help her out of the truck.

Olivia looked around, saw no one. She took his hand and stepped on the pavement. She might as well have grabbed a live wire. She extended her fingers to release his hand but he flexed his tighter, maintaining their connection.

"Gorgeous house." Her voice quivered. She hated showing any weakness. He might have said he wasn't trying to take Adam away, and even though her lawyer had received nothing from Mitch's attorney, she wasn't ready yet to trust him. She'd done that before and look how that had turned out.

Mitch nodded. He led her up the steps onto a sweeping, wraparound porch. He opened the front door and walked in as though they were expected. Olivia hesitated at the door.

"Mitch. I don't understand. Whose house is this?"

She followed him down a wide foyer into a sparsely furnished living room. Water flowed down one wall into a shallow trough where it was collected and returned to the top of the wall to fall again. Olivia had always loved the sound of running water. Had Mitch remembered that, or was the fountain-wall just a happy coincidence?

While the house obviously had electricity—otherwise the fountain wouldn't be running—candles of all sizes, heights, shapes and colors covered every available surface of end tables, coffee table, fireplace mantel and shelves. When tables and shelves were full, candles had been placed all around the room on the floor. Someone had lit every candle, filling the space with a sweet, floral aroma. Candle flames flickered and danced on the walls and ceiling.

Olivia turned in a full circle, took in every carefully placed item. The room vibrated sexual energy. The attention to detail, to make this scene everything she could have dreamed of, exploded the thick wall she'd constructed around her heart.

"This is…is…incredible. Gorgeous." She glanced at Mitch. His drawn face suggested something serious. "What's going on, Mitch?" She pulled her hand from his, suddenly fearful that he'd set the stage to deliver bad news. Her heart beat heavily and she found it difficult to breathe with the band squeezing her chest.

"Sit down." He nodded toward the sofa. "I need to…just sit."

She did as he requested. He didn't join her, but began to pace.

"I'm not sure where to begin so I'll start with I'm sorry." He ran his hand through his hair. "It seems like I say that a lot to you." He walked a couple of steps, turned and walked back. "First, I had no idea what Joanna was up to. I swear. I never asked her to meet with my lawyer about getting custody of Adam. *Never.* That was her lame-brained idea." He shook his head. "I had no idea what you were talking about when you left, telling me to have my lawyer contact yours. When my lawyer called a couple of weeks later about needing my signature on papers and mentioned getting the paperwork going on the custody action, I was stunned. After meeting with Joanna and with him, I pieced together that Joanna had it in her head that if she helped me get custody of Adam, I'd need her to help me raise him so I'd marry her again." He rubbed his eyes. "She was shocked that I didn't agree that was the perfect solution to get us back together. Where she got the idea that I would ever want to get back with her…"

He paced. Olivia waited.

"I had another long talk with my parents about Adam and Mom dropped a bombshell. She said that one of the reasons she and Dad had never told me about Adam was Joanna. They didn't trust her. You want to know the kicker?"

Olivia nodded.

"Neither of my parents believes she was ever pregnant. They think she dreamed up that pregnancy to get James moving on their engagement. Then when James died, she was stuck with the story. I don't think any of us were thinking straight. James's death was such a shock. It was like I went to sleep, and when I woke up I was married to Joanna." He met Olivia's gaze. "I did love her…like a sister. Never like a man should love a woman he's planning on spending the rest of his life with. Do you know what I mean?"

Of course she did. Hadn't she done the same thing with Drake?

"I know what you mean."

Relief rolled across his face. "I don't love Joanna. I love you, Olivia. I've always loved you."

Her heart beat loudly in her ears. Had she heard him right? She was afraid to speak, afraid she'd misunderstood.

He sat on the sofa next to her. "Did you hear me? I love you."

"Is this about Adam? Are you telling me this because we had a son? You don't have to. I'll let you see Adam."

This was a gamble, but Olivia had to know if he loved her or if he loved Adam's mother.

Smiling, he took her hand. "I love you, Olivia Montgomery Gentry. I loved you before Adam was conceived. I loved the girl you were in college and I love the woman you've become. I love you for being the mother of my son."

"So what is it you're wanting, Mitch?"

"I want to marry you. I want us to build a life together. The life we should have had six years ago."

When she hesitated, he added, "I'm not asking you to move away from Dallas and your friends and your family. I'll move here."

She was stunned. He was offering to reorganize his life to accommodate her and Adam. "But what about the Lazy L? Your family?"

"You don't understand. You and Adam are my family. You're what I need, what I can't live without."

"And the Lazy L? What will happen to the ranch?" The guilt of him giving up everything to be with her gnawed at her.

He chuckled. "That's where this story gets crazy."

She arched an eyebrow and waited.

"Mom and Dad held on to the ranch for James, Caleb and me. Caleb has no interest in ranching." When she looked surprised, he said, "I know. Shocked me too. Seems little brother has an interest in becoming a vintner. He's studying agriculture in college, focusing on grapes and wines. With James gone, that just left me and Dad. Dad turned down an offer to sell the Lazy L about ten years ago. Since then, he and Mom have talked about retiring. That would leave the entire Lazy L operation to me to run. It's not that I couldn't do it, but I realized that without my family, without you and Adam, I didn't want to do it.

"When you left, the house felt empty, too quiet. I guess I got used to Adam stomping on the hardwood."

"I'm confused, Mitch. I still don't know whose house this is, and why we're here, or even what you are proposing."

He grinned. "Proposing is the right word." He slid off the couch onto one knee. "I'm proposing marriage. Marry me, Olivia. Live with me here."

"Here? This house, here?"

"This house, yes. I've been talking to your brothers, and let me say, I had no idea Travis could cuss like that." He laughed. "It took me a while to convince them to see me, hear me out. I'm going into business with your brother Cash, raising bulls for the Professional Bull Rider circuit. This ranch is smaller than the Lazy L but a perfect setting for starting a new operation."

"But the Lazy L?"

"Sold. As soon as I knew that's what my parents wanted, and they knew I needed to be here with you, it was a no-brainer. Dad has been turning down offers for years. We finally accepted one."

Olivia was breathlessly overwhelmed. He'd hit her with so much new information. Her head swam with all he'd just told her.

"Olivia."

She looked at him kneeling before her. Being apart from him for the past three months had taught her how much she loved him, and that no other man could take his place in her life. She could see love in his eyes. She could hear the honesty in his voice when he said he loved her. While she had some regrets about their three-month separation, she knew it had given both of them time to think about what was important in life, and she believed they'd come to the same conclusion. Love and family. They shared love. They shared a son.

"Marry me?"

She slid from the sofa to sit beside him. Now they'd share their lives. They were equal partners in this relationship. Neither above or below the other.

"I love you, Mitch. Yes, I'll marry you anywhere and any day. What would you think about giving Adam a sibling?"

He leaned forward and kissed her. "No time like the present."

New York Times and USA Today Bestselling Author Cynthia D'Alba was born and raised in a small Arkansas town. After being gone for a number of years, she's thrilled to be making her home back in Arkansas living on the banks of an eight-thousand acre lake.

Photo by Tom Smarch

When she's not reading or writing or plotting, she's doorman for her spoiled border collie, cook, housekeeper and chief bottle washer for her husband and slave to a noisy, messy parrot. She loves to chat online with friends and fans.

Send snail mail to: Cynthia D'Alba PO Box 2116 Hot Springs, AR 71914

Or better yet! She would for you to take her news-letter. She promises not to spam you, not to fill your inbox with advertising, and not to sell your name and email address to anyone. Check her website for a link to her newsletter.

www.cynthiadalba.com
cynthiadalba@gmail.com

Read on for more
Whispering Springs, Texas books
by
Cynthia D'Alba

TEXAS TANGO

WHISPERING SPRINGS, TEXAS, BOOK 2 © 2013
CYNTHIA D'ALBA

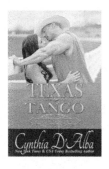

***Sex in a faux marriage can
make things oh so real.***

Dr. Caroline Graham is happy
with her nomadic lifestyle fulfilling
short-term medical contracts. No
emotional commitments, no disap-
pointments. She's always the one to
walk away, never the one left behind.
But now her grandmother is on her
deathbed, more concerned about
Caroline's lack of a husband than her own demise.
What's the harm in a little white lie? If a wedding will
give her grandmother peace, then a wedding she
shall have.

Widower Travis Montgomery devotes his days to
building the ranch he and his late wife planned before he
lost her to breast cancer. The last piece of acreage he
needs is controlled by a lady with a pesky need of her
own. Do her a favor and he can have the land. She needs
a quick, temporary, faux marriage in exchange for the
acreage.

It's a total win-win situation until events begin to
snowball and they find, instead of playacting, they've put
their hearts at risk.

Read on for an excerpt:

Friday afternoon, Travis Montgomery pulled his
truck under the only shade tree in the Montgomery and

Montgomery Law Offices parking lot. He hoped his brother had some news for him about Fitzgerald's place. After ten years of unsuccessfully trying to get Old Man Fitzgerald to sell, Singing Springs Ranch would finally be his. He could feel it in his bones.

He hadn't known Fitzgerald had family, so finding out Caroline Graham was his great-niece was a tad of a surprise, but no big deal. Other than Caroline, no other Fitzgerald family members mentioned in the obit lived here. He couldn't imagine that old tightwad leaving his ranch to any of them. And even if he did, there was no way anyone would up and move to Texas just because they inherited a rundown ranch, especially if that person knew nothing about ranching. Yup. Whoever ended up with Singing Springs would be thrilled to unload it, and Travis wanted to make sure that person unloaded it right into his hands.

He let himself in the back door of his brother's office, stopping long enough to grab a bottle of cold water from the kitchen, then headed for the reception area.

After removing his beige straw cowboy hat, he leaned over the reception desk to give Jason's secretary a wink. "Hi, Mags. Is little brother available?"

"Hey, handsome," Margaret said then sighed. "If only I were twenty years younger and not married..."

Travis slapped his hat across his heart. "My bachelor days would be over."

She smiled and nodded toward the closed door down the hall. "He's on the phone. I'll let him know you're here. I'd offer you something to drink, but you seemed to have helped yourself."

He rolled the dewy bottle on the back of his neck. "Can't decide if I want to drink this or pour it over my head. Man, it's a killer out there. What about KC? Is my lovely cousin around?"

Before Margaret could respond, Jason's door opened. "I thought I heard a reprobate out here. Stop flirting with my secretary and c'mon back. I've got a date with Lydia tonight and you know she hates when I'm late." He ducked back into his office, leaving the door ajar.

Travis groaned. "I'm coming." He looked at Margaret and hitched his thumb toward the door where his brother had just been standing. "He been in this bad mood all day?"

She shook her head. "Nope. He was quite pleasant when KC headed out about thirty minutes ago. Your cousin's got perfect timing. She always knows to clear out and avoid the Montgomery brothers when something's brewing."

"Lucky me. Wish I knew her magic."

Travis entered his brother's office and closed the door behind him. He dropped onto the thick leather sofa running along the office wall then set his hat crown-side down on the cushion beside him. He draped his arm along the back of the sofa. "I hope you've got some good news for me. I've had a bitch of a day."

"What happened?"

"One of the Webster kids spooked a new stallion I'd just unloaded. The bastard almost trampled me, John and a couple of hands before we could get him under control."

Jason frowned. "I'd think your foreman's kids would know better than to get near a stallion, especially one I suspect was antsy to begin with. Which kid?"

Travis's mouth cocked up on one side in a grimace. "Rocky. He had a classmate visiting, and I think he was trying to impress him. But after John and Nadine get done with him, I suspect his ears will be ringing for the next week." He gave a small chuckle. "And I'm getting my stalls mucked out for free for at least a month, maybe two."

"I hated mucking stalls."

"So I remember. What's the good news?"

Jason took a seat closer to the sofa. "Well, I've got good news and bad news."

"Great. Bad news first then."

"Fitzgerald had KC prepare his will about a year ago, so his estate won't be going to the state to resolve."

Travis scowled. "I was afraid of that," he growled. "So what can you tell me now?"

"All the beneficiaries have been notified and the will duly probated. It was fairly straight forward. I don't foresee anyone challenging it."

"So don't keep me waiting. Who do I need to talk to about buying Singing Springs?"

"Dr. Caroline Graham."

TEXAS FANDANGO

WHISPERING SPRINGS, TEXAS BOOK 3 © 2014
CYNTHIA D'ALBA

Two-weeks on the beach can deepened more than tans.

Attorney KC Montgomery has loved family friend Drake Gentry forever, but she never seemed to be on his radar. When Drake's girl-friend dumps him, leaving him with two all-expenses paid tickets to the Sand Castle Resort in the Caribbean, KC seizes the chance and makes him an offer impossible to refuse: two weeks of food, fun, sand, and sex with no strings attached.

University Professor Drake Gentry has noticed his best friend's cousin for years, but KC has always been hands-off, until today. Unable to resist, he agrees to her two-week, no-strings affair.

The vacation more than fulfills both their fantasies. The sun is hot but the sex hotter.

TEXAS TWIST

WHISPERING SPRINGS, TEXAS BOOK 4 © 2014
CYNTHIA D'ALBA

Real bad boys can grow up to be real good men.

Paige Ryan lost everything important in her life. She moves to Whispering Springs, Texas to be near her step-brother. But just as her life is derailed again when the last man in the world she wants to see again moves into her house.

Cash Montgomery is on the cusp of having it all. When a bad bull ride leaves him injured and angry, his only comfort is found at the bottom of a bottle. His family drags him home to Whispering Springs, Texas. With nowhere to go, he moves temporarily into an old ranch house on his brother's property surprised the place is occupied.

The best idea is to move on but sometimes taking the first step out the door is the hardest one.

Loving a bull rider is dangerous, so is falling for him a second time is crazy?

TEXAS BOSSA NOVA

WHISPERING SPRINGS, TEXAS BOOK 5 ©2014
CYNTHIA D'ALBA

A heavy snowstorm can produce a lot of heat

Magda Hobbs loves being a ranch housekeeper. The job keeps her close to her recently discovered father, foreman at the same ranch. She is immune to all the cowboy charms, except for one certain cowboy, who is wreaking havoc on her libido.

Reno Montgomery is determined to make his fledging cattle ranch a success. Dates with Magda Hobbs rocks his world and then she disappears, leaving him confused and angry. He's shocked when he learns the new live-in housekeeper is Magda Hobbs.

When a freak snowstorm cuts off the outside world, the isolation rekindles their desire. But when the weather and the roads clear, Reno has to work hard and fast to keep the woman of his dreams from hitting the road right out of his life again.

TEXAS HUSTLE

WHISPERING SPRINGS, TEXAS BOOK 6 ©2015
CYNTHIA D'ALBA

Watch out for chigger bites, love bites and secrets that bite

Born into a wealthy, Southern family, Porchia Summers builds a good life in Texas until a bad news ex-boyfriend tracks her down. Desperate for time to figure out how to handle the trouble he brings, she looks to the one man who can get her out of town for a few days.

Darren Montgomery has had his eye on the town's sexy, sweet baker for a while but she's never returns his looks until now. He's flattered but suspicious about her quick change in attention.

Sometimes, camping isn't just camping. It's survival.

TEXAS LULLABY

WHISPERING SPRINGS, TEXAS BOOK 7 ©2016
CYNTHIA D'ALBA

Sometimes what you think you don't want is exactly what you need.

After a long four-year engagement, Lydia Henson makes her decision. Forced to choice between having a family or marrying a man who adamantly against fathering children, she chooses the man. She can live without children. She can't live without the man she loves.

Jason Montgomery doesn't want a family, or at least that's his story and he's sticking to it. The falsehood is less emasculating than the truth.

On the eve of their wedding, Jason and Lydia's well-planned life is thrown into chaos. Everything Jason has sworn he doesn't want is within his grasp. But as he reaches for the golden ring, life delivers another twist.

SADDLES AND SOOT

WHISPERING SPRINGS, TEXAS BOOK 8 ©2015
CYNTHIA D'ALBA

Veterinarian Georgina Greyson will only be in Whispering Springs for three months. She isn't looking for love or roots, but some fun with a hunky fireman could help pass the time.

Tanner Marshall loves being a volunteer fireman, maybe more than being a cowboy. At thirty-four, he's ready to put down some roots, including marriage, children and the white picket fence.

When Georgina accidentally sets her yard on fire during a burn ban, the volunteer fire department responds. Tanner hates carelessness with fire, but there's something about his latest firebug that he can't get out of his mind.

Can an uptight firefighter looking to settle down persuade a cute firebug to give up the road for a house and roots?

TEXAS DAZE

WHISPERING SPRINGS, TEXAS BOOK 9 ©2017
CYNTHIA D'ALBA

A quick fling can sure heat up a cowgirl's life

When a devastating discovery ends Marti Jenkins' engagement, she decides to play the field for a while. A ranch accident lands her in the office of Whispering Springs' new orthopedic doctor, Dr. Eli Boone. And yeah, he's as hot as she's been told.

Dr. Eli Boone is temporarily covering his friend's practice and then it's back to New York City and the societal world he's lives. He's not looking for a wife, but he wouldn't say no to a quick tumble in the sheets with the right woman.

Due to ridiculous challenge, Eli has to learn to ride before he leaves town. He turns to the one person who can help him win the bet, Marti Jenkins.

As he learns to ride a horse, Marti does a little riding of her own…and she doesn't need a horse.